DARK HOURS

Ryan David Jahn lives in Louisville, Kentucky, with his wife Jessica and two beautiful little girls, Francine and Matilda. His novel *Acts of Violence* won the Crime Writers' Association John Creasey Dagger. His work has been translated into twelve languages.

Visit his website at www.ryandavidjahn.com
Or follow him on Twitter @ RyanDavidJahn

D0795233

By Ryan David Jahn

Praise for Ryan David Jahn

'Jahn just gets better and better. He's a writer not to be missed'   **Mark Billingham**

'*The Dispatcher* was one of the best thrillers I've ever read'
Simon Kernick

'A one-sitting, fist-in-mouth read'   *Guardian*

'An impressively accomplished performance that never strains for mythic power but nevertheless acquires it'
Sunday Times

'Over the past few years a new generation of crime writers have come perilously close to recreating the jaded mindset of the classic noir thrillers, but no one has succeeded quite like Jahn . . . The author leads the new noir pack with a series of palm-sweating situations that pay homage to the classics of the genre while feeling entirely fresh – in a mean, lean, unclean way'   *Financial Times*

'Jahn's most ambitious and complex novel to date. It's also a mood piece and a homage to 1950s West Coast crime fiction, when the hard-boiled style morphed into the psychologically strained depths of noir . . . Murder, blackmail, execution and betrayal – of one's own integrity and morality – stalk this very fine, multi-layered novel'
Book of the Week, *Daily Mirror*

'The violence is vivid, the tension is high, the imagery of the world often bleak but sometimes beautiful, and the characters get under your skin whether you want them there or not'   **www.spinetinglermag.com**

'A taut novel that upends ideas about heroism and romance'
Sunday Times

'This is the first book I've read in two years that has caused me to sit up until the early hours to finish it . . . I guarantee that if you pick this up, then everything else in your life will immediately be pushed to the margins, and when you've finished you'll resurface as if from an especially corny dream sequence – dazed, confused and with a thin layer of cold sweat on the back of your neck'
Dylan Jones, Editor of *GQ*

'Jahn delivers a nerve-shredding thriller with plenty of energy and a tight plot'   *Big Issue*

'Near pitch perfect. This is human life as we dare not imagine it can be, packaged in an adrenaline-pumped storyline and one that will leave you with your lower jaw resting on your chest. I don't believe anyone else is offering Jahn's insight and style of writing today, so if you can stomach it, do try him out and make sure you allocate sufficient hours to read in one sitting. This continues to be outstanding work from Jahn'   **It's a Crime**

RYAN DAVID JAHN

DARK HOURS

PAN BOOKS

First published 2015 by Pan Books
an imprint of Pan Macmillan
20 New Wharf Road, London N1 9RR
Associated companies throughout the world
www.panmacmillan.com

ISBN 978-0-230-75757-8

1 3 5 7 9 8 6 4 2

A CIP catalogue record for this book is available from the British Library.

Typeset by Ellipsis Digital Limited, Glasgow
Printed and bound by CPI Group (UK) Ltd, Croydon, CR0 4YY

Visit **www.panmacmillan.com** to read more about all our books
and to buy them. You will also find features, author interviews and
news of any author events, and you can sign up for e-newsletters
so that you're always first to hear about our new releases.

For Benjamin Alt,
Barbara Alt
&
Harlan Ellison

ACKNOWLEDGMENTS

Most of this book was written and edited while my wife Jessica was within shouting distance. Whenever I needed help with research or a bothersome sentence her name could be heard echoing through the house. In addition to working for free as my researcher and human dictionary, she listened patiently as I complained about the difficulty of pulling this story from my head, which saved me very expensive sessions with a therapist (I lie to therapists, in any case, so going to one is pointless). Thank you. I love you more than I can say.

Thanks also to Jeremy Trevathan, my publisher; Wayne Brookes and Louise Buckley, who edited the book; Andrew Pagana, who took my phone calls when Jessica was not home to listen to me kvetch; and, finally, my daughters Francine and Matilda, for giving me a reason – two reasons – to get out of bed every morning. In fact, they demand it.

Finally, as always, I'd like to thank you for reading. A book doesn't truly exist until someone turns to page one and reads the first sentence.

RDJ

29 January 2015

I

Lamb was crushing a couple pills with the bottom of a whiskey glass when the woman walked into his office. He looked up from what he was doing and saw her standing just inside the doorway, a pretty brunette in her early thirties with a pixie haircut and nervous brown eyes. She was wearing Levi's and a red blouse with the top three buttons undone. The sun was bright outside and shining in through the smudged glass door so that she almost appeared to be glowing, like a woman in one of those religious paintings from the Middle Ages, or whenever it was.

He pulled open the top drawer of his desk and brushed the blue powder into it so she wouldn't see what he'd been up to, then wiped the bottom of the glass off on his cheap navy slacks. He had another five pairs just like them hanging in his closet at home. He set the glass down on his desk's scratched surface and asked the woman if she was in the right place.

I don't know.

Then maybe you aren't.

I want my daughter back.

Then maybe you are. Have a seat.

The woman took a step, hesitated.

I'm not dangerous.

I heard you were. That's the only reason I came.

Lamb extended an arm toward one of the chairs opposite him, inviting her once more to sit. His clients often came to him this way. Though he had never been indicted for anything his name had been in the *Courier–Journal* more than once and his reputation was one most men in his business would not have wanted though it brought in clients.

It made his life difficult. He had nearly lost his license half a dozen times. He was not a rich man, some months he ate ramen, and he needed the money that his reputation brought him. What he didn't need was the headache. A simple adultery case would have been nice from time to time. Sitting in his car outside motels. Snapping post-coital photos. Delivering them. Click-click and done. Sorry your marriage is dissolving; make the check payable to Damien Lamb.

Yet he was who he was; he was *what* he was.

The woman walked to the chair and sat down. She set her orange doctor's-bag-style purse on her lap and held it like a pet dog. She tapped her right index finger nervously on the purse's gold latch several times before clicking it open and pulling out an unopened soft pack of Marlboro Reds. She knocked the cigarettes against her left wrist, removed the cellophane, peeled away a square of foil.

Lamb had become good at recognizing quality in clothes and other products – he liked to know when real money was walking through his door; it affected his price – and though the woman had the front of the purse turned toward her, he recognized it as Prada. It had likely cost her, or the person who bought it for her, somewhere in the neighborhood of three thousand dollars.

Do you mind if I smoke?

I don't.

Then I will.

She tapped several cigarettes out the top of the pack, selected one with narrow her bird-bone fingers, and drew it out the rest of the way before putting it between her lips. She lighted it with a black Chinese lacquer and gold lighter. Possibly S. T. Dupont. If so it'd cost a grand, at least half that even if she'd picked it up from a pawn shop. The woman took a deep drag. Her hand was shaking. When she pulled the cigarette away from her mouth the filter was stained wine-red with lipstick. Tom Ford's Black Orchid, perhaps. A hundred and thirty dollars. She exhaled with a heavy sigh.

Lamb pushed a glass ashtray across his desk. It was orange and hand-blown and had once belonged to his father, one of the few things he kept around that reminded him of the man he had hated for so many years but now missed. He missed the relationship they'd never had, in any case. Adulthood had brought an understanding of the man with it, and understanding the man, he could forgive him the things he'd done when Lamb was a boy. The bottom of the ashtray was covered already in a thin film of ash, and two butts lay in it like dead soldiers, the end of one stained pink while the other butt was his, a crushed blue camel printed on its paper just above the red line that verged the filter.

How long has your daughter been missing?

She's been gone three months.

Police have any leads?

The woman made no response for some time. Then slowly she shook her head. Her large brown eyes, however, were dancing with something like guilt – they sparkled with it – and though she maintained eye contact her pale cheeks turned blotchy with blood.

I don't work with people who lie to me.

The police can't help me.

Why not?

She's seventeen years old and they say she isn't being held against her will.

Then you know where she is?

The woman nodded.

If you know where she is and she isn't being held against her will—

She *is* being held against her will.

You're certain of this?

As certain as a mother can be.

Have you talked to her?

They won't let me.

Who are they?

The people who run the church.

Enough with the obfuscation.

What?

What church?

The woman hesitated a moment. She knew, he thought, that he would not like the answer though he had no idea what the answer might be. Finally she spoke:

She's with the Children of God.

Lamb pinched the bridge of his nose with index finger and thumb. After a moment he pulled a fifth of Pappy Van Winkle from his bottom right desk drawer. Poured himself three fingers of barrel-stained liquor, set the bottle down on his desktop, took a sip before looking down at the liquid in his glass. He inhaled its heavy scent and felt pain behind his left eye, a pulsating throb that beat with his heart. He blinked and a single tear ran down his left cheek. The pain would probably become a migraine within the hour and just the thought made him wish he had not left his Topamax on the nightstand at home. Instead he would have to settle for a line of Adderall and a few Percocet and those only after he had managed to get this woman out of his office. But he couldn't rush her away because he needed the work, needed the money, and he thought she had plenty.

The police paid a visit?

They did. She told them she was fine, but I know she did it with Father sitting beside her, and nothing anyone says with Father sitting over them can be taken for truth. She'd have told them whatever he wanted her to. She'd have told them she killed Lincoln.

They know who killed Lincoln.

That wasn't my point.

You could have said Kennedy.

They know who killed him too.

If you believe that bullshit. How'd she get involved with them?

My husband.

Your husband is involved with them?

The woman nodded.

In what capacity?

How much do you know about the Children of God?

I know they have a compound in southern Kentucky. I know they deal heroin in order to fund themselves and have dealers in Louisville and Lexington and Frankfort, to name but a few cities out of which they operate. He cleared his throat. I know they're dangerous.

Which is why I'm here talking to you.

But you still haven't told me how your husband is involved with them.

His name is Rhett Mosley. Do you know enough that that answers your question?

Rather than respond, Lamb finished the rest of his bourbon in a single draught, set his glass down on his desk, poured himself another three fingers, and drank that as well. His throat was on fire and he felt a rush of heartburn which he swallowed away – he wished he could eat some chalk tablets but had none here – but he felt a little better as well. Then, after a moment's consideration, he reached into his shirt pocket and fingered two pills that lay at the bottom of it amongst the lint. He decided not to wait after all. He removed one of the Percocet and placed it on his tongue and dry swallowed. He might not be able to do his line, but he could at least start some medicine working on his headache, which was worsening by the minute.

I'll take that as a yes. Are you going to help me?

I haven't decided yet.

What can I do to sway you?

You're about to ash on my floor.

She looked down at her cigarette, flicked the ash into the glass ashtray. Then she leaned forward and looked at Lamb with her nervous brown eyes.

Tell me what I can do to sway you. I'll do anything you want. Anything at all.

I only work for money, lady, and I haven't decided this is worth it.

I could be good to you.

And I could drive over to one of the strip clubs near the airport and get a piece of ass for less than two hundred dollars. But I'd rather keep the money.

I can tell you how to get more money than you could spend in a lifetime.

Lamb poured himself a third glass of bourbon, swirled the liquid, took a sip.

You don't believe me.

I can read people. It's why I'm good at what I do.

Then you should know I'm telling the truth.

I do know it. That's what I find unsettling.

You don't like money?

Everybody likes money, lady, that's why there's no easy way to come by it. A man has to work awful hard to get to a place where he's comfortable. The result of that is that folks who have money, those who've worked to acquire it, they tend to be reluctant to give it up. They tend to work hard to *keep* it. So you telling me there's money involved don't exactly calm my boiling stomach. I need an antacid.

She reached into her purse and removed a roll of Tums, which she handed to him across the desk. He peeled the foil away, pulled two off the roll, handed the remaining antacids back across the desk.

Lamb chewed his tablets. Thank you.

You're welcome. But I didn't say there was money involved.

You said you can tell me where to get money.

I can.

Implying you don't already have it.

The woman looked away from Lamb. She tried to take a drag from her cigarette, but it was already burned down to the filter. She looked at it with something like contempt and then butted it out. She pulled a second from her pack, lighted it, and finally got what she'd been wanting. She took a deep drag, exhaled through her nostrils.

You're not wrong, she said finally. When I left I took some with me, but most of it is gone now. Living isn't cheap.

Lamb nodded toward the purse. Not living how you live anyway.

It isn't what you think.

What do I think?

The money is as much mine as it is his.

You know what they say about possession.

Are you telling me you aren't interested?

I'm interested. What I'm not is committed.

How can I get you committed?

By telling me the truth.

About what?

Is Rhett Mosley her father?

Whose?

Your daughter's.

A long pause. A drag from her cigarette. No.

What is your involvement with the Children of God?

I left the church six months ago.

You left Rhett Mosley six months ago.

She nodded. Left and took my daughter with me.

As well as some money.

It was as much mine—

I'm not concerned with that. Your daughter went back.

She was taken back.

How deeply were you involved before you got out?

She didn't answer for a very long time, simply sat in her chair looking at Lamb and smoking her cigarette. Drag after drag she smoked without taking her eyes off him. He looked back through the cloud of smoke, through the silence, and waited. He was capable of great patience when patience was called for, and he felt it was called for now. She was working herself up to something. Whatever she had to say she needed first to build the courage. He was willing to give her as much time as she needed.

I was lost when I joined his church, she said finally. My father – my real father – was not a good man. He did things to me and my sister. He did things fathers should never do to their little girls. My mother called me a liar when I told her. Called me a liar but also called me a slut. Not because I was lying – or even because she thought I was lying – but because she was jealous of me. She blamed me and she hit me. After that I told no one. But when I was sixteen I finally found the courage to run away. I tried to get my younger sister to come with me but she wouldn't, she was afraid to, so I went alone. I had a little money but you never hold on to a little money. Only people with a lot of money can turn it into more money. I was homeless. I slept in an abandoned building on 28th Street. I did things to get by that I'm still ashamed of. Then one day a girl told me about a place where I could have a bed and three meals a day. An actual bed. She was blonde and pretty, maybe a year or two younger than I was. She said her name was Eunice. She made me feel safe. I agreed to go with her and she walked me to a van. I got into the back. Several other girls were already sitting there in silence. I could tell they were homeless too. The grime on their hands gave them away, and the smell of their unwashed bodies. Street whores have a scent. Did you know that? They smell of unwashed sweat and seawater. Several of them were street whores. Like me. We sat in silence, looking at each other. I could tell we were all questioning our decision. But the promise of a bed and regular meals was too much for any of us. There was a boy behind the wheel, maybe fifteen or sixteen. He started the engine. Eunice looked back at us from the front passenger seat and told us that everything would be better soon. I believed her. We all did. That's why we were there. She had such kind eyes, such a pretty smile. But it took an hour and a half to get to the compound and the stink of fear began to fill the van. We were being taken away from everything we knew, awful as it was, taken to a place where anything might happen. The emptiness outside the van windows was frightening, the complete lack of civilization. Dense woods surrounded us. We could easily have been made to disappear and no one would have missed any of us. Eventually, though, we arrived at a metal gate. The boy behind the wheel honked his horn. Someone pulled the gate open and we rolled up a dirt driveway. It felt like it was at least a quarter-mile long, that driveway, and we rolled along so slowly, moving past a small graveyard and grazing animals and feed sheds and barns. Finally the van stopped for good.

The blonde girl, Eunice, looked over her shoulder for the last time and smiled at us. She told us we were home now. She told us we would meet Father soon, but first we needed to get cleaned up. God's children needed to be cleansed of their filth before they were brought before him. As if he were a deity or a king. We were taken to a large group of cabins near the back of the property – it was like a small neighborhood – and given rooms with beds, two girls to a room, four girls to a cabin. We were given white cotton dresses and white cotton panties and white cotton night-gowns. We were given home-made bars of soap that smelled of lavender and told to wash. Each cabin had its own shower. After we were clean, Eunice walked us to a house with a big farm table in the kitchen. We were given rice and beans and buttermilk biscuits and cherry Kool-Aid. It was the best meal I'd ever eaten. It might still be the best meal I've ever eaten. For three days prior to that the only thing I'd consumed was a candy bar I stole from a Thornton's. We were wiping the last of the food from our plates with our biscuits when Father arrived.

Look at these beautiful children of God, he said.

We all turned to look toward the source of his voice. It was deep and musical and commanded your attention. He stood in the doorway to the kitchen but seemed somehow to fill the entire room with his presence. His eyes were bright with life and so kind you wanted to crawl into his arms and never come out. You knew he could protect you from the devil himself. He seemed somehow to be the opposite of everything I'd ever learned about men, but there was nothing effeminate about him either. I can honestly say I fell in love with him the moment I saw him, and I wasn't the only one.

He walked to the head of the table and sat down with us.

Welcome to my home, he said. Welcome to my table. It is wonderful to be sitting here with you. You are all so beautiful with your freshly scrubbed faces and your clean white clothes. All God's children are beautiful once they've been washed of the filth with which this world has covered them. You have been washed, and so you are beautiful, and as long as you stay clean you will remain beautiful, and you will have a home here. I promise you that. You are under my protection now, which means you are under God's protection, and I will love you for as long as you accept that love. My heart overflows with it. I see you've eaten. You must have been very hungry, which I do understand – these human bodies of ours are frail things with needs that cannot be denied – but you will never again break bread without first bowing your heads with me and thanking the Lord for the meal you are about to receive. If you are to accept God's love you must express your gratitude for that love, and before you can accept my love and be welcome here you *must* accept God's love. Do we understand each other?

We all nodded our understanding.

I think you will find this a wonderful and welcoming

home, he said. There are rules, of course, and you must all work to earn your keep – crops must be harvested, alpacas sheared, soap made – but I think you'll find the rules fair and the work rewarding. You will learn more about all of this tomorrow, as well as pay a visit the medical building to receive a physical and treatment for any ailment with which you might have been afflicted while out on the streets. I just wanted to take a moment to personally welcome you to your new home.

Until we meet again, children.

He got to his feet, turned, and walked out of the room.

Later that night, while in bed, I woke to Eunice shaking me gently and whispering for me to get up, get out of bed, sweetie.

What is it?

Father wants to see you in his chambers.

Are you sure? I couldn't believe that he would know who I was much less want to see me.

She nodded and told me to hurry up.

We tiptoed out of the bedroom, through a small living area, and out into the night. I can still remember how the moon hung in the sky. My little sister used to say it looked like God's smile, that bright white crescent up there in the darkness. To me it looked like a sharp bone. Or a scythe. I thought of her as we walked along a pathway, past several other cabins, then across a field of grass and a garden to Father's house. I thought of her and wished she was with me. I wondered what she was doing. I wondered if Dad was lying in bed beside her, doing the things to her he had once done to me. Was she muffling her cry by putting her face into her My Little Pony pillowcase? I pushed the thoughts away. I didn't want to think them. The wind was warm and the grass felt cool under my feet and I felt that everything was going to be okay for me – but I wanted my sister to be there more than I'd ever wanted anything.

She killed herself two years later, when she was only fifteen. She slit her wrists with one of my dad's safety razors and I wasn't there to stop it. I wasn't there to protect her. I don't even want to know what those two years were like. Having to take all of our father's abuse. Our mother hostile to her because somehow it was her fault.

The woman stopped talking for a moment and looked at her cigarette. She took a drag and then held the cigarette in front of her face and stared at the orange ember glowing at the end of it. She blew on the ember and it brightened; she stopped blowing and it dimmed. After a while she looked once more at Lamb.

The house stood tall in the night, she said, its dimly glowing windows the only light for miles. We walked up the steps to the porch and then across the porch to the front door. Eunice pushed the door open and we stepped inside. She led me through the foyer, down a hallway, to a white door. The door was cracked. It was dark on the other side but for a faint flickering light which turned out to be a candle.

Go in. Eunice motioned toward the white door. I looked

from her to the flickering light in the room. I took a step forward, putting my hand out to push the door aside. It slid across the carpet, making an angel wing.

Look at this beautiful child of God come to offer me salve. Don't think that I am not grateful for your company.

The guttering candle on a nightstand. The flame dancing as it threatened to go out.

I looked from it to the man sitting across from me. Father was in a leather chair in the corner. He was naked. The candlelight made his eyes seem to sparkle. It also illuminated his pale white belly and his skinny legs and the flaccid thing between them which lay across his left thigh like a chicken neck. His pubic hair was thick and graying.

How old are you, girl?

Sixteen.

I have not known sixteen for thirty, but even at my age I am a child. We are all children in the eyes of God. What is forty-six years when compared to an eternity? What is a hundred years? What could any of us say that would seem anything but childish rubbish to the entity that created us all? God is a philosopher while we speak in nursery rhymes. What is your name, girl? Tell me.

Naomi.

Have you been with men before, Naomi?

I wanted to lie. I knew what he wanted to hear, but something about him and the way he was looking at me made it impossible. I nodded.

His face went hard and angry with frightening suddenness. Then yours is the name of a cunt, he said, and it no longer suits you. You have been washed clean of your past transgressions, and so you have been washed clean of your name. I will call you Abigail. His face softened. Does that name please you?

I nodded again. If the name pleased him, it pleased me.

Disrobe, Abigail, so that we might be as innocent as the first man and woman.

I thought of my dad coming into my bedroom when I was thirteen. I thought of the way he'd lie in bed beside me. I thought of the pain and the way he'd stroke my hair and tell me it was okay even while he made certain that it wasn't.

It's okay, sweetheart, don't cry. Daddy loves you so much.

I thought of those things while I pulled off my nightgown and dropped it to the floor.

I wondered if he would see the cigarette-burn scars on my breasts. I wondered if he would find the fact that I'd been used unattractive.

He spoke of purity but I felt dirty inside.

You are a beautiful girl, Abigail, and these human bodies of ours have needs that cannot be denied. You're old enough to realize that, aren't you?

Yes, sir.

Yes, *Father*.

Yes, Father.

That's a good girl, Abigail. Now come to me.

I went to him and he took me and when it was over he told me to get dressed and to leave his house, and I did, but he called me back the next night, and the night after that. By the end of the week I was one of the few girls who got to live in the house with him. There are men and boys in the compound, of course, but none of them get to live in Father's house. Not even Elijah, who has been with Father longer than anyone. They sleep separately from the women and girls as well, even if they're married. They are allowed nudity only under Father's direct supervision. He must be certain that they remain clean in their nudity. Many of the children born of the wives on the compound belong to Father. Fifteen or sixteen of them live there still.

She paused to take yet another drag from her cigarette.

For the next eighteen years I lived in Father's house. There were others, of course, but they came and went while I remained. He grew tired of the others, but never of me. He wouldn't admit it, but I knew he was as much mine as I was his. If it weren't for Lily I would be there with him still, despite the fact I lost faith long ago – if I ever actually had any. I'm not sure, to be honest. I may have only wanted to believe because I loved him – or thought I did.

Lamb sipped his bourbon and looked across the desk. His headache was beginning to subside. He picked up his pack of Camel Filters from his desk, lighted one, inhaled. He watched a ribbon of smoke twist toward his nicotine-stained ceiling.

You're Abigail Mosley.

I heard you were smart.

Lily is your daughter.

She is.

Who is the father if it isn't Rhett Mosley?

Abigail looked down at her lap. She remained silent. Lamb could see shame on her face.

Is Lily also your father's daughter – is she your sister as well as your child? That seems to be the timeline if I'm adding it up right.

Softly: Yes.

Rhett Mosley has taken her into his bed.

He raised her as his daughter and did to her what my dad did to me. I should have known it was coming before it happened. I should have recognized that look in his eyes. I'd seen it before, when I was a girl. I should have seen it on her, too, after it happened the first time. But I didn't. For years it went on and I was blind to it. I can't forgive myself for that, and I can't forgive him. She was beautiful and she had a chance. But after what he did to her, after what he did to her—

She shook her head. There was great sorrow in her eyes.

He did the same thing to you.

I was broken before he laid a hand on me. Lily had a chance.

Lamb nodded his understanding, and he felt something like pity for her – for her and her daughter – but one cannot allow emotions to get in the way of a job. Pity will neither put food on the table nor pay the electric bill.

Tell me more about the money.

It used to be under one of the toolsheds in the armory. Now he keeps it in an upstairs bedroom. He said once that he moved it for safety reasons, but it's less safe now than it was before. The truth is, he needs the money close to him. He says he worships God but what he really worships is the dollar.

Where in the bedroom?

It isn't hidden. It couldn't be.

Tell me this. Do you want your daughter back or do you want the money?

I want my daughter back. I'm telling you about the money as incentive. I don't care if I never see a dime of it.

Okay, Lamb said.

Okay?

I'll get you your daughter back.

Do you mean that?

I do.

A bigail pushed through the fingerprinted glass door of the private detective's office and out into the late spring afternoon, the sun's fading light splashing bright across her smooth, pale face. The clouds' undersides were lighted pink and orange by the sinking sun, which was low in the sky, sitting directly behind the cityscape. She slipped a pair of Burberry sunglasses onto her nose, shading her eyes, walked to the used BMW she had purchased for cash after fleeing the compound, and fell into the leather seat behind the wheel. She started the engine, cracked her window, and then lighted a cigarette and closed her eyes. She tried to picture her daughter's face on the inside of her shuttered lids but the only thing she saw there were the pallets of shrink-wrapped money Rhett had locked away in that spare bedroom on the second floor of his house, so much cash that the floors seemed to sag beneath the weight of it.

Most of what she had told the private detective had been truth. She was smart enough to know that Lamb would have seen through her if she had lied more than was necessary – that he might see through her, anyway, though it so happened that he had not (she believed he had not, in any case) – so she Trojan-horsed her lies, buried them beneath piles of hard truth, sneaked them into his brain under a heap of sad facts, to which detectives, to which decent men in general, were never immune.

It had worked.

She wanted her daughter back and was worried about the girl, these were facts, but she also resented her and had in her heart some hatred for the girl; she had fucked a man she had no right to fuck and in so doing had ruined what had been the best life Abigail had ever known. But that wasn't the right way to look at it. The girl had fucked nobody; she had *been* fucked. So it made no sense to blame her for what had happened and what was happening still. She knew this. She knew she was experiencing the same emotions for which she had resented her own mother. It made her feel ugly inside. Yet Abigail couldn't help but place some of the blame on the girl. If her daughter were neither pretty nor easily manipulated, if her daughter did not need so desperately to feel loved, to feel that human connection, even if it was a negative connection, the life they had both been living six months ago might well be the life they were living today.

But everything had changed. They had left with nearly

$150,000, but the money was quickly dwindling, even without a second mouth to feed. The people she had known all her life, her closest friends, she could know no more. The house she lived in for eighteen years had been traded in for a small apartment with a single small bedroom, a small fridge, and a two-burner stove.

Abigail resented her daughter for causing those things to happen – resented her and hated her, too, a little bit.

Because of those things and others her daughter was not, in reality, despite what she had said, her top priority. The money was. Without it her life on the outside was over. Yet men were protective of women and girls. They responded to sad stories.

If she had gone to Lamb about the money alone he might have bit hard on that green hook, he might have agreed to help her steal it for a cut – twenty percent or forty – but he might also have decided to keep his distance. He might have decided it wasn't worth the risk. Despite his reputation he did not strike her as either reckless or stupid. He was clearly a little bit crazy – you could see madness in his eyes even when he sat expressionless; it was deep below the surface yet visible – but his insanity was tempered, she thought, by intelligence. He was not a stupid man, merely a damaged one, one who might do anything to prove to himself that he was worthy of the air he breathed. Stealing money would prove only that he was weak and greedy, which was something she believed he needed to prove to himself not at all. If the money were secondary to saving the life of a young woman, however, if she could convince him that her motive for coming to him was her daughter rather than the money, was her daughter alone, then that would make him vulnerable to her manipulations. It would also make him vulnerable to his own manipulations. He could tell himself that what he was doing was a good thing. He could pretend his own greed had nothing whatever to do with his decisions.

If you could get a man to lie to himself, it saved you the trouble of telling the lie yourself.

She wanted that money and she needed Lamb to get it for her. Let him believe he was doing a different job altogether, it would motivate him, but in the end that money was hers. She had earned it. For eighteen years she had allowed Rhett Mosley to fuck her even though for fifteen of those at least she had hated him. For eighteen years she had sucked his cock and swallowed his come and listened to the insanity that left his mouth more foul than the shit he pushed out the other end. She had earned every penny and she would have it – even if it meant double-crossing the man who helped her.

She put her car into gear and backed out of her parking spot.

Soon she was rolling along Poplar Level Road, heading toward an early Victorian mansion in Old Louisville that had been converted into apartments in the middle of the last decade. She drove up to Mary Street, onto which she made a left, then she made another left onto 3rd Street, which she took down to Central Park, which bordered the right side of the road. The west side of the road, since she was now heading south. She stopped at the curb, killed the engine, put on the parking brake, got out of her car. She walked across the small lawn – Kentucky bluegrass growing long and thick beneath her feet – to the building's thick wooden front door.

She thought of the three thousand dollars she had left in her underwear drawer, three grand to hold her entire life together. When it was gone there would be nothing else, unless the private detective came through, and she thought he would, was almost certain he would, but even so the hold she had on her new life felt very tenuous indeed. For months her chest had felt as though it had a great weight pressing down upon it. The money was dwindling and if something weren't done soon she might have to go back to the compound, and once there the man she had married but now despised would certainly force upon her a bitter punishment before accepting her back again. If he accepted her at all.

But now she had transferred the weight of all that to someone else. It helped her to feel better. Something would be done and if the right things were done she could see everything working out.

Lamb would get both her daughter and the money out of the compound. How he did that mattered not at all to her so long as they both made it out safely. He might believe the money belonged to him but it would not. It would be hers. She would make sure of that. Lamb would take care of everything and then she would take care of Lamb, and she had no doubts about her ability *to* take care of him. Men like Lamb were merely tools. Hammers you used to smash down a few nails before tossing them aside.

She walked up three flights of stairs. At the top of the third flight, at the back of a small landing, stood her front door, dark mahogany made almost black with age. She keyed open the front door and stepped into her three-room apartment. She closed the door behind her and twisted the deadbolt. She looked around and for a moment felt weight return to her chest. If the private detective failed she would lose even this. She would be left with nothing at all. Her daughter would be gone. The money would be gone. Her friends would be gone. She would be alone in the world with nothing. Mosley might take her back but even that thought filled her with dread.

Her entire future was in the hands of a man she knew only by reputation.

The uncertainty made her feel as she had when she was sixteen, when she had packed some clothes and a small amount of money into her book bag and sneaked out the bedroom window and into the night, leaving her parents and her little sister behind in that little shotgun house in Germantown, leaving everything she had ever known behind. It was difficult to walk away from your life even when your life was miserable; stepping into the unknown was frightening, stepping into the darkness beyond the flashlight of what you knew.

But sometimes lives needed a reboot. You either started over or the virus that was your current life would infect your soul and end up killing you. Her soul had suffered enough damage.

So she was starting over once more.

But she would not do it as she had the first time. She would not sleep in abandoned buildings and suck the sweaty cocks of men in cars for fifty dollars, feeling them thrust into the back of her throat only seconds before they zipped up and drove home to their unknowing wives. She needed money and would have it but was no longer willing to sell herself in order to make that happen. That only caused her to feel cheap and dirty and useless. She also needed her daughter out of that place, if only so that she'd be able to live with herself. She had abandoned her sister and her sister had ended up killing herself. It had left a great hole in her heart and infected her with constant guilt. She would not leave her daughter to the same fate as she had left her sister.

She *could* not.

She walked to an end table and picked up a picture of Lily. She looked at it for a long time and felt a strange juxtaposition of contradictory emotions. Part of the reason she hated Lily was that the girl was so much like her and she hated herself, and part of the reason she loved her was that the girl was purer and held potential for goodness that

Abigail herself had lost long ago if she'd ever had it. Despite the circumstances by which the girl had been conceived she was better than Abigail had ever been, which was probably the reason Rhett had been attracted to her in the first place; he was the sort of man who loved the purity of clean white snow so much that he could not help but trudge all over it in order that he might feel close to that purity.

She set down the picture and walked to her refrigerator and pulled out a bottle of Red Stripe. She opened the beer and took a swallow. There was a time when she had tried to believe in God and His goodness and believe too that Rhett Mosley was the voice of that goodness but she had learned the hard way that Rhett was not only not the voice of God on earth but that, if there was a devil, he might well be his voice or the beast himself.

The private detective had to come through for her or all was lost. She believed that he would but standing there over her small refrigerator with a beer in her hand she decided that she needed to take measures to ensure the fact.

She would pay him a visit tonight and once there would do whatever was necessary to get him fully invested in her cause, and she believed she knew exactly what was necessary.

Men were all the same, and they responded best to one thing.

L amb watched the woman leave. The door swung shut behind her and the evening light slanted in through its smudged glass. Dust motes floated in the air. He turned to the empty chair sitting across from him and wondered why he'd agreed to get the woman her daughter back, why he'd agreed to get involved at all, when he knew that people who got in the way of the Children of God had a bad habit of getting dead, and usually in grisly fashion.

Rhett Mosley tended toward closed-coffin murders.

Some of it was that Lamb simply needed money – he had good periods and bad, the money ebbed and flowed, and this had been a bad three months – but he had turned down jobs before when he needed money, sometimes they simply weren't worth the hassle, so he knew that that wasn't all of it. Perhaps not even most of it. The fact was he was doing the job primarily for the worst reason possible. He felt sorry for the woman sitting across from him and wanted to help her. He tried not to take such jobs. He did not like to get emotionally involved in his work. But sometimes it couldn't be avoided.

Yet he did not think that was the whole story either. There was something else in him that told him to take this job, some soft voice whispering from the darkest corner of his mind, and he had no idea why it had spoken.

Well, fuck it.

He pulled open the top drawer of his desk and with a business card scraped up the blue powder from his crushed pills. He put it on his desktop and cut a line before tapping the dust off the business card and setting it aside. He picked up a rolled dollar bill, one end of which was already crusted with snot and traces of powder. He used the rolled bill to snort his line. He swallowed, tasting the bitter powder as it dripped onto the back of his tongue. He took a drink of bourbon to wash away the taste. He lighted a cigarette, inhaled deeply, and exhaled through his nostrils, watching as the smoke rose toward the ceiling.

It didn't matter why he'd agreed to do it. He'd agreed to do it. All that was left now was to either get it done or fail to get it done, and he was a man who got things done for a living. He might be a failure in life but he was good at his job.

He was a private investigator, of course, but only nominally. The quirks of his personality as well as his reputation had made him something else altogether.

Private investigators could do much of their work in office, using telephones and computers to retrieve information. The work that couldn't be done in that fashion could still be managed from the safety of a vehicle with tinted windows. You parked your car, sat in the passenger seat so that it looked as though you were waiting for someone, and observed what needed observing. You took pictures and informed but you did not get involved, and your lack of involvement meant there was a distance that made the work, usually, fairly safe.

Lamb wasn't sure there was a name for what he did, but it rarely involved safety or distance. It rarely involved working strictly within the confines of the law. Only occasionally did it involve any kind of investigation and when it did the investigation merely preceded his real work, which tended to be messy.

He looked at his watch. It was ten to six. He could have gone home to watch television if he hadn't just snorted amphetamines. He supposed he still could, but he was beginning to feel sweaty and antsy and wanted to do something both monotonous and physical.

He got to his feet, grabbed his suit coat from the back of his chair, walked to the door and then through it. Once he was on the other side he locked it.

A moment later he was in his car.

It didn't even feel as though he'd gotten to his car. He was just there. That was how speed affected him. He'd think to do something and then that something would be done, and there would seem to be no interval between those two events, between thought and goal.

He started his engine and put the car into gear; he parked his car at his destination.

He stepped out of his vehicle, grabbed a pack of cigarettes from his breast pocket. Pulled a cigarette from the pack and tried to stick it between his lips, realizing only then that he was already smoking a cigarette. He pulled it from his mouth and looked at it perplexedly, then took a drag, replaced the old cigarette with the new, and lighted the new with the butt of the old before throwing the butt to the asphalt.

He stepped out the butt as he walked to the back of his car and once there popped the trunk. From within he pulled a baseball bat and a plastic batting helmet. He kept them there for just such occasions. He loosened his tie as he walked toward the cages.

Soon he was swinging. It felt good to connect. He felt focused but loose. For a time he thought about nothing but what he was doing. He was a machine. His life ceased to matter. His lonely house ceased to matter, as did the fact that after this he'd be spending his evening there. The TV dinners stacked in his freezer, the bottle of bourbon on his coffee table, the flickering television flashing frames on the wall, the empty space on the bed next to him: none of those things mattered while he was in the cage.

Nor did his history matter, neither as a lover nor as a soldier. So women had broken him while he had broken other men. Everyone was broken eventually and there was no need to dwell on the fact. You either managed to sweep up the pieces and glue your-self back together or you didn't. It was as simple as that.

The ball provided a focal point and created within him a tunnel vision he liked very much. When he was straight he felt tired and his mind felt scattered. He imagined a truck roaring down the interstate spilling its contents all over the road and those contents shattering as they hit asphalt. This was different. This was what he needed.

A ball flew toward him. He swung, connected – felt the force of the impact ride its way up the bat, into his hands, and up his arms to his shoulders – and watched it fly.

Triple, he said.

Another ball flew at him.

Double.

Another.

Foul tip.

That was followed by a home run which was followed by yet another double.

He found a rhythm he liked very much and he let himself get lost in it. He thought about nothing at all but those balls flying toward him at sixty miles per hour. For a time. He didn't even notice when the pickup truck pulled in and parked next to his old Mercedes; he didn't notice when the four drunken men got out of it, laughing and swigging from a brown-bagged bottle. He simply swung and swung and swung until his shoulders ached, until his right hand was singing with pain, and even then he continued, barely noticing his discomfort.

When he was much younger he had come close to playing in the majors. He played in the minors for two seasons, and during his last season there was talk of the Astros purchasing his contract. But that was eighteen years ago now and still no one knew his name.

He'd been so certain that he was bound for greatness. He was going to be something. He was going to be some*body*. He would make a name for himself, put his mark on this earth. Everything his father had told him would be proven wrong.

But in his penultimate game, as he was stealing home, he shattered his kneecap. It broke into six pieces. The doctors wired it back together but he was never the same. He could still hit, but he couldn't run anymore, and running had been what set him apart. He could steal bases like nobody else. He could turn a single into a triple almost any time he put his mind to it. Before the accident he could. But that had been taken from him. He played one more game in the minors, knew it was over for him, and hung up his jock for good. You'd never catch the dream you were chasing if your knee had been shattered. It would forever outrun you.

He swung and made contact.

Double.

Well, life was full of disappointments. Life was, when boiled down to the bone, nothing but a series of disillusionments. Almost everything you believed as a child – even as a young man – turned out to be a lie. God was not good. Justice was a fable. And almost nobody ended up being the person they'd once believed they would become. The person you were going to be eventually disappeared in order that the person you were could stand in his place, and then, finally, you looked back at the person you once had been, and saw that you hadn't been Ty Cobb. You'd been a gumshoe with worn-out soles and a soul of tin.

So after getting his heart broken by a girl who had said she would never hurt him but love him forever, and after a stint in the army during which he visited more than one desert nation, he was back in Louisville where he'd grown up. He'd been back for twelve years and often ran into people he had gone to high school with while buying groceries at the Highlands Kroger or booze from Gordo at Old Town Wine and Spirits, he ran into people he had told himself he was better than, and it felt as though he had never left. It had been a bitter realization to discover he wasn't better than anybody. There would be no great achievements. There would be no better places. This was it. This was his home. This was the place that produced him and the place he belonged.

He would die here and probably he would die alone.

Women did not tend to stay with ill-tempered alcoholic pill heads who punched holes in walls when they got angry.

He swung and missed.

Fuck.

He slammed his bat against the ground and it split in two, the crack running up the handle and slicing his palm in the process. Usually the cages provided focus. Usually he thought of nothing but what he was doing. Usually he had tunnel vision.

He didn't know why things were different tonight.

Sometimes the brain grabbed onto something and wouldn't let it go. Sometimes the brain was a vicious dog that tore only at itself.

He opened his right hand and looked at the bleeding gash in his palm. He hissed and shook his hand and cursed again. Blood flew from his shaking hand and spattered against the ground and onto his shirt.

It's just the cages, man, don't let it get to you.

He looked toward the men two spots down. One was swinging away while the other three watched. They were young, in their twenties, and appeared to be in good shape. They appeared also to be in good humor. He doubted very much that anyone was trying to start trouble. The words were meant to be friendly. But he didn't want to hear them.

Mind your fuckin business.

What? This from a large blond fellow in a white T-shirt and cargo shorts.

You sure you didn't hear me?

No, why don't you repeat yourself?

I said you should mind your fuckin business.

The man was about three inches taller than Lamb and twenty pounds heavier, but Lamb had taken men his size and greater. He eyed the man, daring him to start something.

You lookin to get your ass kicked?

Lamb stepped from his cage, still holding half a bat in

his left fist. His right, meanwhile, steadily dripped great splashes of blood onto the asphalt.

You know, he said, I think I might be. In fact, it could be just what I need. The cages aren't doin it for me tonight.

You think I won't?

I think you can't.

Look, man, said a squirrely guy in a red T-shirt and cut-off shorts, we aren't looking for trouble. We're just here to hit some balls. Let's drop this shit.

If your friend had kept his cunt mouth shut there wouldn't be anything *to* drop.

He didn't mean nothin by it.

Don't speak for me, Jeremy. This motherfucker wants trouble, he's got it.

Trouble is just what I want.

You sure about that?

I'm fuckin positive.

Then call me a cunt again.

I didn't call you a cunt. I said your mouth looks like a cunt.

His heart was beating fast in his chest. His stomach was in a knot. But this was exactly what he wanted. There was a tight coil of violence within him and it wanted release. It *needed* release. It didn't matter that these kids had done nothing to provoke him. It didn't matter that there were four of them. Some awful part of him demanded this happen.

The blond took a step toward him.

Let it go, the squirrely one said.

He's askin for trouble.

I just want to hit some balls, man.

Then hit your fuckin balls and stay out of it, Jeremy. I don't need your help to take this old man.

Let him kick the guy's ass, said the one in the cage. He's askin for it.

That's right, Lamb said, that's just what I'm doing.

The fuck is wrong with you, the squirrely one said; you got some kind of death wish or something?

Lamb laughed. Who doesn't?

Kick his ass, man.

That's right, kick my ass.

Okay, old man, you got this coming.

The blond walked toward him. Lamb was glad of it. He'd been afraid they'd be talking all night. Now it looked as though something might actually happen. He tossed his stick. It hit the ground and settled with a rattle. The man stopped just out of arm's reach and tried to stare Lamb down. Lamb looked back, unflinching. The man blinked.

Take one more step, Lamb said.

The man took his step.

Lamb sent his fist straight at the guy's face. It hit the nose and he felt the nose bend and then snap. The man stumbled back two steps, blood gushing down his face, and then he fell to a sitting position, his teeth clacking together as he did.

Call me old man again.

Shit.

Goddamn it.

Let's go.

Lamb looked up to see the other three coming toward him.

You stupid fuck.

Then they were on him. He hit the squirrely guy next, sending his fist into the throat. The guy gasped for breath and staggered backwards. But that was the last punch he threw. The other two were on him, punching him in the gut and the back of the head, in the kidneys and the ribs, and he could no longer orient himself. Soon all four were on him, kicking and punching. He hit the ground and they continued, kicking, spitting on him, cursing at him, and the next thing he knew he was alone, lying on the ground, bleeding.

It was silent.

He spit a mouthful of blood and saliva onto the asphalt and was glad to see there were no pieces of teeth in the mix. He laughed.

It was all clear to him now, if it hadn't been before. He knew exactly why he'd agreed to get that woman her daughter back.

He pushed himself up to his hands and knees, and after a few pained curses got to his feet. He looked around the quickly darkening night for his batting helmet, found it on the ground about ten feet away, picked it up, and headed toward his car, limping.

After falling in behind the wheel and tossing the helmet onto his passenger seat he lighted a cigarette, inhaled deeply.

Well, he said to himself, that was fun.

Abigail was sitting at her small dining table drinking her third beer and drawing with blue ink on a white sheet of paper. The world outside her window dimmed to black but for the artificial light from street lamps and windows that splashed across the buildings and asphalt below her. She could hear the sound of traffic on 3rd Street three stories below but paid the sound no mind, nor was she anything but subconsciously aware of the barking of the dogs being walked in the park across the street or the sounds of conversation floating up to her from the pedestrians on the sidewalk below. She wasn't even aware of the apartment around her.

In her mind she was in the compound.

She drew what she saw in her mind's eye, paying special attention to the details she thought might prove useful to the private detective, and while she traveled in her mind through the compound – floated across the land like a ghost, wondering if a part of her might really be there, for it was dark and she could smell the damp hay and the animals – she thought of her experiences there, eighteen years of experiences.

She thought of living under the rule of her dictatorial husband but she thought also of sneaking into the woods behind the compound and drinking homemade blackberry wine with her friends. She thought of laughing with them and talking about everyday concerns and how when they were out there beneath the stars she felt almost normal, felt almost that the life she was living was a good one. She thought of giving birth to her daughter there and breast-feeding while sitting on the front porch of the house as the sun shined down on the beautiful land that surrounded them all green and dewy and as full of promise as the baby cradled in her arms. She thought of her brief affair with a young man who disappeared soon after she first had sex with him and though Rhett never said anything more than that the kid must have decided to forsake the Lord and leave them she could tell by the look in his eyes both malevolent and knowing that he was aware of the affair and that he was responsible for said disappearance. She wondered if the young man – the boy: she had been nineteen and he had been sixteen – was buried somewhere on that land. It was almost certain that he was, that with her need to feel some kind of human warmth she had damned him to an unmarked grave and damned his family to never knowing what had become of him, which she thought must be worse than the certainty of death, for with death you could at least feel some sense of an ending.

Part of her felt nostalgic about her life there, yet she never wanted to return.

A knock at the front door drew her attention. She jumped at the sound, took a swallow from her beer, got to her feet. This apartment had been rented under her childhood name, Naomi Allen-Brown, which meant it was unlikely that Rhett had found her – it was unlikely he was even looking for her, having, as he did, a younger version of her at the compound already – but she still felt nervous about answering the door. She was not expecting company.

She walked across the hardwood floor to the door, unlocked it, and pulled it open. Immediately she felt both relief and frustration. The man on the other side was not dangerous but he was someone with whom she didn't have time to deal.

His name was Michael Thompson and he lived in the apartment below hers. He worked at Fifth Third Bank as a teller but tonight was wearing, rather than a suit, a pair of Levi's and a plain white T-shirt. He looked at her with nervous eyes.

I've called several times.

I know. She glanced toward the telephone and the blinking nine that told her of the messages left there. I've been busy.

Last week, feeling lonely and in need of some sort of connection, she had gone to Nachbar hoping to pick up someone with whom she could spend the evening. There was no room in her life at the moment for love but sex could at least offer some sort of temporary relief, could for a time fill that hollow within that seemed to grow larger and more aching the longer you went without the touch of another person. Michael had been there, sitting at a picnic table in the back, smoking a Newport and drinking a Budweiser, which she had judged cruelly, as men who smoked mentholated cigarettes were in her estimation not men at all and Budweiser was merely beer teenagers stole from liquor stores and drank in parking lots. Probably he had his morning coffee with cream and sugar as well.

But he had recognized her and struck up a conversation and it had been easy so she picked him up while letting him believe he was picking her up and they went back to her place and kissed and undressed and she tried to feel something – tried to feel some sort of connection – as she guided him into her, but she felt nothing at all. He spent three minutes rooting around in her like a blind rodent in a burrow and then came pitifully, making whining noises that she tried to ignore, and when she grabbed him by the hips and tried to keep him moving within her, hoping that she might actually climax, he had gone flaccid and pulled out, and his warm come had seeped out of her and spread on the sheets.

Then he lay with his face in her neck, telling her that she was the most incredible woman he had ever met, that he loved her. But she simply wanted him gone. She had been desperately hoping for something that he had not given her, and now, with him in her bed, she was lonelier than ever.

He left the next morning – he had not picked up on her hints that he should leave that night – and she had been avoiding him since.

Too busy for a phone call?

I'm not interested in getting to know you, Michael.

He said nothing but his face grew red. He turned his head and looked down the hallway, she knew not at what.

I'm not interested in getting to know anybody.

I really like you, he said. I thought we had a connection.

We had a one-night stand, Michael.

But it doesn't have to be a one-night stand. It could become more.

It couldn't – it can't.

I don't understand.

You don't have to understand. You just have to know I'm telling the truth. We had a one-night stand and I'm not interested in extending the length of our relationship.

Why are you being such a bitch?

I'm not having this conversation.

She pushed the door shut in his face and locked it. He banged on her door for another five minutes, but she ignored him, and finally he went away.

After the knocking stopped she went back to drawing her map of the compound. But she didn't get lost in it the way she had before. She was thinking about her one-night stand and how she sometimes hated her own desperate need for physical contact. It created situations like the one she had just experienced. Her daughter was the same, which was the reason she was drawing a map of the compound in the first place. She wondered what was wrong with her, but in the end that train of thought would lead her only to a collapsed bridge, and she knew it, so she pushed the question aside.

In another ten minutes she was finished with her drawing. She folded it up and slipped it into her purse, then walked back to the table and finished her beer.

Finally she walked to her front door and pulled it open. Then stepped through and closed the door behind her.

L amb parked his car and stepped from the vehicle. He flicked his butt into a flower garden (he cleaned it out once a week), walked along a steep path to his house, and up four steps to his front door. He unlocked the door, stepped inside, and closed the door behind him. His right hand was now wrapped in an oil-stained white rag he had found on the passenger floorboard. It had turned red with blood and was now drying to brown.

The glass-shaded floor lamp in the corner was on, lighting the living room. A green couch sat against the back wall, a coffee table in front of it. An old Henry F. Miller piano that never stayed in tune – it desperately needed to be restrung – was pushed against the wall to the left of the couch. A few books rested on the piano, mostly nonfiction, and those mostly war-related, as well as a beer stein he'd picked up during a trip to Germany five years ago and a few pictures from his childhood. Here he was with a fishing pole in hand. Here he was riding a bicycle. Here he was standing between his mother and father, grinning awkwardly because one of his front teeth was missing and he felt self-conscious about it. A television was mounted on the wall opposite the couch.

Lamb picked up the remote from the coffee table, turned on the television, muted it, then grabbed what was left of his bottle of bourbon. A newscaster spoke without sound on the television. Lamb walked to the piano, pulled out the bench, and sat down. He pulled the cork from his bourbon, took a swig, set the bottle on the bench beside him. He looked down at the keys, ran his bloody right hand over them. He played a few random minor chords, letting them ring out. He pulled his hand away and looked at the red smudges on the white keys.

The room seemed very quiet.

After what felt like several minutes, and a few more swigs of bourbon, he brought his hands back up to the keyboard and slowly began playing Beethoven's Piano Sonata #14 in C sharp minor, at first with hesitation and uncertainty, and then, once his fingers had found their rhythm, with the instinct of someone who has had eleven years of piano lessons.

His mother had wanted a pianist. His father had wanted a professional baseball player. He, being the failure that he was, had given them neither. Instead he was a professional thug. A collector for those who, for whatever reason, could not go to the police. After his career in baseball was cut short and his stint in the army ended – with a general discharge that precluded participation in the GI Bill and demanded forfeiture of his signing bonus – he worked mostly menial jobs until becoming a private investigator. He'd been a construction worker, a deckhand on a fishing boat, a short-order cook. He'd also spent many a month collecting unemployment benefits and eating peanut butter sandwiches.

But he played well. He didn't feel anything while he played, not at first – he wanted to, but no feeling would come – he simply played in order to be doing something with his hands, played despite the pain it caused. It sounded nice, sounded as though it was being played with emotion, but the music was a lie, as music so often is. Play the correct three notes together and suddenly sadness is floating on the air. Doesn't matter in the least what you're feeling when you play them. The sadness exists independent of its creator. Free-floating and ready to infect anyone within earshot.

He thought about women he'd loved and lost, and tried to feel sadness. He thought about his dead father and the things between them which remained, and always would remain, unresolved. He thought about his dreams wasted. But he could not bring on sadness. He could not even bring on anything that lived next door to sadness, such as regret.

He felt instead a strange manic self-loathing and a rage so big there was room within him for little else. Yet there was no place but inward to direct that rage, so it only worked to increase his self-loathing.

The mind was a vicious dog that tore only at itself.

He stopped playing on a sour note.

Fuck it, he said, just fuck it. He took another pull from his bottle.

In the bathroom he undressed. It was a painful process and he cringed his way through it as his torn and bloodstained clothes dropped around his feet. Once he was naked he looked at himself in the mirror. He was a mess. His prematurely graying hair – he was thirty-eight but was often assumed by others to be in his late forties – was streaked and clumped together with blood. His left eyebrow was split. His right eye was purple and threatening to swell shut. His nose was swollen and bloody and possibly fractured. His lower lip was split. The inside of his upper lip had been cut by his teeth, the result of a punch to the mouth, he was sure, though he had no idea which punch it might have been or even from whom. His neck was bruised, as was his left shoulder. His ribs were purple and tender to the touch.

And, of course, his hand probably needed stitches.

So he'd got what he wanted but felt no better for it. He felt empty, as one often did after an unfulfilling encounter.

He lighted a cigarette, took a drag, and got the bathtub going. He thought he might settle in, finish his bourbon and, in an hour or so, stumble to bed drunk and slightly faint from too long in a hot bath. Maybe he'd jerk off first, maybe he wouldn't. That part didn't matter. As long as he got drunk enough to sleep he would be okay. He'd be able to fall off the edge of consciousness and into the black pool of sleep below. If he didn't fall asleep the moment his head hit the pillow, however, he would not fall asleep at all. His mind would start going, and once it began it would not stop. The brain was a vicious dog, et cetera.

Lord was he bored with himself. He thought that maybe he should get a pet. He'd had a black lab mix named Oscar Hubbell up until six months ago, but the woman he'd been living with for several months took the dog with her when she moved out, despite it being his before she moved in. He hated her more for that than the many indignities she had subjected him to throughout the course of their relationship. The cheating and the lies came with the territory – this was the type of woman he dated – but her taking his dog broke his heart, and he hated her for it. If she were standing in front of him he'd have no problem putting his fist into her nose. Feeling it break beneath his knuckles.

Oscar's mine now, she'd said when he called her cell phone after returning home and finding both her and the dog gone. You can't even take care of yourself.

He closed his eyes and saw blood pouring down over her mouth and a sick, bloody-toothed smile touched his own.

The tub filled slowly, it seemed, but finally it did fill. He got to his feet, turned off the water, and was about to step into his bath when he heard a knock at the front door.

A sigh escaped his mouth.

The gears of the universe were turning against him.

Lamb grabbed a towel, wrapped it around his waist, and walked out of the bathroom. The hardwood floor felt grimy under his bare feet. He should sweep it. But then he should do a great many things he didn't do – and he shouldn't do a lot of things he did.

That was life. You got one chance and learned as you went. You were bound to make mistakes. But still, you did the best you could.

He walked downstairs and across the living-room floor.

When he reached the front door he looked through the peephole. The porch light was not on, which made it difficult to see the person standing on the other side of his door, but he could tell, at least, that it was a woman. The silhouette was strictly female. He retracted the deadbolt, unlocked the doorknob, and pulled open the wooden door. The light from the living room fell upon the woman's face. Abigail Mosley stood on the other side of his fingerprinted storm door looking back at him. Big brown eyes blinking. Tom Ford lips pursed with humor.

What happened to you?

How'd you find my house?

How many Damien Lambs do you think live in this town?

He pushed open the fingerprinted storm door and stepped aside.

Come on in.

She made her way inside.

Did you fall down a flight of stairs – twice?

Ran into a little trouble at the batting cages.

That's a seriously malfunctioning machine. You should consider a lawsuit.

It was human trouble.

You do seem like that sort of man.

What sort of man is that?

The sort who can go to the batting cages and walk away looking like you look. You did walk, I assume?

I drove.

I meant you weren't crawling.

I was about to take a bath.

That explains the towel. Don't let me stop you.

Okay.

He turned away from her, walked back up the staircase and across the hall to his bathroom. He removed the towel, tossed it onto the sink, stepped into the bathtub. As he sank into it the water turned pink with blood. Several scrapes and scratches he'd not even been aware of began to sting badly once in contact with the hot liquid. He cringed as he adjusted to the feeling, and slowly the stinging faded. He took the last drag from his cigarette and dropped it into the tub. It sizzled out. The filter floated on the pink scrim that lined the water's surface.

Do you expect me to be embarrassed, Mr Lamb?

Abigail Mosley had followed him upstairs and now stood in the bathroom doorway looking down at him, her orange bag hanging from her right hand, her left propping up the wall. There was something bordering on a smile touching her lips.

I have no expectations, lady. I'm just tired and in need of a bath. Do you mind handing me my cigarettes?

She picked them up off the counter and handed them to him.

Thanks. He lighted a cigarette and set the pack down on the tile floor by the tub. I'm guessing you're here for a reason.

I am.

Well, don't keep me in suspense.

She reached into her orange bag and removed a folded-up piece of paper. I drew you a map of the compound. It can be confusing and I thought you might need to know the important details. It isn't to scale.

He put his cigarette between his lips and reached out for the paper. She handed it to him and he examined it. It might not be to scale, but it was detailed, and he thought it might in fact be helpful. He wasn't sure how things would go down. He couldn't even begin to guess. Situations like this were always unpredictable. Humans were unpredictable. But knowing the lay of the land would almost certainly be useful.

He took a drag from his cigarette, ashed into his bath-water. The cylinder of ash disintegrated on the water, a time-lapse decomposition, and spread across its surface.

I appreciate this. Are these tunnels?

Yes. They'll get you from building to building underground.

What is their purpose?

Rhett wanted a way to move illegal product without being exposed.

Who knows about them?

I don't even think Rhett knows I know about them.

Good.

Do you know how you intend to infiltrate the compound?

I don't even know *that* I intend to infiltrate the compound.

Well, what *do* you intend to do?

I intend to take a bath, drink some bourbon, dress my wounds, and sleep on it.

When do you think you'll start?

Your daughter's being held captive. I don't exactly view that as something to be casual about. I'll start tomorrow morning.

There's that at least.

Can you put this on the counter?

He held out the map she'd drawn and she took it and set it where he'd asked her to. He then took a drag from his cigarette and set it on the edge of the tub. He dunked his head. The cuts and scrapes on his face screamed at him, but he made not a sound in reply. He pushed his head back up out of the water, ran his fingers through his hair, and grabbed the soap from the soap dish. A bar of Grandpa's brand pine tar. It smelled of railroad tracks and leather. He began washing, and as he did, the sharp pains increased.

Anything else you want to talk about? This as he scraped crusted blood out of a soapy ear with a fingernail.

Abigail shook her head.

You can let yourself out if you like. I'll update you as things progress. It could take as long as a couple weeks.

Let me at least help dress your wounds before I go. You've got some nasty cuts and scrapes I don't think you'll even be able to reach.

I'll manage.

I insist. I am a trained nurse, you know.

I did not.

I went back to school while living on the compound, tended to people there.

Is that what you do now?

I don't have a job. I took my NCLEX and got my license but never worked.

Maybe you should think about it. Especially if the money is about to run out.

Maybe I should. Her tone made it clear that she would not.

He finished washing, stepped from the tub, let it drain. Bloody water swirled out of sight, and when it was gone only two cigarette butts remained. They lay on the rusted drain cover, yellow and falling apart.

He dried off with a white towel that quickly became dotted with blood.

Abigail stood in the doorway watching.

Can I get a little privacy?

You didn't seem the bashful sort.

I'm not.

Well, then, that's settled. Where do you keep your first-aid supplies?

Top shelf, he said, and nodded toward the linen closet.

Thanks.

I'll be in the bedroom.

He picked up his dirty clothes and walked out of the bathroom, down the hallway, to his bedroom. He threw his clothes into the hamper, though he knew he'd most likely throw them away at some point. It was a place to keep them until then. He walked to his dresser, pulled open the top drawer, and removed a pair of boxer shorts (white with blue silhouettes of dogs). He slipped into them, cringing at the way he had to bend his body to get into them. It hurt his ribs to do so. Already he was very sore, and he knew it would only be worse when he awoke tomorrow.

This Abigail woman was so strange. He was fairly certain he liked her, but he did not understand her. She was unlike anyone he'd met before. He thought that was part of why he couldn't quite get a grip on her. There were few reference points. Usually he had people pinned down within minutes of meeting them – pinned down and labeled – but Abigail Mosley continued to elude him. He simply couldn't get his net around her, much less have her locked down in his mental collection of types.

She walked into the room with a first-aid kit gripped in

her right hand and her orange bag gripped in her left. She set the bag down on his dresser, which was pushed against the wall to the left of the door, and told him to sit on the bed, Lamb.

He did.

She walked to him and set the first-aid kit down beside him and opened it. She pulled out a tube of antibiotic ointment, unscrewed the cap, and began applying it to the various scrapes and cuts on his face. She did it gently with her right index finger.

You really did a number on yourself.

I had a little help.

It's nice that strangers are still willing to do favors for people.

Isn't it?

It restores one's faith in humanity.

She began peeling Band-Aids and applying them to his face. When that was done, she examined the rest of his body, applying antibiotic ointment and bandages to various cuts and scrapes, being very gentle about everything she was doing. She wrapped gauze around his hand and taped the gauze in place.

I could put in a few stitches if you want.

I'll be okay.

If you say so. She taped the gauze. I think you have a broken rib or two.

I suspect you're right.

Stand up and I'll wrap them.

She pulled an elastic bandage from the first-aid kit and held out a hand for him. He took her hand in his own and she helped pull him to his feet. Then she began wrapping the bandage around his ribs, once, and then again.

Not so tight.

It's supposed to be tight. You compress the ribs to minimize movement.

It hurts.

You're the dummy who got your ribs broken.

She continued to wrap the bandage around him, making it tight despite his protests, and when she was done she pinned the end in place.

There. She looked him in the eyes, their faces now only inches apart. All better.

Then a still moment during which neither of them moved or spoke. The moment was intense, charged with an electricity Lamb did not understand. But he never understood what made some people spark while between others existed only dead air.

He broke the stillness by grabbing the back of Abigail's neck and pulling her face toward his own. He kissed her, tasting toothpaste and cigarettes, tasting his own blood and feeling pain in his mouth that he ignored. He smelled perfume on her. Petite Cherie he thought. Seventy-five dollars. Then all conscious thought was cut off. She put a hand up to his chest and scratched him with her fingernails before pushing away.

We shouldn't do this.

I know, he said, unbuttoning her blouse and pulling it off her before unsnapping her bra and sliding its straps down her shoulders. I know we shouldn't.

He threw her blouse and bra to the floor, turned her toward the bed, and pushed her onto it. She lay back on the bed, looking up at him, and he climbed on top of her, kissing her neck and her breasts, biting her hard enough that she cried out in pain, but she also grabbed a fistful of his hair and held his head in place – before pushing it away again.

We have to stop.

I know.

He reached up and put a hand around her throat, gripping it tight, then kissed her mouth hard, tasting more of his own blood.

She ran her hand down his stomach and slipped it into his boxer shorts, stroking him.

I want you to fuck me, she said.

We shouldn't.

We should.

He unbuttoned her pants and slid them down, pulling them off with her shoes and panties in one frantic motion. Then he turned her over on the bed, grabbed her by the hips, and pulled her back to him. He dropped to his knees, burying his face in her ass. She was sweaty and salty and her odor was strong. He liked it very much. She pushed herself against him. After a while he pulled away and kissed his way up her back, rising to his feet. He put himself inside her. As he did this, he reached around and grabbed her once more by the throat, pulling her toward him, and kissed her mouth. He could hear her trying to pull air into her lungs, but his grip would not allow it, yet she put her hand over his and pushed it down tighter.

With her other hand she reached back and pulled him into her harder, providing him with the rhythm he needed. He bit her shoulder as he fucked her and he bit her neck. He grabbed her by the hair and shoved her face into the mattress.

Then all at once he felt himself coming, and he slammed himself into her a last few times. He let go her hair, groaning into her neck as a spasm shook through his body.

And then, all at once, he stopped all over.

He fell onto her and simply lay there breathing hard, his chest heaving, his whole body aching. She lay beneath him with her eyes open and staring at the far wall, her lipstick smeared, her mouth covered with his blood.

After a while he went soft inside her.

He rolled them both onto their sides and cupped a breast in his hand and they lay in silence for a very long time breathing together and their inhalations slowing over time until finally reaching a reasonable resting rate. The silence continued. Lamb began to drift toward sleep, his mind a small rudderless boat on calm waters moving slowly toward the horizon, behind which he might find only—

Do you really think you'll be able to get her back?

He opened his eyes, blinked himself awake, allowed his

mind to process the question. Finally he answered. I know I will.

Really?

Really.

I believe you, she said.

Good.

That night Lamb slept better than he had in years. The comfort of the woman beside him and her warmth, the quiet sound of her breathing, her heart beating slowly under his hand: these things made him feel calm inside, made him feel something other than anger and self-loathing. It had been years since he'd felt anything like this – the women he had been with recently, even those he lived with, had been little more than void fillers, though he gave them what love he could – but he didn't question it. He let himself feel it, this quiet and contented peace, and he let himself fall into sleep.

His sleep was dreamless.

It was still dark when Abigail awoke. Her subconscious awareness of unfamiliar surroundings drew her out of sleep. She opened her eyes and stared at the far wall. It looked gray in the dim light, though she knew that it was in fact a cream color. Perhaps it had once been white, but years of cigarette smoke had painted it with nicotine. She could feel a warm body pressed against her back and her bottom, a sticky cock erupting from untrimmed pubic hair resting warm against her vulva, and a hand draped over her, cupping a breast.

She felt strange. The fact that she had fucked him in order to get him further committed to her cause made her feel like a whore, which feeling was only increased by the fact that she intended to steal from him what he stole from Rhett, and yet she liked him very much and might have slept with him without need for external motive. She'd experienced her first orgasm in a decade last night, her first orgasm that was not self-induced anyway. In a different life they might have had a relationship of some sort, maybe even a good relationship. Like her he had been shattered by life, and like her he refused to fall apart despite having been shattered – determination was the glue that held the pieces together – but the damage made him, for reasons she did not really understand, all the more attractive to her.

Perhaps it was not the damage but her knowledge of the willpower required to keep the pieces together. It indicated a strength most did not possess.

She carefully took the arm that was draped over her in one hand and lifted it away, and then slid off the mattress. The breast he had been holding was still warm enough that she felt the ghost of his touch on her even as she stood several feeT away looking down at him sleeping.

He lay naked on top of the covers, thin but wiry with muscle. Old scars hashed his body with pale lines and crescents, as if his flesh were a canvas and his injuries the art. He was not a particularly handsome man but in his way he was beautiful.

She leaned down and kissed his forehead gently, then got dressed.

Five minutes later she was walking softly down the stairs toward the living room, her shoes in her right hand. When she reached the first floor she slipped into them and then out the front door. Though early morning had arrived the moon was still visible in the sky, a few wisps of cloud floating in front of it, backlighted. Stars dotted the sky. The air was cool and crisp. The windows of the houses that surrounded her were dark and empty as broken television screens.

She walked to her car and keyed open the door and fell in behind the wheel. She looked at the old Mercedes parked in front of her, twenty years old at least, a dent in the rear bumper. She thought of the car's owner lying alone upstairs.

While starting the engine she wondered idly when she might see him again. Then she backed out of the driveway, rolling into the street. She put the car into first, pulled her left foot off the clutch, and pressed the gas with her right. She rolled down the street, cutting her way through the dim morning light.

Somehow she felt simultaneously full and empty. Full of hope. Empty of everything else. The world was a strange place. You never knew how the people you met might affect you, nor how you might affect them. You tried to approach this life with reason and logic, but sometimes it was difficult. Sometimes doing so required you ignore the feeling in your chest.

She liked Lamb, but she did not know him well or owe him anything, so she would do what she needed to do. He had begun to seep into her heart as they lay together last night, but she would force him out, and put a lock on it to keep him out, and she would do what needed doing.

Fuck love. It always ended in pain. What she needed was money.

She pulled into a McDonald's drive-thru and ordered

herself an Egg McMuffin and a large coffee, no cream or sugar, but once she had the sandwich she found she wasn't hungry.

Lamb awoke at half past seven and found that the bed was otherwise empty. He felt the place where Abigail had slept. It was cool to the touch. He looked to the floor where he'd thrown her clothes but her clothes were gone. He wondered when she had slipped out from under his arm, dressed, and sneaked away. It was unpleasant waking up alone after falling asleep beside someone. He sat up in bed, his entire body sore and aching. He looked to the night-stand for his cigarettes but they were not there. After a moment he remembered that he'd left them in the bath-room. He stumbled there, picked them up off the tile floor, and lighted one. He sat on the toilet lid and smoked, thinking about last night. He was tired and his head hurt. His stomach was sour. His body ached, especially his ribs.

What he needed was a pick-me-up, a little something to get him moving again.

After his cigarette was finished, he stood, dropped the

butt into the toilet, and walked to the medicine cabinet. In the medicine cabinet he found toothpaste, a toothbrush, tools for cleaning teeth, whitening strips, a butterfly safety razor, several packages of Feather blades, a bottle of shaving cream, and orange prescription bottles filled with Topamax, Percocet, Xanax, and Adderall. He grabbed the Percocet and the Adderall and shook two pills out of each and into his palm, then walked back to his bedroom. He dry-swallowed the Percocet and then stood at his dresser and crushed the Adderall with the bottom of a water glass.

He'd be feeling better in no time.

At eight o'clock, after brushing his teeth and putting on a clean suit, he stepped from his house and made his way to his old Mercedes, a variety of pills rattling in his pocket while he walked. The day was already hot and he began sweating the moment he stepped out into the morning sun. He unlocked his car and slid in behind the wheel, the vehicle rocking under his weight. The steering wheel was crusted with dried blood, as was the knob of his shifter. He rolled down the window, hoping to get a breeze, and put the key into the ignition. He turned the key. The engine rattled, then roared to life. He put it into gear and backed out of the driveway.

Then he was on his way, heading south toward he knew not what.

Louisville disappeared behind him, growing smaller and smaller until it simply ceased to exist. From then on there were only small pockets of civilization, McDonald's restaurants, Taco Bells, White Castles, gas stations with Mack trucks parked in their lots. Cars thinned out on the interstate until finally there were times when his was the only vehicle rolling along the cracked and faded asphalt and the only sound was the humming of his tires.

The gas gauge's needle drifted left.

He took his exit and found himself on one narrow road after another, surrounded by cornfields and soy beans. Mobile homes ornamented the roadside at great intervals. Cows and horses grazed. Eventually these things gave way to trees, their branches overhanging the road, casting crooked shadows that looked like spider webs. Streams ran under sagging bridges. Dead animals punctuated the roadside, their guts splashed out before them like tangled rope.

After nearly ninety minutes he arrived at the compound – a fenced-off area dotted with buildings – but did not stop. He rolled past and continued on another half mile or so before pulling his car to the side of the road, rolling to a stop on its gravel shoulder. He killed the engine, pulled a pistol from his glove box. The pistol had had its serial number filed away. He checked his side-view mirror and seeing no vehicles pushed open his door and stepped out into the daylight, the sun shining down hot, tucked the pistol into the back of his pants, and used a pressure gauge to let the air out of his left rear tire.

Whether or not Abigail's daughter was being held

against her will she would not be easy to get to, and he had no real plan to speak of. There was no way to form a plan. He hadn't the necessary information. He would simply have to take measure of the situation and do what felt right in the moment. He didn't like such situations, but he was used to them. Probably today would be a day only for reconnoitering. He could check out the lay of the land, see what was what, and tomorrow, depending on what he saw, move in and try to get the girl. First, however, he must find out how he might do that.

He turned back toward the compound and started walking along the shoulder of the road.

Up ahead a deer grazed only a few feet from the asphalt. A formation of birds cast its shadow across the ground as it moved in a northwesterly direction. The deer looked up, startled by the sound of his footsteps. It watched him as he approached, just stood there looking at him for some time, and then all at once darted into the woods, bounding on thin legs. He could hear the leaves and twigs breaking beneath its hoofs for a moment, and then even that sound was gone, and it was as if the deer had never been there.

He lighted a cigarette, took a deep drag, continued to walk.

The compound came into view, fenced off by barbed wire. Many of the buildings were hidden by pockets of trees – Ohio buckeye, shagbark hickory, and others – but he could see cabins set far back on the land, a garage large enough to hold a dozen or more vehicles, though it appeared to be nearly empty, toolsheds, feed sheds, stables, and coops. Big bales of hay jutted from the earth. Tractors sat rusting in the grass like dead dinosaurs. Cows and alpacas and horses grazed. Chickens pecked at the earth for insects and worms. Several large dogs – South African mastiffs – lay on the ground, lazily soaking up the sun and watching the cows and alpacas and chickens go about their business. Men and women in white clothes walked from one place to the next, sometimes empty-handed, sometimes holding Bibles or baskets of goods. Others still tilled the earth or harvested vegetables or repaired barns and feed sheds and horse stalls and fences. From this distance they looked like photocopies of one another, or cardboard cutouts, dressed identically as they were.

Beyond the feed sheds and the stables sat a large white house. To its left was a vegetable garden, to its right a kidney-shaped pond, and behind it, behind everything, was a dense wood that went back as far as the eye could see, the trees for the most part full and summer green, though there were a few patches of brown here and there where a tree had died but not yet fallen. Diseased or struck by lightning.

You could almost forget the place was funded by the heroin trade. You could almost forget it was home to a cult whose leader was, by reputation at least, a brutal murderer who was not above slaughtering women and children if it served his purpose.

Blessed is the one who seizes your infants and dashes their heads against the rocks.

He thought of the map that Abigail had given him – left at home in case he was searched – and tried to make note of what and where everything was. This place was basically a small town, and if he got into trouble he didn't want to find himself lost.

He flicked his cigarette into the street and walked toward the gate. To his right, behind the barbed-wire fence, lay a graveyard with about three dozen headstones. They jutted from the earth at odd angles, like crooked teeth, the ground beneath them having softened and shifted during storms. The grass and weeds were overgrown, hiding birth- and death-dates. An older gentleman was standing on the other side of the gate with his hands clasped behind his back. He was maybe seventy years old and very thin. He wore a pair of white slacks and a white button-up shirt. His mouth was an angrily penciled line on a sheet of bleached paper. His cheeks were hollow. His shoulders were slumped with age and weariness both, giving him the shape of a candle left too long in the summer heat. His eyes were vacant as yesterday – we've all moved on – and it was clear he had some time ago retreated from the world of men. If his head were a birdhouse it would house no birds. A silent hollow with no song.

I got a flat tire about a half-mile up the road and was wondering if I could maybe use your phone to call the auto club.

I don't let in nobody I d'know.

It wouldn't take but five minutes.

The man shook his head, slow but deliberate. Don't matter if it wouldn't take but five *seconds*. I got my instructions.

Could you maybe ask the person who gave you those instructions?

Can't leave my post.

So you can't let me in and you can't leave your post to find out if maybe the person who gave you those instructions might make an exception?

Yes, sir.

Could you tell me where the next closest house is?

I guess I don't know.

You don't know?

Don't really leave the property.

You must go out sometimes.

Reckon I don't. Used to be a house about a mile and a half west of here, but I don't know that anybody lives there no more.

I see. Well, thanks anyway.

Didn't do nothin.

True enough.

God bless.

Lamb turned away from the gate. It looked as though he'd have to sneak onto the compound. He was hoping to avoid that. Walking onto a property invited allowed you freedoms you did not have when you sneaked on. But sometimes there was no other way. He walked out toward the street, reaching into his jacket pocket for his cigarettes.

Is there something we can do for you, friend?

With a cigarette hanging from his lip he turned to see the source of the voice.

Standing near the gatekeeper was a stick-straight man, broad-shouldered but thin save a hard-looking gut like a bowling ball, wearing a white linen suit, no tie though his top button was done, and white bucks with brown soles. He could have been either forty or sixty. His face was somehow ageless. His eyes sparkled with intelligence and kindness and though his face was lined with wrinkles there seemed to be no weariness in him. Lamb had known from the voice alone that it was Rhett Mosley whose mouth had sent vibrations through the air but now he'd confirmed it visually as well. After hearing Abigail speak he'd somehow expected more. This man was just a man.

Yet it was disconcerting to see him standing there all the same. The long driveway was visible all the way to the white house near the back of the property and yet he'd not seen the man approaching. But here he was.

Lamb lighted his cigarette.

Car got a flat about a half-mile up the road, maybe a little more. Was hoping to use your phone to call the auto club.

You do not have a cellular device?

Couldn't get a signal way out here in the country.

You're not from around here then.

No, sir.

Whereabouts you from?

Louisville.

What brings you down here?

My father.

He lives near here?

In a manner of speaking. He's buried near here.

It was true. Somewhere down here was a twenty-acre plot of land on which his father was buried. Once it had held a small house, the house in which Lamb's father had lived for the last five years of his life, once he'd decided to leave Louisville, but a tornado had knocked it down several years back and though he had collected the insurance money – the property became his after his father's death – he had not bothered to rebuild. There was no point. He would never live out here nor would he step foot on the land. Let it go back to nature. Let the deer and the wild turkeys and the plants reclaim it. It was theirs long before it was his, so it might as well become theirs again.

The righteous perish and no one ponders it in his heart; devout men are taken away, and no one understands that the righteous are taken away to be spared from evil. Those who walk uprightly enter into peace; they find rest as they lie in death.

My father was a lot of things, but righteous isn't one of them.

Rhett Mosley smiled. It is appointed unto men once to die, but after this the judgment.

Lamb nodded. If there's a hell he's in it.

I assure you, friend, there is indeed a hell. Open the

gate for our new friend, Amos, so that he might use our telephone.

The old man slowly pulled up on a handle and dragged the gate across the driveway, the pin that locked it into place plowing a groove into the earth, a cloud of dust rising from the ground, and soon the path was clear for Lamb to enter. He did so, and the old man closed the gate behind him.

What is your name, friend?

Lamb.

May I enquire as to your first name?

Damien.

From the Greek *damao*, which means to tame: to tame the lamb. But who is the lamb, I wonder – at first one would think it is you, but I'm not certain – and how might this lamb be tamed: by a stern hand perhaps, or by sacrifice, and if by sacrifice does he rise again as did the Lamb of God? And I beheld in the midst of the throne and of the four beasts, and in the midst of the elders, a lamb with seven horns and seven eyes standing with the wounds of the slain. Standing, you see, for he had risen. Or perhaps this lamb is no lamb at all but a beast in disguise, in which case this lamb may be you after all. Are you familiar with the Gnostic gospels, friend? I do not feel us abandoned myself but there are times, I must admit, when I do wonder. Sometimes, if the light has been absent for a long time – but I suppose this is no place for such a conversation. Please discard your cigarette and follow me so that you might use the telephone.

He pivoted on his right foot and walked with a soldier's gait, shoulders square, back stiff, toward the large white house. Lamb took a final drag from his cigarette, flicked it out toward the street, followed down a long driveway, passing cows and alpacas and donkeys and horses, all grazing in their respective pens.

The mastiffs raised their heads and with dark eyes watched from the ground on which they lay. Their bodies were taut with sinewy muscle. Their brown coats glistened in the sun. Their black muzzles twitched.

Lamb was not afraid of dogs and had never been – dogs had been his friends growing up when he'd had no others – but there was something in the eyes of these animals that made him uneasy. He had no doubt that Mosley had merely to signal and they would be upon him, and were they to fall upon him not even the fifteen rounds tucked into his belt were likely to save him, for these dogs would be coming from all directions and there were many of them and they would show no fear of bullets even if others beside them dropped.

Mosley reached the front porch of the house and walked up its three wooden steps. Lamb followed, and when he walked by the dog lying on the blue-painted pine it growled at him, saliva dripping from its toothy mouth and splashing onto the wood.

The house into which he followed Mosley was nicely

furnished and there were fine paintings on the walls and the hardwood floors were covered in expensive rugs with tight weave patterns. The only religious object in the house appeared to be a leather-bound Bible which rested on an end table. The end table itself sat beside a large beige couch on which lay a pretty brunette girl, no more than seventeen and possibly younger, with sharp features, porcelain skin – and with her mother's eyes. She was listening to music through a small set of ear buds while flipping through a tattered copy of *Nine Stories*. There was something very sad about her. Some piece of her had been removed, he thought, and it might never be replaced. He wondered if she had yet read 'A Perfect Day for Bananafish', and wondered, if she had, how Seymour's suicide had affected her, whether it had affected her at all. She seemed like the sort of girl Salinger had been writing for – an intelligent but damaged post-adolescent.

He did not let himself look at her long, not even when she glanced up at him and smiled her sad-eyed smile, but walked past quickly, following Mosley deeper into the house. They made their way into the kitchen and Mosley pointed to the phone, which was mounted on the back wall between a calendar and a blackboard.

He glanced in that direction. The calendar pinned to the wall had handwritten notes scrawled in the squares of certain dates. The blackboard held a grocery list: sugar, corned beef, flour. Between them, a beige telephone.

Thanks.

He walked to the telephone and pulled his wallet from his right hip pocket and from his wallet pulled a card and from the card read a telephone number which he dialed. He told the woman on the other end of the line that he'd gotten a flat tire and told her too where his car was now parked. She told him someone would try to get there within the next four hours.

It's a bit out of the way, sir.

I understand.

He hung up the telephone.

I doubt they promised a brief wait.

Measured against the age of the universe?

Mosley laughed. Would you care for a glass of sweet tea in the meantime?

That would be great.

Have a seat.

Lamb sat down at a large farm table, the same table, he presumed, at which Abigail had eaten her first meal on the compound. Mosley poured him sweet tea from a blue plastic pitcher, poured it into a green-tinted double-bulge glass, and set it on the table before him.

Thanks.

Would you care for a piece of transparent pie?

Lamb shook his head. Don't really go in for desserts.

You'd have to eat a meal for this to be dessert.

Lost my sweet tooth as a little boy.

I do hope the tooth fairy paid you handsomely for such a loss.

Twenty-five cents.

Silence then filled the kitchen. Lamb sipped his tea and the sound of his swallowing was very loud in his ears. He set the glass down and the sound of that was loud in his ears as well. He looked down at his bruised and split knuckles. He flexed his right hand which was still very sore from last night's fight. When he did he could feel the gash in his palm open.

Do you visit your father's grave often?

I do not.

How long has it been?

I've never visited his grave.

When did he die?

Nine years ago.

That is a while. But I understand. I have never visited my own father's grave. He is no longer there, in any case. That devil has been cast into the lake of fire where he will be tormented forever and ever.

Lamb sipped his tea. I guess we both got issues with our fathers then.

I think we very likely have a great many similarities, friend. Most men do if they take time to discover them. But it is the differences that matter. They are what set us apart. For instance, I would never lie to a man about the nature of my visit to his home.

I don't know what you mean.

I am disappointed in you, friend. Lie on top of lie on top of fucking *lie*. Your mouth is a menstruating cunt spilling only waste, and ye are a physician of no value. Did you really believe you could walk through my front door spewing falsehoods and that I would have no knowledge of what you were doing? Let the lying lips be put to silence.

I think there's been some sort of misunderstanding.

I knew what you were before I let you through my gate.

Lamb got to his feet. Maybe I should go wait by my car.

It is too late for that.

Lamb reached for his gun, felt it cool and comforting in his grip. He let it hang there so that Mosley would see it but did not take aim.

It's never too late.

It is never too late for the Lord for the Lord is not slow in keeping his promise. Instead he is patient, not wanting anyone to perish, but everyone to come to repentance. But it is indeed too late for you. I simply cannot let you walk freely from my home.

You're not gonna stop me.

Elijah.

Lamb turned around in time to see a large man coming at him, bringing the butt of a shotgun down on his forehead. There was no pain, there was nothing. One moment he saw the butt of the gun coming toward him in a great brown streak. The next moment he saw nothing, knew nothing. Nothing but darkness and the echo of his own empty thoughts bouncing around the walls of his skull like pennies in a coffee tin.

Mosley looked down at the man sprawled across his kitchen floor. He wore a navy suit and a nice tie and brown dress shoes but was no gentleman. His face was battered and bruised. Near his bandaged right hand lay a pistol he had drawn. Untruths still clung to his tongue for he'd been stopped short in their spitting. Mosley was tempted to cut his tongue out for him so that he might never lie again – it would increase his chances of seeing Heaven – but resisted the temptation. This man was here for a reason and Mosley wanted to know what that reason was. He needed to know. Perhaps after his tongue had told him all it could he would cut it out like the malignancy it was but not until.

Who is he?

The voice belonged to Lily, sweet Lily, so unlike her mother who had become jaded and unbelieving and mistrustful, whose heart had calcified and whose soul had been corrupted. For years he believed he had helped to wash her clean of worldly filth but in the end she was still the whore he had pulled off the streets, only now she was arrogant and full of partially digested knowledge and confidence in her own righteousness despite his better wisdom.

He looked up and there she stood, his Lily, innocent and beautiful and sad, leaning against the doorframe between the kitchen and the living room, her skin flawless, her doe eyes lacking the nervous intelligence of her mother's but still beautiful, her sex untainted by other men. Unlike the girls he pulled off the streets she was truly innocent and required no cleansing. Born here and raised in his home she was the only true purity he had ever known aside from his daughters, and yet her mother in her arrogance would deny him her as though she had the right. As though he had not earned her.

He wanted her now. The violence of the day had made him crave the purity of her touch – he wanted to exorcise what violence was left in him and to absorb her innocence – but he denied himself access. This was not the time. Later, when this situation had been resolved, then he would have her, but not until, for until it was resolved he must focus his energy elsewhere.

An interloper whose purpose I do not yet know, he said. But you need not be concerned with such matters. They are too much for a delicate flower such as yourself. Why not head back to the living room, or perhaps our sleeping chambers, and avoid being confronted by such ugliness as this?

Okay, Daddy.

She was the only one who could get away with calling him Daddy, but he had such a spot for her in his heart that she could get away with a great many things, with almost anything in fact. She turned and walked away and he watched her go until he could watch her no more, and in those few moments his face was almost boylike in its awe, and then it hardened again and became cruel.

Get a wheelbarrow, Elijah, and help me haul this fabricator out of my house.

Yes, Father.

Once he was gone Mosley sat on his haunches before the interloper. He stroked the man's graying hair. It was coarse yet inexplicably soft. Despite the cuts and the bruises, and despite the lies on his tongue, he was a beautiful man in his way. Most men were – and all women. It was a shame he – and they – had been ruined by the world. It was such a terrible shame.

He blinked and felt the tears that had welled in his eyes roll down his cheeks. He wiped them away with the heels of his palms. One should not feel sorry for the lost that could not be found; they were already gone. But sometimes one could not help it. The waste got to you. So much beauty lost, like a fine painting damned to Nazi flames. It was true that there were things in the world to which most people should not be exposed, but it still made your heart ache.

The man on his floor moaned.

Mosley picked up the pistol that lay beside the man and used it to bash him in the head, one quick and brutal blow behind the ear. He did not want him waking and causing trouble. He stood, tucked the pistol into his own waistband, and with the back of his hands wiped the liquid from his cheeks one last time.

One should not feel sorry for the lost that could not be found.

He was a good-sized muscular man and because of this heavy and difficult to carry, but they hauled the interloper to the front porch, one man on his arms while the other had his legs, his middle drooping between them like a bridge about to collapse, down its three steps, and dropped him into a rusting green wheelbarrow like the pile of waste he was. Mosley looked down at him there, his legs hanging over one end while his head hung over the other, his neck bent back and his mouth open.

Take him to the feed shed by the pigpen. I'll be there in a few minutes.

Elijah nodded, grabbed the wheelbarrow by its wooden handles, and began rolling the man across the green lawn toward the shed and the blood-splattered slaughter tub that sat beside it. The wheelbarrow's inflated rubber wheel was almost flat under the weight of the man within it. Mosley watched for a moment before heading back into his house.

He made his way downstairs, into the basement, and across the unfinished concrete floor to a set of built-in shelves that held paint cans, lacquer-thinner, teak oil, a full gas can, and other such materials. Once he reached the shelves he grabbed the left side of them, fingers wrapping around a thin lip, and pulled to reveal a tunnel barely wide enough for two men to walk down side-by-side. He made his way into the darkness, pulling on thin chains as he went, sixty-watt bulbs lighting the surrounding area as he did so. He was walking beneath one of the two large gardens on the property, making his way toward an underground room that sat hidden beneath a toolshed. Though no earth was exposed – concrete lined the walls and ceiling as well as the floor – the tunnel had about it the smell of moist dirt, the scent having permeated the concrete. It was cool as well, and somehow comforting, like a womb. Mosley believed that there were times in every man's life – and perhaps in every woman's as well, though it was impossible to tell with women; he did not even know if they could love or if they merely pantomimed the love that men felt (he believed it was probably the latter) – when he longed for the safety of the womb. But of course one could never go back; once you left your first home you were expelled from it forever. Forced from that warmth into a cold world.

This tunnel was about a hundred yards long, and he made his way through it rather quickly, arriving finally at a narrow wooden door. He pulled open the door and found himself looking at a dark room, approximately fifteen feet wide by twenty feet deep. He reached up, grabbed a chain, and pulled. A bulb painted the room with light.

Wooden crates lined the walls and a pallet sat in the center of the floor between them. Two trash bags sat on the pallet and within the bags were hundreds of decks of heroin worth, all told, a little more than a million dollars. He was here, however, for enough only to dose a man once.

He reached into one of the trash bags and removed a deck.

When he arrived at the feed shed fifteen minutes later it was with a duffel bag gripped in his right fist. Within the duffel bag he had placed a hammer, a box of nails, a handkerchief, duct tape, and within a small zip-up pouch the heroin he had collected and a kit with which to cook and inject it. He stepped through the doors into the dim shed and found Elijah waiting for him, standing over the interloper who still lay unconscious in the wheelbarrow.

You should leave, Elijah. I will handle things from this point forward.

Elijah nodded and left the shed, closing the doors behind him.

Mosley set the duffel bag on a dusty shelf and walked to the wheelbarrow. He kicked the wheelbarrow over. It crashed onto its side with a loud thud. The man within went sprawling out across the shed's bloodstained pine floor without being brought back to consciousness. When he had ceased to move he lay prostrate with his left arm folded under his body. Mosley flipped him over onto his back and removed his clothes save his underwear and undershirt. He walked to the duffel bag, unzipped it, and from within removed the handkerchief and duct tape.

While looking down at the unconscious man Mosley considered what he was about to do. Not long ago he had told himself that one should not feel sorry for the lost that could not be found, but perhaps this man *could* be found, not through ordinary means, of course, for the world had got to him long ago and he was too far off the path of the righteous to find his way back alone, but through the means he was about to employ for his own ends. The very horror of the situation this man was about to find himself in might work to bring him back to the Lord. Mosley certainly hoped so, for the man would not be leaving here alive, and it would be better to send him to eternal bliss than torment. Mosley knew that God was just, which meant eternal damnation was just as well – for the Lord gave every man ample opportunity to repent his sins – but that did not mean he had to feel good about it. Sometimes even justice could be cruel. A fact he knew all too well.

For in his heart he was a gentle man.

He shoved the handkerchief into the interloper's mouth and used the duct tape to hold it in place. While he did this the man gagged unconsciously, but his eyelids did not so much as flutter. The gagging was simply a physical reaction, nothing more.

Mosley walked back to the duffel bag, threw the duct tape into it, and removed the hammer and the box of nails.

He returned once more to the unconscious man on his floor and before him sat on his haunches and set down the box of nails. He opened the box and removed one of the galvanized four-inch pins. He bent the man's knee to ensure his right foot was resting flat on the floor. He placed the nail over the man's foot, held the hammer in place a moment, aiming, pulled back, and drove the nail home. One hard swing put it through his foot and into the pine floor so the head of the nail was only half an inch or so off the flesh. One more strike put it flush, denying any movement whatsoever.

The man woke up screaming a muffled scream through the handkerchief and flailed about but with one limb pinned down he could do nothing to remedy his situation.

Hush now, Mosley said, screaming will resolve nothing. We're already one fourth of the way through this and once we've got this situation nailed down, excuse the paronomasia, I'll be more than happy to provide you with some medication which will alleviate your pain.

The man tried to say something through the handkerchief and while his words were far too distorted and muffled to be understood there was certainly cursing involved. Motherfucker might have been one of the words. His face was red. Tears streamed down his cheeks.

I can see that you're upset, but you should keep in mind that you are the one who walked into my house with lies on your tongue. Were you an innocent you would not be in this situation. Innocents and those who wish to return to innocence are always welcome here, and can remain here as long as they choose unharmed.

The man tried to grab at Mosley but failed. He pulled on his foot and screamed but could not free himself. Blood pooled beneath his foot as he tore at his own flesh. It ran to the edges of the floorboard and dripped down into the dirt below.

Don't fight it. You'll only cause yourself more pain.

Mosley grabbed a second nail from the box, walked around the body, grabbed the left arm, and, after a struggle, pinned it down with his knee.

Try to remain calm. I know it hurts, I know that, but getting worked up about your situation solves nothing. You are closer to God now than you have been in many years, I assure you, for the Lord is near to the brokenhearted and saves the crushed in spirit. Let yourself go and you will find Him.

Mosley drove the second nail home.

The man began to sob openly, choking on the handkerchief shoved down his throat.

Don't be ashamed of your tears. I know that men often believe tears are a sign of weakness, but in fact it takes a strong man to cry openly. It is only weak men who will not admit their vulnerability. They know that if they reveal it they can be broken. The strong know they will never be broken and so hide nothing. We're halfway through this, and I must say, you're holding up very well. I'm proud of you.

The man simply sobbed. That was quite all right. He was going through a lot and could not be expected to maintain composure. He did, however, maintain consciousness despite the fact that losing it would bring immediate relief. This was a fellow who could take a lot of hurt. But then hard men developed a tolerance for pain. The more they had suffered and withstood the more they could suffer yet.

Mosley drove the last two nails home. It was unpleasant but necessary.

With that job done, he threw the hammer and the box of nails back into the duffel bag and removed the drug kit. He unzipped it and looked down at a small deck of heroin, a needle, a syringe, a spoon, several cotton balls, and a small vial of distilled water. He had shot up only once in his life, in order that he might know his product, but he was familiar enough with the procedure to get it done. Even if he missed the vein a skin pop would still get the man done.

Within five minutes he was walking toward the fabricator nailed to his floor with a loaded syringe in hand. The man watched him with fear in his eyes but did not attempt to squirm away. Mosley could almost admire him for that. He knew his situation now and accepted it. Many men were not capable of understanding their circumstances. It took a man with a firm grasp on reality, a man who did not hide behind false hope, to do so.

It's okay. This will take away your pain.

He removed his belt and wrapped it around the man's arm, cinching it tight. He tapped at a vein, and, satisfied, slid the needle in. He thumbed down the plunger.

The man's eyes rolled back in his head and his body slackened.

There. Isn't that better?

Mosley took back his belt and slid it through his loops. He tossed the drug kit into the duffel bag and zipped it up. He walked to the man's clothes which lay on the floor in a pile and went through the pockets, finding cigarettes, a lighter, a cell phone, a bottle of prescription pills, a set of keys, a well-worn leather wallet. He opened the wallet and looked inside. The man had twenty-eight dollars in cash, two credit cards, several business cards identifying him as a private investigator, and a driver's license.

He had been truthful about his name.

Mosley wondered who had hired him to come here, what he was investigating.

Soon enough he would find out.

He folded the man's clothes up and set them on the dusty shelf. Beside the clothes he placed the wallet and its contents save the auto club card, and beside the wallet the phone and the cigarettes and the lighter and the pills. He removed the pistol from his waistband and set that down as well. It wasn't as if the man could get to it. The keys, however, he held on to.

I'll be back in a little while to talk, he said. For now you should try to rest. Pain is exhausting, I know, and you have suffered a great deal of it.

He walked out of the shed and into the bright daylight.

His next task was to get the interloper's car off the road. He got into a powder-blue Ford pickup truck and drove up the driveway toward the gate. By the time he reached it it was already swung wide and he rolled through, making a right onto the narrow gray strip of asphalt that curled past the front of his property. Soon enough he came to the old Mercedes and parked behind it. The car did indeed have a flat, as he'd already known, but he suspected as well that there was a perfectly good spare in the trunk. The man had let the air out of the tire himself – his people had watched him do it – and a man wouldn't do such a thing if he couldn't remedy his situation, auto club or no. Not out here in the middle of nowhere.

He walked to the trunk and popped it and within found what he'd been sure would be there. He removed the spare tire and the jack and got to work, unhappy that he was dirtying his suit, but knowing it must be done. Already it had been spattered with blood.

Sometimes a man had to get dirty to keep himself clean.

The outside world would not come in. His fences represented a separation from the filth out there, and he would maintain that separation at all costs. It was true he had to use the outside world. A church such as his could not survive on faith alone. Money was necessary and that money must come from the world apart, but that did not mean the filth of the world had to come with it. He had experienced more than enough filth in his youth. Living under his dictatorial father's roof he had known little else. The man was vile and godless and without a single redeeming quality save the ability to die, and after the man killed his mother when he was only eight – everyone knew he had done it, though even the police failed to prove it – he had no one to protect him from the fat, drunken, violent beast. He had no one to protect him and no way to escape, for though they were not behind bars children were inmates, completely at the mercy of those that birthed them. He knew he was much more like his father than he wanted to be, but his faith in God had tempered some of the worst of the traits he had inherited from the son of a bitch. Sometimes when he looked at himself in the mirror all he could see was his father. His mental image of himself was as a twenty-five-year-old man, full of energy and sex, but when he looked in the mirror he saw something else. He saw the man who had beaten him with belts and fists and switches. The man who had kicked him until his ribs were broken and called him a useless piece of shit. The man who had enslaved him until he had finally done the world a favor and died a miserable death, choking on his own drunk-vomit in his sleep.

Soon after that Mosley had first heard the voice of God. It was late at night and he was lying in bed in an otherwise empty house. He was staring at the ceiling. From his left he heard a voice. Deep and melodious. Startled, he turned toward the sound and saw a light glowing in the otherwise dark room, glowing like a gas lantern, and the light spoke to him. It said that it had great plans for him. It said that it had chosen him to help guide its people toward Heaven. Sometimes it spoke to him still. There were times when he neither saw the light nor heard its voice – it could be years and when it was he felt abandoned – but it always returned. He saw its glow and felt its warmth and was comforted. He heard its voice and knew that it was the voice of God and that voice gave him guidance.

Yet there were those who believed he did what he did for money alone. They were wrongheaded cynics. The money was necessary only that his church might survive. So he provided sinners with the means of their own destruction. Yet they destroyed themselves. If they were clean in spirit his product would never reach their veins. There was he believed an ironic righteousness to the heroin trade as he ran it. Using filth to cleanse the world. If these junkies were to understand that their bodies were holy, if they were to respect this gift the Lord had given them, never would they fall prey to their own weakness. It was their blindness to the holy that killed them, and that blindness meant they deserved the death they were so often dealt. For the holy was right before their faces if only they would open their eyes.

Sometimes you had to put filth into the world in order that the world might be cleansed.

He threw the flat and the jack into the trunk and dropped in behind the wheel. He started the engine of the Mercedes and put the car into gear. He drove it off the shoulder of the road and into the woods as far as he could, tree branches scratching at the paint and the windows like reaching fingers. He stopped the car and killed the engine. He stepped from the vehicle and walked back out toward the road and when he reached the road he looked toward the car. He could just see it, light splashing against the glass of the rear window, but believed he could only because he was looking for it. No one driving along this stretch of asphalt would accidently spy it, and even if they did they very likely would think nothing of it. People abandoned cars all the time. Even the police would drive on by.

He walked back to his truck and stepped up into it. He started the engine. He turned the truck around, rolling through the grass on the shoulder of the road to do so, and headed back toward home. The drive was a short one.

What he wanted more than anything as he pushed through the front door was to take a shower and cleanse himself of this day's filth, but the filth would remain with him a short while longer. One more thing needed his immediate attention. He walked to the kitchen and once in the kitchen walked to the telephone. He removed the auto club card from his pocket and dialed the number. He told the woman who answered that he'd called earlier about a flat tire but that the auto club's services were no longer required as a nice fellow driving by had stopped and got him in order. He hung up the telephone, exhaled.

He believed he now had a few hours.

He walked to the bedroom and closed the door behind him. Lily lay in bed watching television. He did not like her to do so, he thought it best if she maintained distance from the secular world, but as with everything else he could not deny her this small pleasure. She was such a sad girl and it offered her some minor salve. How could anyone deny her such a thing?

He removed his clothes and dropped them to the floor at his feet and, standing naked before Lily, asked her to have Elijah burn them.

They are filthy.

What happened?

Nothing with which you need be concerned.

I'm not concerned, I'm curious.

Curiosity should be one of the deadly sins.

But it isn't.

A sin, no, but very often it is deadly.

I'll take my chances.

I wish you wouldn't speak like that.

Why?

It reminds me too much of your mother.

But I came back.

I took you back. He held a hand out toward her, his palm open. Come, help me to once more get clean.

She nodded without looking him in the eye, then rolled out of bed and walked to him. She gave him her hand and together they went into the bathroom.

Undress, he said.

She did, slowly and sadly, and while she did he turned on the shower and waited for the water to get hot. He liked it scalding. Steam rose toward the high ceiling.

He pulled open the shower door and stepped onto the blue tile and turned toward Lily. She stood naked on the carpet, her body firm and young and untainted by the world. It had been tainted by him. This was true. And he was aware that there was some contradiction in his using her pure body to exorcise his demons – he would thrash about inside her until he could expel them, thereby corrupting that purity – but some things were too beautiful for their own good. He could live with the contradiction if it meant having her.

Come, he said.

She walked to him.

Lily stood naked in the bathroom, her clothes discarded on the floor. The carpet felt coarse and unpleasant beneath her feet. She looked across the room to the blue-tiled shower into which Father was stepping. Steam rose toward the ceiling and fogged up the glass. Father was such a frightening figure when clothed. He seemed as solid as a brick. But when he was nude she could see the age and the frailty in him. He was shaped like an avocado pit on a pair of toothpicks, his legs thin and white. Blue veins lined the pale flesh, creating a horrible roadmap. He turned toward her, his white stone of a belly protruding, his penis like a walnut in a bird's nest, his face sweaty and his eyes full of sad desperation.

She feared him. She hated him. She felt sorry for him.

When she was a very little girl – five years old, six – he used to bring her back lollipops when he went on trips to Louisville or Lexington or Frankfort. He would set her on his knee and bounce her, and even now she believed that there had been nothing sexual in his actions. He would read her bedtime stories and if she woke in the night crying – she used to have terrible dreams about the devil stepping from her closet and coming for her, pitchfork in hand, forked tongue protruding lecherously, coming to take her to Hell – he would come into her room and comfort her. He would wipe the tears from her eyes and kiss her forehead and tell her she was safe from the devil.

If he tries to get you, I'll punch him in the nose.

She had believed him. She had trusted him. She had loved him.

She supposed she loved him still.

But things were different now. They had been different for years. Something changed in the way Father looked at her when she was fourteen years old. He no longer had the eyes of a father but instead the eyes of a predator. Like a lion in a nature film. The way he touched her changed as well. There was no longer innocence in his fingertips. Instead it had been replaced by a desire she did not yet fully understand. She had secretly kissed a few boys in the woods and let them touch her breasts and given one a handjob – she was fourteen, not a *little* kid – but the boys were her own age and as confused by what they were doing as she was. The way they touched her was hesitant and somehow innocent and exploratory despite the desperation in their fingers. The way Father touched her made her feel dirty. He told her she was pure and innocent and he needed innocence in his life. He told her he loved her so much and she was beautiful. But the gentleness and the kind words gave way to force and frantic brutal shoving that left her with tears in her eyes, feeling raw and hollow.

She wished things had never changed. She had loved him so completely once and though she loved him still she hated him too. Part of her wanted simply to bash in his head with something hard and heavy. A wrench or a stone. She felt betrayed by him. With his behavior he had promised to be one thing to her, but as she developed breasts and hips, as she began menstruating, he had proved the lie in that promise. It made all the good moments feel false as scenes from a sitcom. She could imagine a canned laugh-track echoing hollow over her most cherished memories. There she is getting a Band-Aid placed on her scraped knee by Father. She sits on her bed and he kneels before her.

I'll always be here to kiss your booboos.

Cue laughter.

When she had cried after the first time he held her in his arms and asked what had brought the tears to her eyes. She told him that she felt awful – it had hurt and made her feel sick and now she felt used and ashamed. She felt that God must be looking down at her angry and disappointed.

He told her that what she had done for him was a good thing. These human bodies of ours were frail things with needs that could not be denied.

When she was fifteen he had gotten her pregnant. She had known within weeks of it happening, had felt her body changing and had known without need for a pregnancy test, but she had not wanted to tell him. She had been afraid to tell him, and as it turned out, she had been right to be afraid, for when she did tell him his face went red and he cursed and called her a cunt and a whore and asked her how she could have done this to him. He slapped her hard across the face. Then he stopped and looked at her. Her cheek was stinging with pain and tears streamed from her eyes. He told her he was sorry and he held out his arms. She walked to him and he wrapped her in an embrace and told her it would be okay. We'll take care of it. I promise.

Six weeks later Father'd had the fetus cut out of her.

A large part of her – most of her – had been glad of the procedure, for she was not ready to be a mother. She knew that down to her bones. But the relief only worked to increase the guilt, which was corrosive, creating a black cavity in her heart.

She told herself there was no reason to feel guilty. She told herself that Father was the voice of God on earth and what he did and said was by definition good and correct, and oftentimes she could even make herself believe it. She had to make herself believe it. If she didn't she would be unable to live with herself.

Come, Father said, standing in the steaming shower, looking at her with desperation in his large, kind, lying eyes.

She hesitated – and then walked to him.

*

Mosley put on a clean suit, combed his hair, looked at himself in the mirror. It was now nearly five o'clock, which meant his boys would soon be returning. It seemed this day would offer little reprieve from the corruption of the outside world. Always there was something with which he had to deal. Never could he find peace.

Hide your face from my sins and blot out all my iniquity. Create in me a pure heart, God, and renew a steadfast spirit within me. Do not cast me from your presence or take your Holy Spirit from me. Amen.

Stepping over his dirty clothes to get to the bedroom door he reminded Lily that Elijah needed to burn them.

I want the fire hot.

I'll tell him.

Do.

He made his way to the front porch to await the arrival of his boys, and standing there he looked at what he had built. It was something to be proud of, and all so that he might spread the word of the Lord. This had been nothing but an empty 120 acres when he purchased it, but look at it now. Teeming with life and the love of God. He brought in the lost, the filthy, the loveless, and he showed them the way and he cleaned them and he revealed to them God's kindness to which they had for so long been blind. God was merciful but He also had a sense of humor. If you did not understand His actions you might mistake His kindness for cruelty. Many on the streets did. But he brought them into the fold and gave them a place to call home that they might never again wander blind through the shadows.

Three hundred people lived here, and while some might view that as a failure, he did not, for very few men could claim to have saved three hundred souls, and there were thousands of others who had traveled through this land and been made better by their time here. It was true that televangelists reached millions, but their words were not pure. They did not speak with faith and honesty. So many of them were cocksuckers and boy-fuckers and drug addicts who had so little respect for truth that the lies in their mouths did not even taste bad on their tongues. To him even a necessary lie had the taste of shit. You could see the cynicism in their eyes, and while he was cynical about a great many things, he was not cynical about the word of the Lord. His heart was pure and when he spoke to his flock it was with honesty and conviction. The light of God spoke through him even when he could not see it.

And it had been a long time since he'd seen that lantern's glow.

The vans began to arrive, coming in from various cities and towns throughout the state, and with them they brought the day's collection plates. Most so-called men of God required a tithe of their congregation but he believed in no such thing. A man of God should provide for his people, not only spiritually but a haven from the world, and that meant he should not put a tithe on them but on everyone else. It was the outside world that must pay so that this world apart could survive.

Amos opened the gate, dragging it across the dry earth of the driveway, raising a small cloud of dust, and the vans began rolling toward the house. The first two arrived within a minute of one another, their drivers parking and stepping from their vehicles with black duffel bags in hand. Each of them had made at least a dozen stops, dropping off product and collecting payments of one to five thousand dollars from hub dealers. Those dealers each had another dozen or so boys and men working for them, most of the street hustlers being black, but they were of no concern or interest to Mosley. No one who lived outside these fences was of any concern or interest to him unless they got in his way.

Cyrus walked up the porch steps with his duffel bag in hand.

Did everything go well?

Yes, Father.

Good.

Cyrus set the duffel bag down at his feet, turned, and walked away. He stepped back into his van, put it into gear, turned it around, and drove it to the garage, which sat between the church proper and the road.

This happened ten more times, each man setting his duffel bag to the left of the one set down before it until there was a row of them, each containing anywhere from twenty-five to forty thousand dollars. All told, there was somewhere in the neighborhood of four hundred thousand dollars resting at his feet.

One might think this a great sum of money, but it was not cheap to feed and clothe and offer spiritual nourishment to three hundred people. It did not cost four hundred thousand dollars a month, of course, so there was always some surplus, but that only went into savings. Things could always go bad and one needed to be prepared for such an occurrence.

Finally the twelfth and final van arrived. It came to a stop. The engine died. The door swung open and a young man stepped out with a duffel bag in hand. Mosley could tell before the young man said a word that something had gone wrong. It was in his posture and in his refusal to make eye contact as he approached. He walked across the dirt to the steps carrying his duffel bag, and the duffel bag seemed to be of some weight, but Mosley still knew what the young man's mouth had yet to speak.

What happened, Oliver?

Ulysses refused payment.

Did he say why?

He did not.

How much did he owe?

Eight thousand dollars. If you recall, he delayed the last payment as well, promising to pay this month.

What was his demeanor?

I don't understand.

Did he say he would pay when he could?

This time he refused payment altogether and threatened

to kill me if I didn't leave the product with him, so I did. I'm sorry. I was scared.

You needn't be sorry, son, for you made the right decision. It is not your fault that others are less honest in their dealings than are we. No point in putting yourself in unnecessary danger.

The young man nodded.

We won't be working with Ulysses again, so don't bother with him come the next delivery date, okay?

Okay.

Leave the bag and get cleaned up for dinner.

The young man set down the bag, turned, and walked away.

When Mosley was too long absent people ceased to fear him and when that happened he knew it was time for his return. The first offense had to be the last or word got round that one could get away with anything, and when that happened things could quickly get out of control. It began with a dealer refusing payment but it ended with his vans getting jacked by common hoodlums and this, of course, was unacceptable.

It resulted in far too great a financial loss and far too much bloodshed, and when the bloodshed was indiscriminate innocents got killed. His heart could not stand this. There were those who believed him cruel but when it came to innocents he was very soft indeed. In fact he was not cruel at all. He was merely pragmatic, doing what was necessary. But even this did not mean he would break from biblical code, for he would not. All of his actions he was certain were within his rights as a man of God and none of them a sin.

The day was just getting worse. He had a drive ahead of him now and would once more have to resort to violence.

Sometimes a man had to get dirty in order that he might remain clean.

But that was for later. Some deeds were best done in darkness.

Elijah carried the duffel bags upstairs and set them in the hallway to the left of the locked door, one beside the other in a neat row, before turning once more toward the stairs and trudging down them. Mosley unlocked the door – knob as well as padlock – and pushed it open, revealing the room behind it. Bundles of ten- and twenty- and hundred-dollar bills were stacked there, standing as high as the window sills. Each stack was approximately four foot wide by four foot deep. Because of the various denominations, the stacks were worth varying amounts, but Mosley kept a ledger, noting all monies which went into and out of the room. Currently it contained $16,325,000.

There was another million stored in safe-deposit boxes to which only he had access. This money he would use only if he had to escape the law by way of leaving the country, which he did not want to do, for it would mean abandoning his people, and he thought he would rather die than do that. Yet he had purchased a different identity – driver's license, social security number, passport – which he stored in the nearest safe-deposit box in Louisville in case things ever went sideways. No one had ever died regretting the presence of an escape hatch.

This money too he knew he should keep elsewhere, even if elsewhere was underground – in fact he once had kept it underground – but somehow its presence in his home provided comfort. He grew up extremely poor, had often eaten only ketchup sandwiches on day-old bread for supper, and there were times when he felt he needed to walk upstairs simply to look at the money, to remind himself that he was somebody, that he was not the unkempt little boy he once had been – that little boy with home-cut hair and home-sewn clothes who had been beat up on his way to and from school, that little boy who had resorted to theft before finding God and allowing Him into his heart. Probably there was something wrong with that need, it certainly made him feel unholy, but it was one he could not deny. He might be a man of God, but a man of God was still a man, try as he might to be something more. He would only be truly pure once he had shed this husk that made him human and become spirit alone.

He reached down, picked up the first duffel bag, and carried it into the room. He set it on a block of money, unzipped it, inhaled – he loved the scent of money – and began removing the bundles of cash. He counted the money as he removed it, noted its presence in his ledger, and set it on the smallest block. Once this block reached the size of the others he would shrink-wrap it, but that would take some time, as he always had expenses – heroin, arms, police payoffs, vans, gas, and of course the expenses that came with running his church. This all amounted to just under $3 million a year, $250,000 a month, and since he brought in only $4.5 million to $5.5 million a year he was looking at years of income, years of careful, incremental savings.

In an hour he was finished.

He stepped out of the room, locked the door, both the knob and the padlock, which he ran through a thick stainless steel staple after swinging home the hasp. He trusted his people, but not so much that he would leave this room unsecure. If the serpent in the garden had revealed anything about human nature it was that temptation was the one thing man could not resist. So long as a man's view was only of the holy he would not be tempted and would therefore remain clean in thought as well as deed.

He carried the empty duffel bags downstairs and dropped them on the front porch beside the door. Elijah would know what to do with them from there.

He stepped off the front porch and began walking toward the feed shed.

Lily stood at the bedroom window and watched as Father walked from the house to the nearest feed shed. It was a small rectangular structure made from plywood siding and four-by-fours. It had been painted red but the paint was weathered and peeling away. The corrugated metal roof, which slanted down from left to right, was spotted with rust, and leaves and debris lay in its grooves, though they would certainly be washed away by the next rain. To the left of the feed shed sat an ancient claw-foot tub that was used for slaughtering pigs, and blood had dried to its sides. Weed grass grew tall around its feet, pointing toward the clear blue sky, waving in the hot summer breeze, lawnmowers unable to cut it down.

There was a man in the feed shed who would almost certainly be dead by the end of the day, dead and buried out in the woods rather than in the graveyard near the road. Lily had heard tell of such things happening before, though the details had always been kept from her. Father thought her too delicate to be exposed to such ugliness. But she was stronger than he thought. She knew more than he thought.

She contemplated the way the man in the suit had looked at her as she lay on the couch with her book. His face had been bruised and cut and covered by Band-Aids but there had been kindness in his eyes. There had also been something like recognition. It had felt as though he knew her but she could not imagine why he would. She was certain she had never seen him before. Yet she thought of that look in his eyes and she thought of him dead and felt sad. She did not understand how Father could snuff out life in the way he did, like throwing dirt over a campfire, with no emotional involvement at all.

It was strange to her how he seemed to be two men. How he could be simultaneously gentle and coldblooded.

She thought about how sometimes after sex he would lie in bed staring at the ceiling and talk to her quietly about his childhood. How tears would stand out in his eyes as he spoke of his mother and how she had loved him and held him to her bosom. How his father was jealous of their relationship. How he beat both of them. How they would hide together to avoid those beatings. How his mother would talk to him of God and salvation and assure him that this life was a test – a trial – and that when they died they would find eternal peace. How they must not despair of this life for they would come forth as gold. He spoke to her of how his father had finally killed his mother and with her no longer there to protect him he had been tormented by the man.

On those nights Lily tried to imagine the man beside her as a boy but found she could not. She had seen pictures of him as a child, old black-and-white photos, and she tried to imagine the man within the boy, and the boy within the man, but her imagination failed her. Somehow, despite the fact he was flesh and blood, Father seemed to her to have been chiseled from stone. The boy and the man were two different people, each immutable, and when Father spoke of the boy he was speaking of someone else.

She turned away from the window and walked to the bathroom. She turned on the shower and stepped under its spray. She washed away the stink of the man who had just been inside her and she cried. She let the spray wash away the seed that was running down the inside of her thighs. She hated herself. She hated herself for wanting so badly to be loved that she would allow a man she hated inside of her. She told herself that he was a man of God. Part of her, most of her, even believed it to be true. She had been told it since she was a small girl. But somewhere she did not believe it. In her marrow she did not believe it. She knew it was wrong to doubt. But she did doubt, and her doubt made her hate herself even more. For if he was not a man of God – if he was not the voice of God on earth, if he was not all the things he and those around him claimed he was – then he was simply a dirty old man who had raped her, and she had stayed by his side, and what kind of person would stay by the side of her rapist? So he must be what he claimed to be. It was the only way that her standing by his side made sense. It was the only way her lying in his bed made sense. If he was not what he claimed to be then she should not be here.

Yet here she was.

She stepped from the shower and dried off.

But if he was what he claimed to be why did she feel so awful after he had been inside her? Why did she feel used and sick to her stomach? If he was what he claimed to be shouldn't she feel as though she had been filled with love and light rather than stuffed with foul earth, with compost?

She put on a white T-shirt and a pair of panties and walked to the vent in the floor. She lifted the vent and reached down into the air conditioning duct. She pulled out a small plastic bag that held a fold of rolling papers, a lighter, and an eighth of marijuana. She rolled a joint – dropping seeds and stems back into the bag – and returned to the steam-filled bathroom and opened a window. She looked out at the woods and lighted the joint and took a deep drag, holding the smoke within her lungs. She exhaled lazily, watching the smoke drift out the window before being carried away on the hot summer breeze.

It was wrong to smoke marijuana, the body was a temple that one should not corrupt, but it made her feel better. When she was stoned she found she could live with herself, and shouldn't a person be allowed a little bit of peace?

She no longer found peace in God or religion. She found turmoil there. Her stomach felt sick and her heart felt heavy when she thought of God witnessing the things she did with Father. She felt dirty. If she could convince herself that Father was what he claimed to be she might be able to live with herself without the use of drugs, but no matter how hard she tried to do that she found that she still had doubt within her.

Shouldn't a person be allowed a little bit of peace?

She took another hit and looked out at the woods and thought about running through them, thought about running away from all of this. As her mother had. But this was the only life she'd ever known. This was her world entire and she knew so long as this world existed she would never be able to leave it. She was afraid of what lay beyond. She was afraid of admitting that her entire life thus far had been a lie. If she did that she would have to acknowledge that she had been a stupid little girl, a stupid little whore, who had allowed herself to be used by a man who was not what he claimed to be, and she did not know how to do that. She did not know how to live with that. So she suppressed her doubts in the only way she knew how.

But still that thought was there. Running through the woods and escaping all of this for good. As her mother had done.

She wondered what it would feel like to be free of this life. Though this place was comforting it was also a prison.

It made her chest feel tight when she thought about it.

It made her stomach feel sick.

Sometimes she wished she had the courage to kill herself. Then she would be free of everything. But those who killed themselves were denied Heaven, were denied the sight of God. So she was stuck here. She would be stuck here forever, and either she would manage to finally suppress her doubts and her self-hatred or she would not.

But she did not see herself ever escaping this life.

It was her world entire.

Mosley stepped into the feed shed and smelled immediately the stench of human waste. The interloper had shit himself. He walked toward the man and the man watched him with watery, glazed-over eyes. He pulled the duct tape away, unwinding it from the man's sweaty head, and removed the now saturated handkerchief, which he allowed to drop gingerly from his fingertips to the bloodstained pine floor.

Out of life's school of war: what does not destroy me makes me stronger. This is but one of the many times that Nietzsche spoke something which sounded profound but which was in fact false. I would bet green money that you do not feel particularly strong at the moment, yet you are not yet destroyed. Am I correct in my assessment?

Fuck you: the two words spoken in an angry whisper, spittle on the man's lips and chin.

Mosley ignored this and continued:

Sometimes what does not destroy us takes away a great chunk of what makes us human. Men can have their humanity shattered and still breathe, can they not? I would suspect that men in war know this with certainty though I have never seen a battlefield but this one we are all born to by the act of conception. But fucking gets us all here, so I don't feel privileged in my knowledge. Am I speaking truths you do not already know?

Let me go now – the man inhaled, exhaled – and I might let you live.

Mosley smiled. I admire your bravery.

It isn't bravery.

Mosley cocked an eyebrow. What is it, pray tell?

A simple fact.

So it is delusion rather than bravery. Who sent you here?

The man turned his head away.

Mosley walked to him, put the sole of his shoe upon the nail in the man's left foot, and pushed down. The man gritted his teeth and began breathing hard, chest heaving, but he refused to cry out though a cry was clearly in his throat. Refused to allow it to escape. That wild bird would remain in its cage.

I know the injection I gave you alleviated some of your pain, but I see that you are still capable of feeling something. Tell me why you are here and I'll alleviate all your suffering.

The man turned back toward him and there was surprising calm in his glassy eyes. He smiled, looking sickly, almost ghostly, as if he had already died without moving on.

Do you really believe – the words seemed to be coming with difficulty, as if each were a stone he had first to push to the top of a hill before cresting it and allowing it to roll off his tongue – do you really believe you're a righteous man?

Mosley removed his foot from the nail and walked to the dusty shelf. He picked up the man's cigarettes and lighter, lighted a cigarette, walked back to the man nailed to his floor. He sat on his haunches and put the cigarette to the man's lips. The man inhaled.

Cigarettes and alcohol are not permitted here but I believe I can make an exception. You intrigue me. I don't believe I've ever come across a man quite like you.

The man was far away for a moment, but blinked several times, forcing himself to find focus. You didn't – he cleared his throat – you didn't answer my question.

Trying to play mind games despite the pain you're in. Trying to find the upper hand. You will not find it, friend. You intrigue me, as I said, but you are at a disadvantage and will not be able to reverse your circumstances. But to answer your question: yes, I am as righteous as a man born of this earth can be. I live without hypocrisy.

Thou shalt not kill.

You'll have to do better than that, friend. The correct translation is thou shalt not murder, and I have not once been guilty of that sin.

You've killed women and children. I've heard stories.

I merely sent them home. There was never murder in my touch nor and especially in my heart. Can you say the same thing? I doubt very much that you can, for I see what kind of man you are. The scars on your body tell a tale, as does the look in your eyes, glassy though they are. I see that you are not a man meant to live in this century. You are not a man meant to live in a world of shopping malls and salad forks. You crave violence. You need both blunt force and tools for cutting. Death calls to you, which makes you brave in the face of it. Are you saved, friend? Have you found God?

God is a bullet. Why don't you help him – help him find me?

Mosley smiled again. In other circumstances, in another life, I suspect we could have been great friends. I would like to meet you in Heaven so that we might talk.

You think you're strong but you're not.

Mosley removed the cigarette from the man's lips, ashed on the floor, replaced it. Is this another tactic?

No, the man said, it's another fact.

Do you think you're strong nailed to my floor and bleeding?

I'm strong enough – strong enough to admit what I am. I'm strong enough to lie here knowing you're going to kill me without craving salvation which will never come.

But salvation can come, friend, and it can set you free. All you have to do is accept God as your personal savior. Let Him into your heart and He will erase your pain and replace it with love, and when the time comes, which I assure you will be soon, He will welcome you home.

You're a child, the man said, and you have childish beliefs.

Some people must deny the holy for they cannot accept anything greater than themselves. Dogs howl at the moon but if the moon howls back the dogs will cower. You are just such a dog – and for reasons I do not understand you must deny the light in the sky.

At least dogs howl at something that actually exists. The moon is there for everyone to see. Where is your god?

Mosley felt a surge of anger rush up within him and he slapped the man across the face, knocking the cigarette out of his mouth and sending it flying across the feed shed.

Don't you degrade the holy in my presence, you filthy motherfucker.

The man turned his head back toward him, a smile on his now bloody mouth. His glassy eyes sparkled.

You know it's true and that's what makes you angry. You've dedicated your life to something and yet you doubt. In quiet moments – he coughed – in quiet moments your faith falters. As it should.

Mosley walked to the gun on the shelf and brought it back, shoved it brutally into the man's mouth, hearing and feeling his teeth scrape on the metal.

You're about to find out how wrong you are.

The man's glassy, pained eyes were aglow with victory. It gave Mosley pause. It made him realize the man was intentionally pushing him toward murder. He might not want to die, but he certainly wanted not to talk. This was his way out.

Mosley forced himself to calm down. He pulled the pistol from the man's mouth. He combed his fingers through his hair, dragging his bangs from over his eyes. He exhaled.

You almost had me, friend.

I did have you. You're weak.

We will see how brave you are when the effects of your anesthesia have ceased to ease your suffering. A man in agony tends to say what he must in order to stop that agony. You may be in pain, but more will come over you in the next several hours. You will reach a point, I assure you, when you will tell me what I want to know only that I might put a bullet through your brain, and when that time comes I will relieve you of your life that you might discover the truth of what lies beyond, and you will find yourself both shocked and horrified, for your life will have proven to be a waste, and you will writhe for eternity in agony greater than anything I have shown you here or am capable of showing you, for the torments of Hell cannot be replicated on earth.

Mosley got to his feet. He walked the gun to the shelf and set it down. He looked at his hand as if it were an alien thing, clenching and unclenching his fist. He inhaled and exhaled. He looked at his watch. It was nearly time for evening prayer. His flock would be waiting for him in the dining hall.

We will continue our conversation later. I suspect you'll be rather more willing to divulge information then, and I am keen to hear what you will say.

He turned and walked out of the feed shed, heart still thumping angrily in his chest, despite his calm, fluid movements.

How he wished to murder that godless son of a bitch.

Lamb watched Mosley walk out of the feed shed, and as soon as he was gone dropped his head to the floorboards and allowed himself tears, for he was exhausted and in pain and had never before struggled so hard to maintain something like normalcy, never before had to draw up from within himself so much willpower and then utilize it. He'd wanted so badly to answer the man's questions, to end his pain in that way, but he would not give in. He would not have words pried from his mouth. He might be killed but he would not be beaten. Would not be broken. There was something within him that would not allow it, something stronger than flesh or bone, something that would never bleed or break even if the rest of him did. All his limbs might be amputated but this part at his center would never be destroyed, not until he was dead.

His hands and feet throbbed painfully with the beat of his heart.

But if it weren't for the pain he'd have been unable to focus himself at all. The pain had given him something in the here and now on to which he could hold, on to which he could cling, as sharp as it was at the edges, and clinging on to it he had been able to taunt the man, to play with his head, almost to get himself killed without the man having further opportunities to pry words from his lips, and for that he was glad, but now that Mosley was gone he allowed himself once more to drift. The pain was too great to do otherwise. He needed to float away from it. The heroin was a temporary comfort and he needed reprieve, so he allowed his mind to drift out onto the dark sea of the needle. He thought of sharks swimming beneath him. He wondered where the moon might be for it was not in the sky, not the one at which he was looking in any case. Occasionally his body would twitch and throb with pain and he would be wrenched back to reality, back to the feed shed, but after a time he would once more close his eyes and drift into the darkness. He wondered if he would die out here on this endless needle sea. He wondered if the sharks would take him. He wondered if there *were* sharks. He could neither see them nor sense their presence yet somehow he thought they were there beneath the surface, waiting for him to sink down to their depth. They need not attack. They fed frequently enough that they could afford patience. He wanted to find land but the shore to which he was closest held only misery. It seemed difficult to believe that only last night he had lain in his own bed and slept beside the warmth of a beautiful companion. It couldn't be true and yet he knew that it was. That was life. It was strange and ugly and painful and beautiful and so full of joy that sometimes you thought your head might explode. Anything could happen. Maybe he would find God out here in the darkness. He wondered if there was a god. God was a bullet. Someone should save him from this ceaseless drifting. He wondered where his god might be, where his bullet might be, but did not truly want a bullet. He knew that now. Faced with darkness he wanted light. He wanted light.

He wanted—

He opened his eyes and saw darkness, but in time he found focus. His eyes adjusted to the night and he began to see his surroundings. He was in the feed shed once more, the needle sea gone. His hands and his feet throbbed with an almost unbearable pain but he let himself feel it. He had to feel it so that he might remain in the present, and he must remain in the present at all costs, for he had to get himself out of this situation. He had to save himself and he knew not how much time he might have in which to do it. He turned his head to look at his right hand. It was covered in blood and the blood looked black in the night. He forced his hand up against the nail head as hard as he could, but the nail gave not at all. Instead it dug into his palm. He tried to wrench his hand left and then right. There was no movement doing that either but plenty of pain. The nail was firmly in place, embedded deeply into the floor. He stopped and a sob escaped him. Drool hung from his mouth. He was going to die here. He was certain of it. He was going to die here because he could not stand this pain. He was going to die here because the nail would not move. It didn't matter why; he was going to die here.

He inhaled and exhaled and told himself to stop thinking that way. He told himself that he would die here only if he believed it, only if he gave up. He told himself he was stronger than this situation, dire as it might be. He told himself he could get out of this.

He closed his eyes. Tears rolled down his cheeks. He once more forced his right hand against the nail. If he could not move the nail from the floor, then he would have to move his hand past the nail. That was his one option. If only he had access to that hammer and could pry the nails out of the floorboards things would be different, if only he had access to that hammer and a third hand with which to wield it. But that was dreaming. That was the delirious fantasy of a man suffering from dehydration out on the needle sea. He was pinned here to the floor like an insect and there was only one way to unpin himself. He pushed up against the nail head as hard as he could, feeling it sink deeper into his palm.

Fresh blood began to pour from his hand and run down his arm.

He wondered why he couldn't have made this attempt when he was in less pain. But he knew the answer to that. He had been drifting. The pain was what brought him back, that and his desire to live, and the pain was what allowed him to function even now. Without it he would be nowhere, which was where he had spent hours.

He pushed against the nail head with everything he had in him, gritting his teeth, tears rolling down his cheeks. For a long time he felt as though he were trying to push a mountain. Nothing would move, nothing at all.

But then he felt a pop and heard a scraping of metal on bone.

He stopped. He looked at his hand and saw there was now half an inch of space between the back of his hand and the floorboard. He could hear his blood dripping between the floorboards to the ground below. He heard movement down there, the shifting of some animal. He imagined rats scurrying in the darkness, finding his blood, licking it from the earth.

He felt sick. He wanted to vomit.

There was no going back now. The nail head was inside him. He would have to force it out one direction or the other, and there was only one direction to go. He would have to rip it through the back of his hand. There was no other way to get free.

He wanted to die. He had thought earlier that he didn't, but he'd been wrong. He wanted to die so he could stop feeling this. There was nothing but pain. It filled his head entirely. It was a constant scream and he wanted it silenced. If he could die it would be silenced.

He told himself to stop his bellyaching. He told himself to get his head right. He told himself the pain would be over sooner if he got out of this. He could get out now, or he could suffer for days, maybe weeks, nailed to a madman's shed floor. The man would drug him and feed him and keep him alive until he talked. He could remain here in agony indefinitely or he could free himself. That was his choice and if he wanted to get out of this he had to take action. He had to take action now, not ten minutes from now but right this goddamned second.

With every bit of willpower he had left within him he pushed up against the nail. He could feel the head pressing against bone on the inside of his hand. But there was no movement. His eyes watered. He gritted his teeth. His stomach was tight with nausea. He wasn't going to get his hand free. He would be stuck here for—

A scraping of bone, a tearing of flesh, an excruciating pain: then movement.

He held his throbbing hand over his face and looked at it in the darkness. It dripped blood into his open mouth as he breathed heavily, his chest heaving, but he did not care. He had done it. He had actually managed to wrench his hand free. The proof of it was floating there before his eyes like a pale but bloody ghost. He moved his fingers. It caused him pain, but it was worth it. Seeing them move made it real. That was his hand. He thought to bend the fingers and the fingers bent, so it really *was* his hand.

He let it drop to the floor and closed his eyes. He allowed himself a moment to breathe. He opened his eyes and turned his head to the left. He looked at the hand still nailed to the floor and felt an overwhelming sense of dread. He was hot and covered in sweat but felt himself shivering all over. His muscles were cramping terribly. His stomach was a sick knot. He did not care. His thoughts were only on freeing his left hand. He knew now what it would feel like and did not want to ever feel that again. He wanted only to lie here in this pain rather than force agony upon himself, but he knew he could not. He knew that in passivity lay death. His circumstances required movement. They required action.

He closed his eyes and tried to calm himself. The pain in his extremities continued to throb to the beat of his heart and his heart was pounding. He tried to slow it but it was difficult. All he could think about was dragging that second nail head through the meat of his hand. He might try to wrench out the nail with his free hand, but it had been hammered down so tight against his palm that he could not even grab it. Which meant, as with the first nail, this one had to go clean through.

You can do it. You've done it once so you know you can do it again.

He once more raised his right hand and looked at it, as if to prove to himself that it could be done because it had been done. He blinked at it.

Perhaps he could wait awhile. He had already done so much.

But he knew he could not. He knew there was no time at all. He knew neither how long he'd been swimming in darkness nor when Mosley might return.

In passivity lay only death.

He clenched his teeth and pulled up on his left hand.

He lay motionless, his hands resting on his stomach, warm blood soaking into his undershirt. The faint sound of chirping crickets came to him from outside. The snorting of a pig. Wind blowing through trees. He didn't think he had it in him to free his feet in the same manner. He knew he didn't have it in him and doubted it was possible anyway. The feet contained larger bones, much more meat. He felt completely drained, completely empty, but knew he had to find it within himself to get free somehow.

He sat up, looking at the feed shed by which he was surrounded. There were bags of pig feed on the floor to his right, a few bales of hay, and in front of him a shelf on which rested several empty Mason jars, hacksaws and bell scrapers, a flashlight, and of course his belongings and the duffel bag Mosley had brought in. To his left, the latched shed doors. He turned and looked over his shoulder and saw a push broom leaning against the wall.

For a moment he was still. Then he lay back down and reached for the broom. If he could extend his legs he knew he could reach it, but he could only extend them so far with his feet nailed flat to the floor, and doing even that caused great pain. Yet he had no choice. He pushed against the nails. It was his only chance to escape. He pushed with his legs, gritting his teeth at the pain, and finally his fingers were able to brush against the broom. He gripped a few of its bristles between his fingers and pulled the broom toward him. It came forward only inches, but it was enough. It allowed him to grab hold of it and pull. The broom fell to his side with a loud thwack. He grabbed it and pulled it to his chest, gripping it tight.

A strange exhilaration came over him. He might actually be able to do this. He was doing it. He had come so far. He was almost free.

Holding the broom he sat up once more. He felt dizzy and sick but did not care, for he was getting ever nearer escape. The next thing he needed to do was stand.

He exhaled and pushed himself to his feet. It took great effort with them nailed to the floor. He had to lift himself up entirely with only the use of his upper body, as he was unable to position himself with his legs under him, and he didn't think he'd manage at all but for the fact that he could use the broom as well. He pushed himself off the floor, using the handle to keep himself upright, ignoring the pain in his hands and back.

Finally he was standing.

Black dots floated before his eyes and his numb head felt light as a balloon. He imagined the dots were tiny black holes. If he got too near the verge of any one of them it would suck away his consciousness. He stood very still and let the blood flow back to his head. The dots floating before his eyes faded away, spiraled out of existence, and he found that he was able to find focus. He looked toward the shelf and the duffel bag resting there. He raised the broom in his hands and moved the end toward the duffel bag, trying to put the handle through its straps.

After three attempts he finally managed. He lifted the end of the broom. It was difficult to do, as his arms felt rubbery and weak, but he managed, and the duffel bag came sliding toward him along the broom handle. He grabbed it and pulled the broom out of the straps. He threw the broom aside, reached into the duffel bag, and from within pulled the hammer. It was very heavy in his hand. Its metal must be very dense, for it seemed to weigh fifty pounds.

Looking down at his bloody feet he told himself he could do this. He told himself he could do this and he believed it. He leaned down and carefully tried to slide the hammer claw between his flesh and the nail head. There was very little room between the two, there was no room at all, and he had to dig into the flesh to hook the claw under the nail head. His foot throbbed terribly. The handle of the hammer was slick with blood and sweat from his hands and difficult to grip. He wiped his hands off one at a time on his shirt. He pulled the handle to the right, the neck and poll putting great pressure on the cuboid bone as he tried to lever out the nail. He cringed and pulled and felt the nail begin to lift, he believed he did, and he heard a screech as the nail began to slip from the grip of the wood floor. He wondered if he might break a bone in his foot prying the nail loose, but did not care. If he did he did. So long as he got himself free he would be okay. Then the hammer slipped from his hand, bounced back, and went falling forward. He reached for it, afraid it would slide out of reach, and lost his balance. He tried to catch himself but there was nothing to grab. Sharp pain shot up his legs from his feet. He waved his arms. He felt himself going down, falling forward.

Next thing he knew he was prostrate on the floor.

He looked over his shoulder to his feet. The nails had pulled loose from the floor. His feet were free. All he had to do was force the nails up through his flesh now, force them back out the way they had gone in. This would have to be less painful than what he'd endured with his hands.

He rolled over and lay on his back a moment. He looked at the roof of the feed shed. Moonlight slanted in through a few small holes in the corrugated roof. In the distance a large dog barked and his bark was answered by a smaller dog. Nearby pigs were wallowing in the mud, grunting to one another. A young girl laughed somewhere. Crickets continued to chirp.

He sat up and looked down at his feet. They barely seemed to belong to him. Even the pain was somehow distant. For the moment it was. But that was about to change. He drew his right foot up and placed it on his left knee. He looked at the nail driven through it, at the point of the nail protruding about an inch and a half from the arch of his foot. He exhaled. He reached out and grabbed the point of the nail. Just doing this sent fresh pain shooting through his foot and up his leg like a great surge of electricity. Into the ends of his toes, which twitched involuntarily. He pushed, sliding the nail up out of his foot. Then he pulled from the other side. He tried going slowly at first, but the pain was tremendous, so he paused, waited a moment, exhaled, and then simply yanked. An involuntary gasp escaped him. He let go the nail and the nail hit the floor and rolled in a half circle, leaving a thin trail of blood behind it, before falling into a crack between the floorboards and going still and silent.

He looked to his left foot.

Almost there, he said.

Lily stood at the window and watched through the narrow gaps between the now-closed blinds as Father got into his truck, started the engine, and headed down the driveway to the faded asphalt which would carry him away from here. His taillights grew smaller and then – poof – disappeared. She felt a weight lift off her chest. He was gone. At least for this short time she was free of his watchful eye. Part of her hoped that he ended up in a car accident, that a tractor trailer hauling twenty tons of goods t-boned his vehicle at seventy miles per hour. He would be slammed first into the door of his Ford and then the truck would roll, compressing the cab until there was no more room for human life within it, until the life was squeezed out of it, leaving only a battered corpse behind, the blood motionless within its arteries. But as soon as she had the thought she felt guilty for thinking it. Father was a man of God, he was the voice of God on earth, and a person capable of having such thoughts about the voice of God must be an instrument of Satan. Must at the very least be weak or evil enough to fall prey to him and become his instrument.

Then her eyes were drawn from the shadow-covered length of the driveway, and her thoughts cut off, by movement to her right. She turned her head and watched as the feed shed doors swung open. A man stood in the open doorway. He wore wrinkled slacks and an unbuttoned shirt. His gray hair hung down over his forehead in sweaty clumps. His hands were covered in something dark. She thought it was blood. They glistened beneath the moonlight. He took an unsteady step out into the night and looked in her direction. For a moment she was afraid that he was looking directly at her, but she did not think that was possible. The only light in the bedroom was that of the TV, which was not enough to backlight her, and the blinds were closed. He would not be able to see her through them, not from that distance anyway.

He turned around and closed the feed shed doors. Then started walking toward the northwest corner, toward the far back corner, of the compound. She watched him limp away from her and the house for some time before she decided to follow. She put on a pair of boots and left the bedroom, thinking that she was being stupid, thinking that this man might be dangerous and she would be safest if she remained right where she was.

But then she thought of his kind eyes and the recognition she believed she saw in them. She wanted to know what he was doing here. She wanted to know what it had to do with her. For she was almost certain that it did have something to do with her, though she had no idea what.

She walked down the hallway, through the foyer, and out the front door, stepping onto the front porch. The air conditioner was on in the house and though it was less than eighty degrees outside now the sun had gone down the air felt very warm as it enveloped her.

She turned her head and watched the stranger limp down toward the cabins in which the Children of God lay sleeping. She walked down the wooden porch steps and followed him, trudging through the tall grass covering the ground. She kept her distance. Her heart was thumping wildly in her chest. It occurred to her that the stranger might be looking for someone in one of those cabins. It occurred to her that he might be here to kill one of them. But he walked past the cabins without more than a glance in their direction. Instead he made his way to the cinder-block medical building and stepped inside. The light switched on and splashed out the back window, illuminating the trees behind the compound. There was movement there, a rustle of leaves, and for a moment she saw a pair of eyes that she thought might belong to the devil. They were close-set and yellow and somehow malignant. She froze. She was afraid to go nearer. Perhaps this man was luring her toward that beast. Perhaps this was all part of his plan.

She thought of the conversation she'd earlier had with Father.

Curiosity should be one of the deadly sins.

But it isn't.

A sin, no, but very often it is deadly.

She should have remained in the house. She could see that now. Anybody could see that. Danger lurked in the shadows and she had only become aware of it by chance. The eyes blinked. Then the possum turned around and scurried into the woods.

Her relief was so great that she almost laughed out loud. But she slapped a hand over her mouth and managed to stifle it. She could be so stupid and childish. To think that the devil might be in those woods. The stranger had been luring her nowhere. He was not even aware of her presence. He was wounded and going to the one place he knew he might be able to find supplies with which to treat himself. She had no idea how he might know where the medical building was, but clearly he did. She wondered what else he might know.

She took a step forward.

This step was followed by others.

She stood in the night, looking through the medical building's single window, and watched as the stranger washed and bandaged his wounds, his face a constant cringe. When he was done he replaced his shoes, turned toward the door, and stepped through it.

Now she would find out why he was here. Now he would do what he was here to do.

She walked around the perimeter of the gray cinder-block building, and when she reached the front corner she stopped. She poked her head around. She saw the stranger limping toward Father's house. One of the dogs growled at him. He drew a gun, but did not ready it to fire. Instead he sat down on his haunches and spoke softly to the dog and petted its head. This made her like him a great deal. Father in similar circumstances would have killed the creature. Of this she was almost certain. She stood still and watched him. She was out in the open, and if he turned around he would see her standing there in her white T-shirt, her panties, and her boots, but she made no attempt to hide. There was a part of her that hoped he did turn around. There was a part of her that wanted to know what would happen.

But he did not turn around. He stood up once more and continued toward the house, limping badly but not faltering. The gun hung from his hand as he walked through the tall grass, up the porch steps, and arrived at the front door.

He grabbed the doorknob, turned it, and pushed open the door.

A moment later he disappeared inside.

She wondered what he wanted in the house. There was only one way to find out. She followed him in.

Lamb limped to the feed shed shelf. Blood dripped from his hands and feet as he went. His graying hair hung sweaty in his pale, ghostly face. He ran his fingers through it, streaking it with blood, but it fell again over his eyes. He removed his soiled underwear and his T-shirt and used the T-shirt to wipe himself clean. He slipped into his pants and his shirt, though he did not button the shirt. Doing so would cause him too much pain. It wouldn't be worth the effort. His hands felt fat and hot and ached every time he used them. He was not certain he hadn't broken a few small bones. He put on his shoes but did not tie the laces. He put his wallet into his right hip pocket. He chewed two Adderall and put the bottle into his left hip pocket. He tucked his pistol into his waistband. He picked up his cell phone and looked at it. He could call the police now and end this, but if he did he was also giving up any chance at the money. This he would not do, not after what he'd been through. He had bled for that cash and he would have it. For years he had lived hand-to-mouth and this was very likely the only opportunity in his life he would have to free himself from such circumstances. He thought of those lean weeks during which he ate noodles and margarine. During which he could not afford a bottle. He thought of late electric bills and his ancient Mercedes, bought used. He thought of his closetful of cheap suits. He thought of his expensive work shoes, now ten years old, newspaper stuffed into them because there were holes in the soles.

He had once thought he was going to be somebody, and the fact he realized now he never would be did not erase his hunger for something more.

But mostly he thought about being able to breathe without tightness in his chest. Being able to lie in bed at night without the constant money worries. Which bills would he be able to pay this month? Which ones could he put off a little longer without suffering for it?

People who said money did not buy happiness had always had enough to buy some. Everyone else knew better. He knew better.

He put his cell phone into the inside pocket of his jacket, let it slip down to the bottom. He lighted a cigarette and inhaled.

His shoes began to fill with blood.

He believed today was easily the longest of his life and yet it was not over. He turned toward the feed shed doors. He looked at them. He felt off-balance. He exhaled. He walked forward. His legs felt wobbly beneath him, as if he were walking on rubber stilts, and each step sent pain shooting up from the floor to his groin. His balls were pulled up right against his body despite the heat.

Through a crack between the doors he could see out into the night. It was quiet and still. For a moment. Then the front door of the white house opened and Mosley stepped out onto the porch. He wore a white linen suit, but on his feet, rather than white bucks, he wore a pair of rubber rain boots, and draped over his arm he carried a transparent raincoat. Yet the sky was clear of clouds, stars visible as far as the eyes could see. Lamb forgot to breathe. He wondered if the man was coming to pay him a visit. He pulled the pistol from his waistband and watched through the crack. He felt both fear and exhilaration. This might be over in a matter of minutes.

Mosley walked across the porch to the steps and down the steps to a blue Ford pickup truck. He stood at the truck for a moment, looking off into the distance. Then he pulled open the truck door, tossed the raincoat onto the seat, and followed it in. A moment later the engine sputtered to life. The noise was very loud in the quiet country night. It echoed off the low hills and trees and doubled, then tripled. The crickets ceased to chirp. One of the South African mastiffs barked twice, then went silent.

The truck rolled down the driveway toward the gate.

Lamb wondered where the man might be going. He wondered how much time he had. There was really nothing nearby, so he thought he probably had thirty minutes at a minimum. He hoped so.

He tucked the pistol back into his waistband.

After a few moments of silence he unlatched the feed shed doors.

They swung wide to reveal the night. The air was cool and crisp. The moon fat in the sky, like a bloated corpse floating in dark waters. It illuminated the land and the buildings that lay before him. Stars punctured the darkness like backlighted pinpricks in a sheet of construction paper. A satellite blinked its way across the sky. He wished he were on it. He wished he were anywhere but here.

The pigs looked up and snorted grumpily from their muddy pits in the earth. They were fat and mean and had stupid black eyes he wished to gouge out.

Shut your fucking mouths.

One of them snorted in reply.

He closed the feed shed doors and limped away, limped toward the medical building. He'd only briefly studied the map Abigail had given him but his memory was good. He would be fine so long as he had time to tend to his wounds before Mosley returned. He was afraid that the time wasn't there to take but didn't see that he had a choice but to try. He was bleeding steadily and was in so much pain it was difficult to think. Both of these things needed to be addressed.

He walked toward the back woods, passing the pigpen and a large vegetable garden, a tractor and a toolshed, and dozens of small cabins in which the Children of God slept and dreamed the dreams of the saved. He felt a strong hatred for every one of them. They were as responsible for Rhett Mosley as the man was for himself. Without them he was nothing but a lunatic shouting from Hallelujah Square, bullhorn echoing out multisyllabic nonsense, but by believing in him they had helped to create a man of power and importance. At least in this small corner of the world.

Yet there was also a part of him that envied them. He felt lost in the world, lost in the universe, alone. Entropy was the only thing of which he was certain – things would fall apart – but these people had not only comforting answers but a hand to hold. Their answers were almost certainly the wrong answers, but that did not change the fact that they felt secure in them. It was a neat trick. They had an imaginary blanket that somehow managed to keep them warm. They looked at the sky and felt the presence of a loving god. He looked at the sky and felt vast emptiness. There was no presence, and in fact, the universe was actively breaking apart, growing emptier by the minute as the space between debris grew larger. He longed to feel secure, to feel safe, to believe that there was something better after this life. But he did not and could not no matter how hard he tried. His mind refused to accept even the premise, forget its consequences.

So he was left alone.

He walked behind the cabins before reaching the medical building, a twenty-by-ten cinderblock structure with a single window and an asphalt-shingle roof. He tried the doorknob and found the door unlocked. He pushed into the dark building and closed the door behind him. He found a light switch and, after considering the risk, flipped it. The fluorescent bulbs in the ceiling immediately painted his surroundings with light. The room held not only a standard hospital bed but an exam table and a stirruped birthing bed. The walls were lined with white cupboards and below the cupboards to his right were a counter and sink. The counter held defibrillators, towels, a stack of pink emesis basins, a manual vacuum aspiration syringe, cotton swabs, antibiotic ointments, cortisone cream, gauze, and medical tape.

He looked down at the palms of his hands, at the holes torn into them. He thought he might be able to see through them to the floor on the other side, but saw only blood and meat. They throbbed terribly. Blood dripped from them in great drops and splashed on the white vinyl floor tiles. He moved his fingers slowly and the pain increased. He looked at his feet, at the blood leaking through the seams of his shoes. He could do nothing but clean and dress his wounds and hope that he might find some pain medication in one of the cupboards. Something stronger than what he had on him. It was time to get started.

He walked to the sink, turned on the faucet. Cold water splashed into the metal basin. He waited until steam was rising into the air before putting his hands under the spray. The water washed the blood away. It swirled down the drain pink. The pain was great and he hissed, but he did not pull his hands away for some time. He dried his hands with a white towel, turning it red, and packed his wounds with gauze before wrapping them. Almost as soon as the hands were wrapped red dots appeared above the wounds front and back and spread across the white gauze. He looked again at his feet, at the blood leaking out through the seams of his shoes and puddling on the white floor.

Fuck, he sighed.

Then reached down and pulled the shoes from his feet.

He stepped back out into the night, now bandaged up. He had found a bottle of 8mg Dilaudid tablets and taken one – while putting another dozen into his pocket – but hadn't yet noticed any relief. The pain remained tremendous. He had also taken another two Adderall to keep himself sharp. The effect of these he had noticed. His heart was thumping fast in his chest and he felt nervous and sweaty and irritable but he also felt that he could keep going and after the pain of washing out his wounds, packing them, and bandaging them he had wanted nothing more than to sleep, despite knowing that if he did he would be discovered and once more put into captivity. Sleep would at least temporarily erase his pain, make him forget it. The Adderall helped to push him forward. Without it he would have had to stop by now. But he could not stop. He must continue forward. He must continue forward until he was finished.

He limped toward the house, each step sending a sharp

pain coursing up his leg to his groin. The house stood still in the night, silent as stone. The rectangles of the windows revealed nothing, their blinds all closed. It did not matter. He would go in. He would go in and get the girl and the money and with luck he would leave with them and be done with this godforsaken place. He supposed that Mosley might come after him – he almost certainly would come after him – but that did not matter. It was a problem for another time. It was a problem for tomorrow. Tonight he merely needed to get what he had come here for and leave with breath still in his lungs, for if he didn't do it tonight he would never do it.

His trapped-animal heart thumped in his chest, pounding madly at the walls that surrounded it. His mouth was dry. A breeze blew against the sweat standing out on his chest and his face and this, combined with his exhaustion, made him shiver.

But he continued forward through the quiet night.

Then to his right he heard a low mean growl. He blinked and looked toward the sound. A large South African mastiff stood looking at him, its eyes mean, its muscles tense, its teeth bared. Strings of saliva hung from its mouth and dripped to the ground.

Lamb took a cautious step.

It's okay, doggy.

The dog only growled again.

Lamb reached for the pistol in his waistband.

Good dog – you're a good doggy.

He did not want to shoot for shooting would mean waking people, and this he could not afford to do, not if he wanted to get out of here alive. But he doubted he would get out of here alive, either, with a dog's teeth sunk in his throat.

With the gun in his right hand he reached out with his left and lowered himself so that he would not appear threatening. He brushed his left hand across the dog's head, making soothing sounds. The dog continued to growl for a moment, and then it ceased to growl. It licked his hand.

Good boy, he said.

After petting the dog for some time he got once more to his feet. Dizziness briefly overwhelmed him. A black sheet fluttered in front of his eyes. He blinked away the feeling and began walking again toward the house. The dog followed him up the three porch steps and then sat watching him.

He grabbed the doorknob and turned it and the door opened.

Mosley felt secure enough in his compound that he believed he had no need to lock his doors. This was good. This was very good indeed.

He stepped into the house and though nothing had changed it felt very different being here than it had earlier. It felt dangerous. He knew not who might be in the house nor how many of them there were. Yet this was where the girl and the money could be found, so this was where he had to be too.

With his pistol hanging from his right hand he walked into the house, looking first into the living room and finding it empty, and then looking into the kitchen. It too was unpeopled. Illuminated only by what moonlight splashed in through the kitchen window in the west wall, the counters and appliances as well as the large farm table were blanketed in shadow. He turned away and walked toward the hallway and then down it, stopping when he reached a door. If he continued forward he would arrive at the stairs and could make his way to the second floor, but he needed first to know what was behind this door. He grabbed the knob and felt it cool against his fingertips. He turned the knob and pushed the door and the door slid across the carpet. On the other side of the door he found a bedroom. But the bedroom was empty.

The girl should have been in there. If she was neither in the living room nor the kitchen she should have been in the bedroom. But the bedroom held only a dresser on which rested a television, a chair, a large bed, and two nightstands.

The television flashed frames on the wall.

Then he heard a voice behind him:

Who are you?

He turned around quickly and saw at the mouth of the hallway the girl. She was wearing a white T-shirt, panties, and a pair of boots. Her hair was damp, perhaps from a recent shower. She held a large stone in her right hand.

He looked at her in silence.

Who are you?

He swallowed. Your mother sent me. Is there anyone else in the house?

M osley stood by his truck with his keys hanging from his hooked index finger and looked toward the dark horizon. On his feet he wore a pair of rain boots. He had a raincoat draped over his left arm though he did not expect weather. He was glad it was night. He believed it was best to do dark work during dark hours – God put a blanket over the world for a reason and it was not so the weary could rest – and the work he had in front of him would almost certainly be very dark work indeed.

He pulled open the door, tossed the rain slicker into the passenger seat, and stepped up into the driver's seat. He pulled the door shut behind him and turned the key in the ignition. The engine rattled, and then, after a moment, roared to life.

For God so loved the world that He sacrificed His only begotten son in order that—

He turned off the radio. Sometimes he liked to listen to

such things in order that he might know the lies being told to the world at large, but tonight he was in no mood. He felt heavy with dread and found no amusement in the falsehoods told by those claiming to speak for the Lord.

He put the truck into gear and rolled up the dirt driveway toward the gate and the ugly world beyond it.

This world was full of untrustworthy men. He had known it for many years, almost his entire life, having been born to the father he had been, but every time he came across another one he felt a great sadness in his heart. It confirmed once again that this world was corrupt beyond saving. It had been flung out into the darkness and was now overwhelmed by it. God still lived here. He believed that. But sometimes He was very hard to see in this shadowed place; sometimes the darkness overwhelmed His light. Mosley kept his small pocket of existence as clean and pure as possible, of course, but perfection was unattainable. In this world it was. He longed for the Lord's return and hoped desperately that it happened in his lifetime. He saw signs that it might. And I saw a new heaven and a new earth: for the first heaven and the first earth were passed away; and there was no more sea. The next world, he was certain, would be beautiful. He needed that beauty. He needed to feel calm in his heart. He needed to hear the singing of angels. Instead he felt constant turmoil at the uncomfortable juxtaposition of his actions and his ideals. He did what he could to make them fit together. But in his heart he knew they never could. Not completely. He liked to tell himself that he was without sin, and he could find justifications for his actions in the Bible, but sometimes he wondered if those justifications were just that: excuses for doing the things he would do anyway. On nights like tonight, on drives like this one, he wasn't at all certain.

He parked his Ford at the curb and killed the engine. The trip to Louisville had gone by quickly, perhaps because he was dreading what lay ahead of him and did not want to meet it square. He wished he could put it off indefinitely but of course could not. Life was structured in such a way that, no matter how much you dreaded what was to come, you had to keep moving toward it. Life could not stop, and like a shark in water, if you were not moving forward through it, you were dead. For only the dead ceased to move ahead.

The dead were stopped watches. Everyone else must tick on.

On days like today he welcomed death yet he would never walk into it knowingly. There were so many things he had left to do here, so many people to whom he must show the light before it was too late and they were lost forever.

His heart felt momentarily soft as he thought of the Children of God sleeping soundly beneath white sheets. What beauty he had shown them. What ugliness he had hidden from them.

God put a blanket over the world for a reason and it was not so the weary could rest.

He stepped from his truck, slipped into his raincoat, buttoned it.

From his back pocket he removed a pair of yellow dishwashing gloves and slipped them onto his hands, flexing his fingers once they were surrounded by rubber. He walked around the back of the truck, up onto the sidewalk, and up a set of concrete steps that led to the apartment he intended to visit. The apartment door was green.

He knocked on it.

Who is it?

Open the door that we might speak face-to-face as men.

It's late.

Necessity knows not the hour, friend.

The sound of a chain being unlatched followed by that of a deadbolt retracting. A moment later the apartment door was pulled open.

Why you gotta talk in riddles?

I speak with great clarity. If you hear riddles it is only because the truth is wasted on the lost and the damned. Clear speech becomes babel to those who refuse to hear.

Ulysses was a skinny young man of perhaps twenty-five years. He stood just over five and a half feet tall and wore a white T-shirt and cargo shorts and Nikes. His arms were sleeved with tattoos. His blond hair was shaggy and hung in his face. Black-framed glasses surrounded his eyes. His right front tooth was chipped and gray. He had blue eyes that revealed no emotion. In his right hand he held a pistol of some sort. Mosley was no expert on such matters; while he maintained a cache of arms and insisted certain of his men know how to use them he did not like distance weapons for himself. He preferred the intimacy of close encounters. If he was going to commit an act of violence he wanted to face that violence like a man. He wanted to own it and hold it in his heart forever, painful though it might be.

What do you want?

Might I come in so that we can discuss matters with a modicum of privacy?

I'd like to know why you're here first.

You know why I'm here.

If I knew why you was here I wouldn't be askin, man.

Perhaps it is best if I explain inside.

I think it's best if you explain from where you are.

I'm coming in.

Ulysses stood firm for a moment and then, perhaps recognizing that there was no way to avoid what was coming, stepped aside. Mosley entered the large apartment.

The place was lighted only by a floor lamp in the corner. It revealed a room furnished with a black leather couch, two matching chairs, and a condensation-ringed glass coffee table on which stood several empty beer bottles. One of them was half-filled with cigarette butts. A pack of Marlboros and a Bic lighter rested beside it. A large flat-screen television hung on the wall that faced the couch. A Mario Bros game was paused, Mario himself in mid-jump, coin bouncing from a block his head was bumping against as he hung frozen in the air.

I do not follow video games, as I'm certain you could guess, but even I have seen this one.

The classics never get old. My big brother got an NES in 1985 and the fuckin thing still works if you can believe it.

I'm sure I can.

Thing is five years older than I am and still goin strong.

I suspect it will be operating well even after you are dead.

Ulysses laughed – nervously. You may be right. I picked up Battletoads from that place on Bardstown Road earlier. The one next to the guitar store. If you wanna give it a try I can—

We are not friends, Ulysses.

Lots of people aren't friends before they are. You're a weird dude but I don't see no reason we can't get along, being business partners and all.

We are not business partners, you cunt.

Whoa. The young man took a step back as if the final word Mosley spoke had struck a physical blow. He looked both confused and hurt. I was just trying to talk to you, man.

There are hardworking people in this town, hardworking people all over the world, who pull double shifts under dreadful conditions, and many of them are in untenable living situations nonetheless, yet here you are with a nice apartment and leather furniture and a large television and an NES, as you called it, and you have only to wait for the money to come to you – because of the product I provide –

and yet you so clearly wish to die, which is very curious to me.

I don't know what you're talking about.

Then why the precaution of a pistol?

Only way I ever answer the door. Man can't hold thousands of dollars in product and sit around unprotected. Likely to get a bullet in the eye.

You stole from me.

What are you talking about?

It is quite simple. You have my product yet I do not have your money.

If you don't have the cash, take it up with your delivery boy.

You did not pay and we both know it. You may, however, remedy the situation now.

I'm not paying you twice.

This is a fact. But you will pay me once.

Man, you aren't listening. I paid and I won't pay again.

One way or another, the money is leaving here with me.

I'm the one standing here with a gun.

Mosley smiled. I do not need a gun to take care of a drip like you.

Ulysses raised the pistol and pointed it at Mosley's face. How about I drop you right here so I never have to worry about your dumb ass again?

Mosley reached out and pulled the gun from the young man's hand, and then used the weapon to break his nose, smashing the butt against his face like a hammer. Blood poured down his mouth from both nostrils and the split bridge.

He grabbed his nose, tears streaming down his cheeks.

If you provide to me now the money I am owed I will merely cut off your left hand. This will help you remember that I am not to be trifled with. If you do not provide to me the money I am owed, however, I will not leave here until you are dead, and once you are dead I will collect the money in any case. That is the situation spoken as plainly as I know how to speak it so that even ears which hear only babel might understand. What is your decision?

I'm not paying you twice.

Mosley let a sigh escape him, then nodded his understanding.

He reached out and grabbed the young man by the throat with his left hand. With the gun in his right he beat Ulysses about the face and the head. The young man's arms flailed as he tried to defend himself, but he struck no blows but weak and ineffectual ones, and soon enough he stopped fighting altogether. His body went limp as he lost consciousness. Mosley let go his grip on the young man's throat and the young man fell to the floor in a heap.

Mosley tossed the gun aside and walked to the kitchen. From a block on the counter he drew a large chef's knife. It had a fine blade and though he'd have preferred a ripsaw he believed in working with tools that were handy, and with a little effort it would do the job. He returned to the living room and sat on his haunches before Ulysses.

The young man moaned.

If a thief is found and is struck so that he dies there shall be no bloodguilt.

The eyes opened and the young man reached a hand up toward Mosley beseechingly.

I didn't – I didn't steal from you.

Mosley held the knife over the young man's throat, held it with both hands, pointing the thing down as if he were going to attempt a tracheotomy, and then, after a brief stillness, after a please, he brought down the blade with all the force he could. The young man tried to gasp for air but only a gurgling sound came out, and a moment later the eyes went glassy and faraway.

May your journey be a pleasant one, friend, for the destination will not be.

Blood pooled beneath the young man's head.

Mosley began cutting at veins and arteries and tendons, chopping when he had to. In less than five minutes he had managed to remove the head, which rolled to the left, the eyes staring blankly at the back of the leather couch.

He stabbed the knife into the oak floor, picked up the head by the hair, and got to his feet.

Ulysses was now discovering exactly what lay beyond what we call life, and while Mosley thought he knew what it would look like, part of him was envious, for this young man who had held no faith was discovering the afterlife earlier than he. Of course his own journey would be different for while this man was unsaved he was himself a child of God.

He walked to the kitchen, stepped on the trash can's pedal, and threw the head into the bin.

He stepped out of the apartment with a blue backpack strapped over his shoulder. The backpack contained the product that had been stolen from him as well as what money he'd found in the apartment, approximately seven thousand dollars.

He walked down the steps leading to the sidewalk. The headless body would be discovered soon, and those in the business would know what it meant. It meant that Mosley was a man with whom one did not fuck. This young man had certainly bragged about having stolen from him – his type could never commit such a brazen act in silence – and his brutal death was Mosley's response to that sort of behavior. Word would get around quickly, which was good. It would save lives. People would hesitate now before doing anything stupid.

The act itself had been unpleasant – he found no joy in violence despite its occasional necessity – but it had also been required. Sometimes you must resort to violence in order that further violence be avoided. This had been one of those times.

He walked to his truck, set the backpack on its roof, and took off the boots and gloves and raincoat. He threw them into the bed of his truck. He dusted off his white linen suit and pulled open the door. He grabbed the backpack and stepped up into his vehicle.

He stopped at the White Castle on Preston Highway before heading home. Though he had joined his flock for their evening prayer he had not yet eaten dinner. Knowing what duties lay ahead of him had meant that he'd had no appetite, but now that it was finished he found that he was quite hungry. It was also a rare occasion that he found himself in Louisville and he figured he might as well take advantage of the situation. So rarely did he have the opportunity to eat fast food. He stepped out of his truck and walked into the small building.

At the counter he ordered the Double Cheese Slider Meal with onion rings instead of fries and an individual order of chicken rings with ranch dip. While waiting for his food he filled his paper cup with ice and Big Red. He found a table and sat down and sipped his soda through a straw. He watched the traffic roll by on Preston Highway and listened to the people around him talking. It seemed that only banalities fell from people's mouths these days, like rotten apples from diseased trees. He wondered how anyone could stand speaking with anyone else when all anyone said was nothing.

So I was, like, dude, don't just reach into my purse to—
I can't believe you don't like ketchup on your—

We're gonna see a movie this weekend and afterwards I think I'll invite him back—

A woman called his name and he stood, walked to the counter, and collected his food. The woman smiled at him and told him to have a good evening. He told her it was too late for that and walked back to his table.

He ate his food in silence, chewing methodically, his eyes half-lidded.

When the food and the soda were gone he got to his feet and walked out the door, leaving his trash behind on the table.

It was almost midnight when he pulled his truck off the street and drove up to the house. He was very tired and wanted nothing but another shower and the comfort of his bed. He stepped from the vehicle and looked toward the feed shed. He wanted his bed but thought it would have to wait. There were other things besides sleep that required his attention. He slammed shut the truck door and walked toward the feed shed, passing the pigpen on the way.

He unlatched the feed shed doors and opened them. He stepped onto the blood-stained pine floor – and saw that the private investigator was gone. There were still two bloody nails in the floor where his hands had been but the nails driven through his feet had been pulled up. His clothes were gone, as well as his gun and his other belongings.

At least half a dozen men had been nailed to that same floor over the years and not one of them had ever walked away. Yet Mosley believed that this man had probably done just that. There had been something about him that made Mosley believe it was not only possible but that it was the only explanation for his not being here.

This man had been no man at all but a devil, a devil sent to destroy him and what he had spent so many years building. He could not allow it to happen.

He turned around, putting his back to the shed's interior, and looked out at the night.

Where are you, you cocksucker?

Your mother sent me. Is there anyone else in the house?

The girl blinked, staring back at him in silence. She looked terribly young and innocent standing there in the darkness. She looked almost like a child.

Lamb wondered briefly what he might look like to her, his eyes wide and frantic, pupils dilated, his lank hair hanging down in his face, blood seeping through the bandages wrapped around his hands, his unbuttoned shirt revealing his sweaty torso and graying chest hair and splotches of drying blood. Probably he looked something like a walking corpse.

The girl's expression certainly suggested this.

Is there anyone else in the house?

I – I don't think so.

Do you know how long before Mosley returns?

She shook her head.

I'm gonna get you out of here, but you need to wait. I'll be back.

He turned toward the hallway.

Where are you going?

To take care of some business.

He walked up the stairs. They led to a hallway on the second floor, and the wall there was interrupted by two white doors. One of the doors was held shut by a staple with a padlock running through it, and he knew that behind it must be the room he wanted. He walked across the beige carpet to the door, leaving a trail of bloody footprints behind him. He had bandaged his feet but blood was still seeping out between the seams of his shoes, leaving an outline of the soles wherever he went.

When he reached the door he bashed at the lock with the butt of his gun. This sent a tremendous pain shooting up his arm from his hand, but despite the pain he did it again and again and again. The lock did not break but the staple was beginning to bend downward. The metal was beginning to crack near the base. He continued to hit it until finally the staple fell away and the padlock with it. They hit the floor with a thud.

By this point his right hand was once more a constant scream of pain, but he pushed it to the back of his mind – pushed it as far back as he could anyway – despite the tears running down his cheeks, grabbed the doorknob, and pushed his way into the room.

His pain was immediately forgotten.

It didn't seem real, the amount of money present. There was so much of it that it simply couldn't be real. Pallets of cash stacked and shrink-wrapped in great blocks filled the back half of the room. There had to be enough here to get him through ten lifetimes.

He brought home about twenty-four thousand dollars a year after taxes and expenses, which meant his business was a successful one, but twenty-four thousand dollars was such an insignificant percentage of the cache in this room that he could probably take twice that amount and no one would even notice its absence. Fortunately for him he was not concerned with being noticed. He intended to take as much as he could carry.

He stepped into the room, wondering exactly how he was supposed to haul this money away. Somehow he had not envisioned it like this despite Abigail's description. He knew he could not take it all but he wanted a million, at least a million. That wasn't as much money as it used to be, but if he continued to work until he was fifty and found ways to invest it in the meantime he would be able to retire and live the last twenty years of his life in comfort. But of course his belief that he might live even to fifty was blind optimism. There was more than a small possibility that he would not make it through the night.

I'm not coming with you.

Lamb started at the sound and turned around.

Lily stood in the doorway behind him in her T-shirt and panties. He could not believe he hadn't heard her approach.

Had it been Mosley he would be dead. He was slipping. It was true that he was tired and in pain and on far too many drugs but he was slipping nonetheless. Those things had not caused his failure of awareness; that had been caused by the fact that he had been thinking only about money. He needed to get his head right.

She set a burgundy suitcase down at his feet.

It's empty. Take what you're going to take and leave. Give half to my mother. I know she needs it. She doesn't know how to make money but she does know how to spend it.

You have to come with me.

Be careful. Elijah's house is in the back. If he sees you in the window he'll know something's wrong. Punch me in the face.

What?

Punch me in the face. Daddy can't believe I helped you.

You need to come with me.

I belong here.

You don't know where you belong. You're a child.

I'm seventeen years old.

You don't belong here.

How would you know?

Because no one belongs here.

I was born and raised here. This is my home.

Your home is with your mother.

You don't know her.

I know she isn't a homicidal heroin dealer.

You don't know Daddy either. He's only protecting what's his.

You need to leave with me. You need to get out of this place.

I'm not gonna argue with you. I'm letting you take the money and trusting that you'll do the right thing and give half of it to Mother. But I will never come with you. My home is here. Now punch me in the face. I don't know when Daddy might return.

Lamb looked at the girl in silence for a long moment. She looked back unflinching. Her eyes were big and bright and determined. He doubted that he could convince her to come with him. He doubted there was anything he might say that would make her agree to leave this place. He was a stranger and this was the only home she had ever known. It might be a broken home, the relationship she had with Mosley might be a sick one, but because she knew no other life she knew not how wrong this one was. There was safety here. There was the comfort of familiarity. She lived now in the same house she had lived in as a child. She was surrounded by the same trees and the same people. This compound was her hometown and she did not want to leave it. She would not leave it.

He looked at her. He swallowed. He made a decision.

He threw a punch. It connected with her nose. Her head whipped back, blood began gushing from her nostrils, and she collapsed to the floor, where she lay motionless. Her head tilted to the right and blood ran down her cheek and dripped onto the carpet.

His hand throbbed with pain and tears welled in his eyes. He put his forehead against the wall, cursing under his breath. Once the pain had subsided he stood upright again and looked down at the unconscious girl on his floor.

You're coming with me.

This time she did not argue.

She might not know what was good for her but he did. If he left her, she would wake up ten years from now hating herself for being here. She would look around and realize this place held no potential. She would understand that pious hypocrisy held no holiness.

She was young. She could build a life out in the real world. She could make friends and have boyfriends whom she did not call Daddy, boyfriends her own age. She could still be saved from this life.

You're coming with me, he said again.

He unzipped the suitcase and began loading money into it. He knew he did not have time to count what he was grabbing, but he did take the time to ensure he was grabbing bundles of hundreds and to stack them as neatly as possible, knowing the tighter was his stack the more he could get into the suitcase. Once the suitcase was full, he zipped it up once more and looked down at it.

Now he had to figure out how to get out of here with both the girl and the money, and he had no clue how to proceed. It was weight on top of weight, and though he was a strong man he knew he could not haul several hundred pounds around, not even uninjured, certainly not in his current state.

He stood motionless a moment, trying to figure out what to do. Then he heard the creak of the front door opening downstairs.

He drew his pistol from his waistband and walked down the hallway.

Footsteps coming up the stairs. The sound of breathing. A gun being cocked.

A head rose into view, then a face: Elijah.

Don't move another fucking inch.

Elijah looked up at him with a dull-dumb expression. His eyes were blank as summer chalkboards, revealing nothing.

Drop your rifle.

I won't.

If you don't you die.

If I do I die.

I'll tell you one more time. Drop your weapon or—

The man swung the rifle around toward Lamb.

Lamb squeezed his trigger.

The head snapped hard to the right and the wall behind it was suddenly spattered with blood and spongy pieces of brain, the heavier bits of which slid down its surface and fell away. The man continued to stand there motionless for a moment and then fell out of view.

The sound of him tumbling down the steps.

Lamb walked to the stairwell and looked down. The rifle lay on a step halfway up. The body lay at the bottom of the stairs. Blood leaked from the head, staining the carpet. The eyes were open but saw nothing.

It was now impossible to bring the police into this if it hadn't been before. He'd shot a man dead in a house he had no right to be in. The only good thing about the situation was that he doubted Mosley would want the police here either. Probably the man would simply make the body disappear. Were he in Mosley's shoes that was what he would do. If the police did end up getting involved Lamb was certain to end up in prison. He supposed he might get something less than murder, the situation being what it was, but he would certainly do time. He'd have to hide the money somewhere safe. He could claim it when he got out of prison – but first he'd have to be in prison, which was something he did not want.

But that was a worry for another time.

He walked back to the bedroom that held both the girl and the money. He could not carry them both but was determined not to leave either behind. He closed his eyes and pictured the map that Abigail had drawn for him. He pictured the underground tunnels and where they led. This could be made to work. So long as Mosley did not return this could be made to work.

He walked to the suitcase, grabbed the handle, and hoisted it up. It must have weighed a hundred pounds, perhaps more. He thought about that a moment: a hundred pounds in hundred-dollar bills when usually what he made in a week could easily be folded into his pocket. He read once that an American bill weighed a gram. A pound was 454 grams. So a pound of hundred-dollar bills would be worth over forty-five thousand dollars. Multiply that by a hundred and you could figure he was holding four and a half million dollars. More money than he had spent in his entire life up to this point.

He headed toward the stairs, and then down them, stepping over the rifle and then, at the foot of the stairs, the body.

He headed toward the basement.

L ily sat up on the carpeted floor and blinked several times. Her face was throbbing with pain, which radiated out from her nose. She reached up and touched it. It was tender and her fingers came away bloody. She looked at the blood on her fingertips for a long moment, then wiped it off on the floor. She got to her feet disoriented and dizzy. The world was both too bright and out of focus. The wall before her seemed to be made of fog. She stood motionless, waiting for her vision to clear. Finally texture rose out of the wall as it took a solid form.

The stranger was gone.

Part of her was disappointed by this fact but most of her was relieved. The part of her that was disappointed was the part that wanted to be convinced to go, the part that knew this life she was living was a bad one and ultimately unsustainable. But most of her wanted to stay. Most of her wanted to remain here forever, surrounded by everything she had ever known. It might be a bad life she was living, but it was a familiar one. Everything outside the compound was unknown, and the unknown frightened her. Sometimes one did not want to crawl out from under the blankets, even if the night had been full of bad dreams.

She walked along the hallway and down to the first floor. Elijah lay supine at the foot of the stairs. His head was tilted to the left. The back right third of his skull was a hollow bowl. Bone shards lay on the ground behind him. It looked to her, for a moment, as if his head were a vase that had been dropped. Then reality hit her. She retched and began to cry simultaneously. It might have almost been funny if it weren't so horrible. She stepped around the body, looked back over her shoulder. Elijah with no thoughts in his head. Elijah with no voice in his throat. Elijah still and lifeless as a mountain. The exit wound in his skull big enough to put your fist into. Destroyed brain matter held within like a bowl of Jell-O with a great scoop missing.

She ran to the kitchen and vomited into the steel basin, all of her emotion leaving her in three great spasms that clenched down on her stomach. She cried while she vomited. Then it was over and she turned on the water and rinsed her leavings down the drain. She also rinsed out her mouth and spit. She wiped the tears from her eyes with the heels of her hands, but more came. She could not believe that Elijah was actually dead, but didn't know why she was crying. She'd never liked the man. He worshipped Daddy in a way that made her believe he was mentally weak. He worshipped

Daddy without reservation. Many people in the compound did, but of them only Elijah also demanded respect he had no right to. Yet the fact that he was dead did something to her that she did not understand. It was as if a building she had looked at since she was a child were razed. Suddenly there was nothing where before there had been something, and that alone was a tragedy.

Then a noise behind her.

She spun around to face the kitchen doorway. The opening was empty. Only a living room beyond that framed hole in the wall.

The sound of the basement door swinging shut and latching. She stepped back into shadows, leaving the moonlight that was slanting in through the kitchen window, both anemic and cool.

The stranger passed the doorway, gun in hand. His eyes shifted toward her as he walked by. He seemed to look right at her, if only briefly, but he must not have seen her at all for he continued on. She looked toward the counter and saw the knife block and from it slid a knife. She gripped it tight in her sweaty fist, knuckles white. For a time she ceased to breathe. Then she stepped forward, needing to know what the stranger was doing. As she walked toward the wide doorway she bumped the farm table. Its legs scraped across the tile floor. She clenched her eyes shut and cursed under her breath. She had just announced her location. The choice now was to wait for the man to come to her or step through the door.

She stepped forward.

When Lamb entered the house once more he did so cautiously, uncertain about whether Mosley might have returned during his absence. The house was quiet, but he walked through it with his gun at the ready. His heart pounded in his chest as he did so but he came across no one. He walked to a window and looked out. The driveway remained empty.

He started toward the stairs. But stopped when he heard a noise coming from the kitchen. The scuff of a chair or table across the tile floor.

He turned quickly to see Lily step into the hallway with a knife in her hand. She looked dazed, and her mouth was covered in blood now drying to brown.

You weren't supposed to come back.

I'm not leaving without you.

You don't have a choice.

He tucked the pistol into his waistband and took a step toward her. She took a step back.

Don't come any closer.

I'm trying to help you.

I don't want your help.

But you need it.

You don't know what I need.

He took another step forward. You need to get away from this place.

Everyone I love is here.

Not your mother.

She could have stayed. She could have stayed and had a good life here. That was her decision, not mine. It was her decision to leave, but I made my own. I miss her, but I belong here. This is the only place I know.

There's a whole world out there.

An evil world full of godless people who have no understanding of the holy.

You think Mosley knows what is holy?

I know he does.

Is it holy to fuck little girls?

Her bottom lip trembled briefly, then stiffened. He loves me.

He uses you and manipulates you like he used and manipulated your mother – only your mother finally saw what was happening and tried to get you away from it.

Mother was jealous. She saw that Daddy loved me more.

Daddy saw that she had been corrupted while I had not. He loves me.

Lamb took another step toward her, moving slowly, carefully. You were a little girl and you didn't know any better, but what he did was not love. I promise you that. What he did had nothing to do with love.

What do you know about love?

I know that love is not about judgment or control. He isn't protecting you from the world, Lily. He's protecting himself from the world. He keeps you here because if this is all you know then he cannot be threatened. He's afraid of the world. It's why he did what he did to me when I had done nothing to threaten him.

He saw through you. He knew you were dangerous without you having to do anything.

Lamb took yet another step forward without taking his eyes off Lily. Tears were running down her cheeks.

Your mother misses you. She wants you to come home.

You're trying to confuse me.

I'm trying to make you understand that Mosley is not what you think he is. If he loved you he would not have done to you what he did. He would not have stolen that from you.

Don't come any closer. Don't.

He was now within arm's reach of the young woman. Her eyes were bright with sadness and confusion. It made him feel soft toward her, and it made him hate Mosley more than he already had. This poor beautiful girl had been made to believe that his raping her when she was a child was love. He had made her believe that he was protecting her when he was what she needed protection from. He could think of little else as evil as that. The man was a monster who did not even know what he was. He was a monster who had managed to convince himself that he was holy.

Your home is with your mother. It isn't here. It never was.

You don't know what you're talking about.

Mosley knows nothing about love. He knows nothing about God. He knows only how to justify his actions in order that he might get what he wants and still believe himself to be something other than what he is.

She said nothing for some time, but confusion and conflicting emotion swam in her eyes, which were glistening with tears. She sniffled. Then she looked at Lamb directly and spoke:

Then why did she let him do that to me?

She didn't know, and once she did she tried to take you away from it.

I'm so sorry. I knew it was wrong but I let him do—

You didn't let him do anything, Lily. You were a little girl.

She began weeping openly now, and as she did she let the knife drop from her hand. It fell blade-down to the floor and stuck into the hardwood, wobbling back and forth before finally going still. She put her fists to her eyes like a small child and bawled, gasping for breath.

Lamb took another step forward and put his arms around her. She hugged him back, putting her face in his neck.

I'm so scared.

I know that, Lily, but the world out there is a beautiful place. It's ugly and mean, too, and I can't say it won't hurt you – but it is a beautiful place.

Okay.

Let's get out of here. Let's get you to your mother.

She nodded and sniffled, trying to put herself back together. After a moment she pulled away from him and wiped at her eyes. She blinked several times, exhaled in a long shaky sigh.

It wasn't your fault.

He told me he loved me. He told me I was pure and beautiful and the only one clean enough to be with him. He told me—

It wasn't your fault.

He took her hand in his, ignoring the pain this caused. You're going to be okay. It might take a long time, but you're a strong girl – I can see it in your eyes – and you're going to be okay.

What if I'm not?

You will be. I'll see to it.

Promise me.

I promise.

Okay.

Okay. We need to leave.

She nodded.

It was then that he heard the truck pull up the driveway.

*

Lamb walked to the window. The blue Ford pickup was parked in the driveway. Mosley had already stepped from the vehicle and was now walking toward the feed shed. He pulled open the doors, stepped inside, and then froze. For a long time he did not move. Then he turned around and looked out at his compound, eyes scanning the area.

He spoke words but Lamb could not hear them.

Then the man's eyes locked on the house and, after a moment, he began walking toward it with great purpose.

Lamb aimed and fired.

The window shattered and the dirt at Mosley's feet kicked up. The man dove behind his pickup truck.

Come on out, motherfucker.

But the man did not come out and Lamb did not think he would. Still he waited for a very long time. He saw no movement. He saw nothing but the dark night and heard nothing but – after a few moments of utter silence – the crickets chirping in the emptiness.

He knew that he could not wait here forever, and that in fact waiting might get him into trouble as it would allow Mosley to come at him in some unexpected way, from some unexpected direction, so he turned away from the window, walked toward Lily, grabbed her hand, and pulled her toward the basement door.

They made their way through the door and down the white-painted steps to the cool room underground.

What are we doing?

Getting out of here.

We'll be trapped down here.

We won't.

He walked them toward the built-in shelves but stopped when he reached them. On the top shelf was a red plastic gas can.

Wait here.

What are you going to do?

I'll be right back.

He grabbed the gas can and headed up the stairs.

Once he reached the living room he began dousing the place with gasoline. He splashed it on the floor and the couch and the walls and the curtains. The fumes made his eyes water, but he continued anyway until the gas can was empty, at which point he threw it to the ground.

He pulled his lighter from his pocket, thumbed a spark, and set the couch on fire.

The fire spread quickly and the flames burned hot, sending great clouds of black smoke into the air. They hid the ceiling and began to fill the room.

Lamb made his way back to the basement.

The pain in his hands and feet was constant, and his head was beginning to throb as well, but he knew that he could not stop. He had to keep moving forward or soon he would move no more. He grabbed the left side of the shelves and pulled. They swung open on a hinge, revealing a concrete tunnel.

Let's go.

They stepped inside.

Mosley lay behind his truck for some time and waited for further shots to ring out but all that came from the house now was silence. He shifted and looked toward the window from which the shot had come but saw no movement. Only pale yellow light seeped through the glass but no human shadow. After a time he got to his feet and made his way hesitantly toward the house, taking deliberate steps, waiting for something to happen. But nothing did happen except that he continued to walk toward the house. He did not know what he might do once he reached it – the private investigator was armed while he was not and that put him in a position he did not want to be in – but he knew that he must do something. He could not merely wait to see what the man did next, could not wait to be put on the defensive.

He reached the front door, grabbed the doorknob and, after a brief hesitation, turned it. He pushed open the door to find his house in flames. The living room was full of fire and smoke. He could feel the heat from the front door and the smoke was crowding the ceiling, pushing toward him, black and malevolent. The smell was horrible. Plastic burned and lacquered woods and many other things that were never meant to burn. The air became toxic.

His first thought was not for the money upstairs but for Lily, sweet Lily who had been here when he left. If that man had done anything to her, if he had harmed a hair on her beautiful head . . . but he told himself that such a thing had not happened. He told himself that God would not allow anything to happen to such a pure creature.

He called her name but heard only the crackle of flames chewing at his home and his furniture, consuming everything around them. Devouring everything they touched.

He stepped into the house and moved down the hallway toward the bedroom but was stopped short by the sight of Elijah dead at the foot of the stairs. He lay on his back staring blindly at the wall to his right. His right arm was bent in an unnatural direction. There was a hole in the left side of his forehead, a small hole which could be plugged with a birthday candle – he imagined one there, pink, a small teardrop flame glowing atop it – but the back of his head had been blown away. His most faithful servant killed like a beast of prey. The light of God had left this place. He must now fend for himself.

He turned away and went into the bedroom and called Lily's name once more but received no response other than the silence he'd heard before, but even that was an answer of sorts, was it not? It might not be the answer he wanted but it *was* an answer.

It told him something but what it told him only raised more questions. She had not responded which meant either that she could not hear his call or could not respond. Or both. She was not here or she was here but dead. Perhaps the flames in the living room had already consumed her. Fire was so unlike any other thing on this earth. The more it ate the hungrier it became. One day it was certain to consume all of the world.

Perhaps Damien Lamb had shot Lily in the kitchen. Perhaps she had escaped through the back door and was now hiding in the woods and waiting for the sound of his voice to call her to safety. Perhaps the man had taken her with him.

But having no answers he knew these were things to think about later, for with no answers he could not take action, and this moment required immediate action. He made his way up the stairs, aware that he was risking his life but not caring, and hurried down the carpeted hallway following the bloody footsteps of the private investigator to the upstairs bedroom. If he could not save his money he would lose more than Lily. He would lose his entire way of life. He would lose all his people for he would be unable to care for them. The lock had been broken off the bedroom door. Several million dollars were missing. But all of the money would be gone if he did not move and quickly. He made his way into the room, the floor sagging beneath his feet, its strength already failing, and knocked out the window. He could feel the heat through the floor. He could feel it on the soles of his feet. Hellfire reaching for him. He took a step toward one of the pallets. His foot went through the carpet and the hardwood beneath it and he fell to his knee. He looked down and could see flames below. He had to leave. He would be unable to save anything. God was testing him. He did not know why but God was surely testing him.

Then the Lord answered Job out of the whirlwind, and said, Who is this that darkeneth counsel by words without knowledge? Gird up now thy loins like a man; for I will demand of thee, and answer thou me. Where wast thou when I laid the foundations of the earth? Whereupon are the foundations thereof fastened? Hast thou commanded the morning since thy days; and caused the dayspring to know his place that it might take hold of the ends of the earth, that the wicked might be shaken out of it? It is turned as clay to the seal; and they stand as a garment. And from the wicked their light is withholden, and the high arm shall be broken. Hast thou entered into the springs of the sea? Have the gates of death been opened unto thee? Hast thou perceived the breadth of the earth? Declare if thou knowest it all. Where is the way where light dwelleth and darkness? By what way is the light parted? Hath the rain a father? Out of whose womb came the ice? Canst thou bind the sweet influences of Pleiades, or loose the bands of Orion? Canst thou bring forth Mazzaroth in his season? Knowest thou the ordinances of Heaven? Canst thou lift up thy voice to the clouds, that abundance of waters may cover thee? Canst thou send lightnings, that they may go, and say unto thee, Here we be? Who provideth for the raven his food? When his young ones cry unto God, they wander for lack of meat.

Gird up now thy loins like a man.

He had held Mammon sacred in his house and God was punishing him for this. His faith was being tested and Damien Lamb was the source of that test. The Lord wanted to know whether he held material things in higher regard than spiritual, and he would show the Lord that his heart was pure. He would rebuild from the ashes. But first he must escape this inferno.

He pulled his leg from the hole in the floor, flames licking at him. He looked down and saw his living room destroyed. Black smoke pushed up through the floor, a pillar of it which broke apart as a breeze wafted in through the shattered window.

He made his way to the bottom of the stairs, stepped over Elijah's body, and found the exit blocked by a wall of flame. But he would not perish. His faith was strong. He would walk through the fire and emerge unscathed.

Be on your guard; stand firm in the faith; be men of courage; be strong.

He stepped toward the flames. Sweat beaded on his flesh and ran down his face. The heat was tremendous. But he had no choice but to walk into the fire, so he did. He stepped into the flames and the flames enveloped him, and he felt them trying to consume him, but he told himself that God would not allow it, God would protect him, God would keep him whole, and he made his way blindly – with blind faith – toward his front door, his heart pounding in his chest, the heat hotter than anything he had felt before, and he reached for his doorknob though he could not see it, and it scalded his palm, but he turned it, and he felt the flames explode behind him as they were exposed to fresh oxygen, and when next he was aware of anything he was aware of himself lying face down on his own cool lawn, out of the fire, the left sleeve of his white linen suit in flames.

He slapped the flames away and picked himself up.

He turned and watched his house burn, unable to believe that the man who had stumbled onto his land only this morning had managed to do this.

God had not done this as he'd earlier believed but the devil. Damien Lamb was a tool of the Lord's fallen angel sent here to destroy what he had spent so many years building. He was himself the lamb which Damien had been sent here to tame, which he had been sent here to destroy. But he would not be destroyed for his faith was strong and those who had faith could say to a mountain, Fall into the ocean, and it would be so.

He believed that the private investigator – the devil's tool or perhaps the devil himself – had set his house on fire and gone into the back woods. Perhaps he was waiting there now for Mosley's arrival so that this man of God might finally be destroyed. But this would not happen. It could not happen.

Had he not only moments ago walked through fire and come away unharmed?

He looked at the blister forming on the palm of his hand larger than a silver dollar.

The army of God would rise victorious.

He made his way through the dark night to the cabins in which his people slept. Crickets chirped at him from every direction, and though he wished to curse them he did not, for they were God's creatures, same as him. There was only one devil in the woods tonight and he would have his head on a pike.

Behind him his house burned, lighting up the night, but he ignored it, for it was gone, and one should not dwell on that which was already lost.

He arrived at the cabins. Several people were standing outside looking at him with fear and confusion in their eyes, hoping for answers, but when the first asked him what was happening he said only, Go back inside. Then he turned to all of them and repeated this command. There were men he needed but none of them had yet left their cabins. Even as some of his people went inside, he knocked on doors to draw others out.

There would be a hunt tonight and a devil would be slain.

*

He stood before them in the flickering light of his burning home, six men dressed all in white. They looked at him, waiting for him to speak, stealing glances at the house in the silence. The sound of the fire was loud. The crackling of wood being consumed. The sound of walls collapsing. The heat was tremendous, drawing out sweat from every pore on every man's body. Mosley was glad of this. He wanted his men to feel the heat of Hell as he spoke. He wanted them to understand exactly what was at stake.

A devil disguised as a man came onto our land today, into my home, and tried to destroy what we have spent so many years building. My house is burning to the ground because of him. Our way of life is threatened because of him. He must be found and he must be brought to justice and the only justice for devils is death, for their home is not on earth but in Hell. Ours is a place of peace. God lives here with us but destroying a house will not cause Him to move out, for He lives not in our houses but in our hearts, and while God loves peace He also understands the need for violence. He knows that we are fighting a holy war. It is why each of you was trained in the way of the gun. Violence is called for tonight. Vengeance is called for. This devil killed Elijah and he may have killed young Lily. If she is not dead he may have her in his possession. These matters are uncertain. What is certain is that something must be done and it must be done now. It is time to arm ourselves and hunt this devil down so that he might learn that one does not fuck with the Lord – or His people.

Let us make haste.

Mosley pivoted on his right foot and marched toward the garage where the vans were parked. Under normal circumstances he would reach the armory through the house, but this was no longer possible.

His men followed through the night.

When he reached the garage – a long structure in which fourteen white vans were parked – he turned on the lights and walked to the back right corner. A red toolbox should have been covering a hatch there, but the toolbox had been moved and the hatch was already uncovered. Was it possible that the devil had somehow learned of these tunnels? It could not be and yet he thought it might be nonetheless. He opened the hatch, revealing a hole that led down into the darkness. The first three rungs of a ladder were visible before said darkness enveloped it.

Let us head down.

He crawled down the ladder and into the darkness. When he arrived at the ground below he reached around blindly for a chain, finally finding it and giving it a pull. A sixty-watt bulb lighted the surrounding area and revealed several feet of tunnel leading toward the back of the property, then the light faded and the tunnel continued in darkness. As soon as his men had all descended the ladder he led them down the tunnel, into the darkness, and each time the light from the last bulb grew too dim to see by there was another chain on which to pull, another light bulb to illuminate the way.

Together they made their way toward the armory. The men behind him walked in silence. Their footsteps echoed against the concrete walls, making it sound as if there were two dozen of them rather than a mere seven.

Then, in the darkness, Mosley heard a sound that did not belong to his men. The devil. He was down here after all. He was down here waiting for them.

Silence.

Deep in the darkness there were voices.

I'm so scared.

You don't need to be. This will all be over soon.

The devil was not in the woods but down here in the darkness, unwittingly walking toward him. How the beast knew about these tunnels Mosley did not know, but he supposed it didn't matter. As it had always been, the devil had his ways. He was like a whitewashed tomb which outwardly appeared beautiful but within was full of bones and uncleanliness. But what mattered most was that the beast not only had Lily with him as he had feared but that she was with him willingly. He could tell this merely from the tone of her voice. Yet he should have suspected this was a possibility for had not the serpent deceived Eve in the garden? As it had always been, the devil had his ways.

Mosley did not have any guns, while the devil did, but he was determined that he would kill the beast tonight nonetheless. It would be finished.

Did you think you could steal and destroy what was mine and get away with it?

His voice echoed through the tunnel and when the echoes finally stopped his call was greeted only by silence. The silence stretched out for a long time.

You need not respond. Behind you there are only flames, which means you must come to me. I will be here waiting for you, and when you arrive I will kill you.

His faith was strong. He was a man of God.

He had walked through fire.

He turned to his men and looked at them in the dim light. They looked back. He spoke in an angry whisper:

Leave this place. Shatter every light bulb as you head back to the ladder. If a man emerges and he is not me I want the dogs upon him. I want them to tear at his flesh until there is no flesh at which to tear. I want his screams to echo into the next four counties. I want the motherfucker dead.

Mosley stood in utter darkness and waited. Several bulbs both in front of him and behind him had been shattered. The lack of visibility heightened his awareness of sounds and smells and even the cool, damp air on his skin. He could hear his own heartbeat and feel his pulse in his ears. He could smell the dirt on the other side of the concrete walls seeping through its pores. Nervous sweat ran in a line down the side of his head. In front of him he could hear careful footsteps as well as their echoes so that with each one he counted three. They were still a good distance off but drawing nearer, and with every twenty feet of progress they made he heard the click of a light cord being pulled.

We should go back.

We can't go back.

He's going to kill us.

Not if I kill him first.

This followed by yet more careful footsteps until finally they reached the first shattered bulb and the devil cursed under his breath.

Take off your shoes, but mind the glass.

Then even the sound of footsteps was gone. For what felt a very long time Mosley stood in utter silence but for the beating of his heart. This was so loud in his ears he thought it impossible that the devil could not also hear it. He'd been standing in darkness long enough now that if there were any light his eyes would have adjusted to it and he'd be able to see something but there was no light at all. It was amazing how claustrophobic darkness could feel even when you knew there was open air in front of you. It made your chest feel tight, as though you were in your own tomb.

He told himself that the darkness was not empty. He told himself that God's love surrounded him even now. He told himself that he was protected. He could not see the light but it must be here. The devil might be attempting to destroy him but God was with him always and would not allow it. If he was in a tomb it belonged to the man – to the devil – who was slowly approaching.

He waited.

Soon he thought he could hear the sound of breathing

and the breathing was not his own. He froze, waiting, willing his heart to stop pounding so hard in his chest. Socks brushed against the concrete floor. Inhalations were followed by exhalations. Someone licked dry lips.

They approached and then, nearly brushing against him even as he tried to disappear into the wall, pressing his back to it, they passed him by, leaving him to stand behind them. He listened to their soft footsteps and tried to determine which was the devil and which was the girl. He needed to attack hard and fast and true. He pushed himself away from the wall.

One of his shoes scraped against the concrete.

Someone gasped and spun.

A shot rang out. A flash of light illuminating two human silhouettes.

But the shot missed and Mosley went for the devil.

L amb opened a crate and found several M16s lying on a bed of shredded newspaper. These were weapons with which he was familiar, having both been trained on one during basic in Fort Leonard Wood, Missouri, and issued one when deployed to Kosovo. He removed one of the weapons and stole magazines from two of the others before looking through several additional crates for ammunition, which he finally found. He loaded the magazines, pocketing the ones he did not slam into his weapon.

He set down the rifle, found his pain pills, and chewed two more of them. They were bitter in his mouth, but the pain was constant and exhausting and he was afraid that if he did not numb it he would fail before they managed to escape this compound. His body was breaking down and only drugs would keep him going, that and force of will, but will could only take one so far. If the body was unwilling desire would accomplish nothing.

Despite the cool air underground he was sweaty and clammy. He felt too that he was walking through a dream – or a nightmare. His mind was no longer what it had been this morning. But given what he had been through he was not surprised. In another couple hours he could let himself go – he could simply lose his grip on himself and fall away – but not yet. Not until this was finished.

He picked up the weapon and turned toward Lily who was still standing by the door through which they entered the armory. Her arms were crossed and her eyes downcast. She looked scared.

Let's go.

She nodded, silent, and walked toward him.

When she reached him he lifted her chin with his hand so that she had to look him in the eye, and after a moment of silence he spoke:

I made you a promise, he said, and I always keep my promises.

She nodded.

I *always* keep my promises.

Okay.

This time she looked as though she believed him.

Okay.

They left the armory.

They walked through the tunnel, Lamb turning on lights as he reached them, the bulbs illuminating the stark concrete walls. He wondered what was happening aboveground and hoped that he could make it to the garage and the van in which he'd placed the suitcase without encountering any trouble. It was a small hope – the way things had gone for him so far he doubted it would happen – but a hope nonetheless.

But more than anything he wanted Lily safely away from this compound.

His priority had once been the money but things had changed since he had met the girl. She was a beautiful child, but she was a child – innocent and sweet – and it was unforgivable that Mosley had done to her what he had. He must get her away from here. He must open the world to her so that she could see the light beyond this dark place. This had for so long been everything she'd known – despite her instinctive repulsion she had convinced herself of its rightness. The only father she had ever known told her it was right and it was good and not only that but it was the will of the Lord – and she was afraid of what lay beyond. This created within her a conflict that was heartbreaking to witness. She hated what had been done to her but was secure in it for it was all she knew; the outside world on the other hand was unknown and frightening.

Lamb wanted to protect her.

He was not a father and had never had the desire to become one but felt something paternal rising up within him now.

This girl deserved someone on whom she could rely.

She deserved someone she could trust, someone who would not use her.

I'm so scared.

You don't need to be. This will all be over soon.

She took his hand in hers and squeezed it. It hurt like hell, and forced blood from his wound, but he not only allowed it but squeezed hers in return. She looked at him with gratitude in her eyes.

Then the sound of Mosley's voice echoed through the tunnel:

Did you think you could steal and destroy what was mine and get away with it?

Lily's expression became fearful.

It will be okay, he whispered low. It will be okay.

You need not respond. Behind you there are only flames, which means you must come to me. I will be here waiting for you, and when you arrive I will kill you.

Lamb shook his head at Lily.

We'll get out of this.

Tears streamed down her cheeks.

Lamb told her again that they would get out of this though he was not at all certain he was telling the truth. He was certain, however, that they would not get out of it unless she believed in him. She needed to trust him and do what he said when he said it.

Let's go, Lamb whispered.

Lily nodded.

They continued walking in silence, the tunnel stretching

out before them. Around every bend Lamb expected to see Mosley but never did. With every step they took he could feel the girl's fear increasing. He wanted to say something that might make it better for her but did not know what to say. Finally she spoke:

We should go back.

We can't go back.

He's going to kill us.

Not if I kill him first.

She stopped walking and looked at him for a long time. He looked back knowing that she was trying to decide whether this was something she trusted him to do but knowing too that there was nothing he could say or do in order that she reach the decision he wished her to. Still, after a time, she nodded and began walking again.

They went another ninety feet or so, Lamb illuminating another three bulbs by pulling their chains, before they reached a light that would not switch on.

Shit.

His first thought was simply that the bulb had burned out since last he'd gone through the tunnel, but that thought lasted a very short time, for when he tried to take his next step the ball of his foot rolled across thin glass, which crunched beneath the sole of his shoe. When that happened he knew that Mosley had shattered the bulb, knew that the man wanted them in darkness. Then he would have them in darkness, but he would not also hear them coming.

Take off your shoes, but mind the glass.

Lily looked at him in the remnants of the light from the bulb behind them and there was a question on her face, but she did not ask it. She simply removed her shoes as she was told.

He removed his as well, leaning his rifle against the concrete wall and bending over to pull them from his swollen, bandaged feet. He wanted to cry out as he did so, and tears streamed down his cheeks, but he managed to remain silent. He did not want Lily to know how badly his injuries hurt. He did not want her to doubt him. If she doubted him she might question him when the time came that she absolutely must listen.

Once his shoes were off he stood up and leaned against the wall, his feet throbbing with fresh pain now that blood flow was not constricted by his shoes. Were the wall not there he was certain he would fall, but it was there so he did not. He allowed it to hold him up until he could hold himself up and once he could he pushed himself off the wall. He stood a moment unsure whether he would stay upright and when he did he picked up the rifle and began walking.

Lily walked beside him.

Soon they were enveloped by darkness, no light reaching them at all. Lamb dragged his fingers gently across the rough texture of the concrete walls to keep them heading in the right direction, to keep them pushing forward.

He wondered what they might be walking into and though he could imagine any number of terrible scenarios he knew they had no choice. There was only one way out of this and that was the way they were going. Either they survived or they did not. That was all.

For a moment he considered shooting blindly into the darkness but decided against it. They were surrounded by concrete. The sound would be deafening. The risk of ricochet far too great. The chances of hitting Mosley far too small.

Firing the rifle might also reveal to him their location, which Lamb did not want to do.

As they walked Lamb began to sense that they were not alone, though because of the darkness he could see no other presence. He might as well have been blindfolded. Or his eyes gouged out. He listened carefully but heard nothing but himself and the girl beside him, both their quiet inhalations and the sound of their stocking feet on the rough surface of the concrete floor.

Then came a scraping sound behind them.

Lamb turned quickly and fired into the darkness.

The brief flash illuminating Mosley who had been standing only a few feet behind them. The sound of the shot echoing in his head. After a fraction of a second darkness once more fell over them all and he knew not where he was in relation to anyone else.

A high-pitched tone hummed in his ears from the gunshot.

Something large slammed into him, knocking him to the ground, but not before he reached back to catch himself. His wounds began screaming anew.

The girl let out a frightened cry.

Hands gripped his throat.

Did you really believe you could destroy me, you cunt? Did you really believe that?

Warm spittle hit his face. As did a gust of hot, rancid breath.

He grabbed the man's wrists and tried to pull the hands away from his throat but could not. He was too weak and his pain was too great. He swung his head forward and felt it smash against the man's nose. The nose broke with a crack and the grip on his neck loosened. He reached blindly for the rifle but felt only concrete. A fist slammed into his forehead. Another hit his ear. Finally he found the gun and swung it around, slamming the butt into something soft and meaty. The other man grunted. He turned the rifle around and fired, the flash illuminating the tunnel once more. He saw that his aim was off, adjusted, and fired again. He heard a grunt of pain, the sound of a man being punched in the gut, and hoped like hell he'd in fact managed a gutshot. The other man fell to the ground. Lamb got to his feet and fired three more times into the darkness, aiming for where he believed the man lay, wanting to make certain the son of a bitch was dead. Then he stopped firing and listened. Heard only the sound of his own breathing and Lily's soft crying. Mosley made no sound at all.

Lily.

Her response was something between a yelp and a whimper.

Take my hand.

A hand fell upon his shoulder and he felt it run its way down his arm before lacing its fingers between his fingers. He squeezed her hand, ignoring his pain.

We're almost out of here, he said.

As he and Lily walked through the tunnel holding hands Lamb felt exhaustion begin to overwhelm him. He knew the day was not finished and would not be finished until he was far away from this godforsaken place yet the fact that Mosley lay on the ground behind him bleeding and mortally wounded or dead did something to his mind that he did not like – it caused it to lose focus.

The pain and the exhaustion began once more to take over and he found he wanted more than anything to swallow half a dozen pain pills and sleep through an entire day and night, but that should have been far from his mind since he did not know what he would find when he emerged from the tunnel. He needed to center himself. He needed to find focus. He had not only himself to worry about now but Lily.

He stopped about fifteen feet from the ladder which would take them aboveground and Lily, holding his hand, stopped too. He waited and listened. He could hear muffled speaking, the sound of footsteps, dog nails clicking on the concrete.

The world shrank again.

All that existed now existed at the other end of that ladder. At the top of that lighted hole that looked so much like the thing you walked into when you were dead. If the stories were to be believed. Absorbed by the light and dispersed once more across the universe. All the dead spread across an expanse so large it might as well be infinite.

He shook his head and forced himself to find focus. He'd been drifting.

The hole above them was the only way out of here – out of this darkness and into the light – but getting off the compound would not be a simple task. That much was obvious.

Wait here, he whispered.

He took a step forward and this step was followed by a second and a third and a fourth. He looked up into the light, squinting, and he could see men up there waiting for him. He thumbed a switch on his rifle, setting it to fire in three-shot bursts. He watched a blond-haired man walk by and took aim but the man was too soon out of sight. Another man stepped into view, this one bald. He aimed, held his breath, worked with the rhythm of his heartbeat rather than fighting it – for he could not slow it, as speeded-up as he was – and squeezed his trigger.

Three quick shots sounded and half the man's head tore away, like a hatchet taken to a coconut, and the man crumpled to the ground, falling out of sight.

Immediately there was yelling.

Dogs began barking ferociously.

One of them came into view, snarling down at him, growling, barking with drool hanging from the hinge of its strong jaw, its eyes black as the future and cruel as a knife.

He shot it. It yelped once and fell into the hole, landing at his feet with a wet thud that made his stomach turn.

But when he tried to shoot again the rifle jammed and he couldn't clear it, so he threw the fucking thing aside, cursing his luck, pulled the pistol from his waistband, and began his way up the ladder, looking for targets.

When another dog came into view he shot it.

It fell down, whimpering and howling in pain, a sound he could not stand even in this current situation, so he fired again, wasting a bullet to put it out of its misery. This left him with thirteen rounds, but the dog went silent, finding peace.

The next moment his head was aboveground.

He looked in every direction, trying to assess the situation. There were five men up here now and half a dozen dogs that he could see, eleven shots if every one of his was true and no one was hiding, but the men were armed with hammers and crowbars not with guns, so his hope was that he would not have to shoot them.

A third dog came at him from behind. He heard it coming, heard it rushing up at him, snarling and barking, turned and tried to fire, but missed. The thing sunk its teeth into his left arm and he lost his grip on both his pistol and the ladder. He fell back down into the tunnel, landing flat on his back beside the dog he had shot, the air rushing out of his lungs in a great gush. He simultaneously gasped for air and tried to fight off the mastiff. The thing's teeth were deep in his arm and it was shaking its head back and forth, attempting to tear off a piece of flesh. Not knowing where the gun was he punched it in the head repeatedly, trying to force the thing to let go its grip, but it would not let go.

The pain in his hand was near to making him pass out. Black dots swam before his eyes, blocking the light of the garage above him and his view of the dog he was fighting. He blinked but found no focus.

Finally he grabbed the dog by the throat and squeezed, and though it had no air getting to its muscles or brain it continued to fight for over a minute before succumbing.

He let go of the dog's throat and it fell to the ground beside him. He lay on his back, looking up at the light above him. He sat up and looked around for the pistol but the pistol was not there.

Come on up.

A man stood at the top of the ladder holding his pistol. It had not fallen with him but landed on the floor of the garage, arming his enemy. The man was tall and broad-shouldered with clipped brown hair and blue eyes. He was pointing the pistol at Lamb's head, holding it as steady as his shaking hands would allow.

Lamb rolled out of the line of fire, got to his feet, and limped to the M16 he had thrown to the ground. He once more tried to clear the jam but could not do it. His only way out of this situation now – Lily's only way out – was if he could bluff his way through.

But he'd never been much of a poker player, his emotions always too near the surface to hide completely. They were revealed often before he was even aware of them.

Still he must try.

It was his last and only play.

With his useless rifle at the ready he stepped once more toward the ladder. The man with the pistol still stood there, and when he saw Lamb he again took aim. So did Lamb. The man's hands continued to shake badly.

Drop it or you're dead.

You drop it.

Lamb shook his head. You know damn well I won't hesitate. Can you say the same? I don't think you can. How many men have you killed? Drop the weapon down here.

The man stepped out of the line of fire.

Shit.

Lamb looked toward Lily. She was watching him with moist wide eyes.

Come to me.

She walked toward him and he took her hand in his.

You know I wouldn't hurt you, right?

She nodded.

You need to trust me. If you do I think I can still get us out of this.

Okay.

He looked up to the light, and though he saw no one he could still hear the dogs barking and the hushed tones of frantic speech. Lily's coming up, he said loudly. Call off the dogs and stand back. Answer that you understand!

We understand. The voice of the man with his pistol.

I'll be right behind you.

She nodded and walked to the ladder and slowly climbed up. He climbed up behind her, knowing that what happened in the moment they emerged was of great importance. As soon as her feet touched the concrete of the garage floor he swung the gun around and told the men standing there to stay back. The dogs barked and growled.

One of the men told them to stay, boys, stay.

They listened, but they were tight coils ready to spring at any moment, their muscles tense, their eyes bright with fury. This was what they had been trained for and they were eager for release, eager to use their sharp teeth and their sinewy muscles at last.

As soon as his feet were on solid ground he grabbed Lily, using her as a shield, and told everyone to stay back, you crazy motherfuckers.

Nobody else has to die, said the man with the pistol.

That's entirely up to you. Drop the gun.

Let the girl go.

We both know that if I do the dogs will be on me in an instant. She stays with me. Now drop the fucking gun.

The man nodded and let go the pistol. It hit the ground with a loud clack and one of the dogs began to bark again in response.

Hush now. Stay.

All eyes were on him and Lily as they made their way toward one of the vans. They walked slowly but Lamb's eyes darted in every direction as he tried to keep tabs on each breathing creature in the garage. His heart was pounding in his chest and he could feel that Lily's was racing as well. His arm was wrapped around her shoulder, hand resting above her breasts, and he could feel her heart pounding against his palm as if there were no breastplate separating the two. But she was moving with him, following his lead, and this was good. This was necessary. It was a dance that they must perform well to survive, and their performances demanded she follow his lead smoothly, picking up on each subtle movement so that she always remained in front of him, standing as his shield even as he moved them both toward safety.

He guided Lily to the driver-side door of the nearest white van.

Open the door.

She did.

Climb in.

As soon as she stepped into the van someone shouted for the dogs to attack. The nearest one, only ten feet away, came rushing at him quickly, barking ferociously, but when it arrived he bashed it in the head with the butt of his rifle and stepped into the van, slamming the door shut behind him. He turned the key in the ignition and the engine roared to life. He grabbed the gearshift on the steering column and yanked it into reverse and backed out of the garage as quickly as possible, wanting nothing more than to be far away from here.

As he was backing up, though, the man with his pistol picked it up from the floor and opened fire on the windshield, letting loose six shots. They punched holes in the glass and flew through the van's interior but he felt no pain so he did not slow in his movements.

He spun the van around and slammed it into drive and skidded toward the gate. He looked over at Lily. She was strapping her seatbelt into place, and though her face looked pale and her eyes looked frantic she appeared to be unharmed.

You okay?

She nodded.

They slammed through the gate, the steel ripping from its hinges and flying into the road, flipping end over end before they finally ran over the thing and it was visible only in their rearview mirror, rocking on the asphalt before going still.

Lamb reached into his pocket, found his cigarettes, and lighted one.

The compound was behind them now.

IV

For the next twenty minutes they drove without speaking, the dark night pushing in all around them. Only the shadows of trees were visible on either side of the road and the stars in the sky seemed dim, as if they might flicker out. Kiss me goodbye before I go. Wind blew in through Lamb's cracked window while he smoked and the tires hummed their constant note, but they were otherwise in silence. Lily sat beside him looking out the passenger window. He tried to read her expression in the reflection on the glass but could not. She seemed pensive and faraway but what was going on in her mind was a mystery as great as anything which lay beyond in the darkness – perhaps greater, for what lay within was a result of intelligence and thought while what lay without was a dark expanse of beautiful thoughtlessness.

Do you think he's dead?

It took Lamb a moment before he understood what she

was asking, his mind had been elsewhere, but once he did he answered honestly.

Dead or dying, he said.

It feels strange.

What does?

Thinking about that.

In what way?

He was the only father I ever knew and – and even though I guess I hated him for what he did to me, I think I loved him too. I know I did. It doesn't make sense. I shouldn't have a place for him in my heart. I know that. But even now I do.

Of course you do.

But how can you love someone who's done to you what he did to me?

Because you have to love somebody – nobody can live without any love at all – so if that's who you have to love then that's who you love.

I shouldn't have loved him. I shouldn't now.

You wouldn't be human if you could live without love.

I didn't like being with him in that way. It made me feel dirty. He told me I was clean and pure and beautiful but he made me feel the opposite. I would cry sometimes afterwards. I would cry sometimes during. At first I would. But I believed him when he told me it was God's will. I made myself believe him.

You don't have to explain yourself. You didn't do anything wrong.

You keep telling me that but—

You didn't do anything wrong. You were never given the chance to exist outside the life into which you were born. Children are not behind bars but they're prisoners all the same: for eighteen years they are prisoners of the circumstances into which they were born, and that as a prison can be far worse than one with bars, for escaping who you are is impossible. With guards and cyclone fence at least there's a chance.

Then why do I feel so terrible – why do I feel like it was my fault for staying there and allowing him to, to . . .

She shook her head and looked out the window again.

I don't know the answer to that. I only know that it wasn't your fault. If there is one innocent in this situation that innocent is you.

By the time they reached his house the sky was streaked pink with sunrise, though stars were still visible, and the sun itself had yet to breach the horizon. He pulled into his oil-spotted driveway and put the transmission into park and killed the engine. He stepped from the van and walked around to the back of the vehicle. He swung open the rear doors and grabbed the suitcase from the gray-carpeted floor. He hefted it from the van, set it in the driveway, and closed the doors. He lifted it once more and walked around the van and by the time he did Lily was standing by the passenger side waiting for him. She looked out of place in his suburban neighborhood, wearing only an oversized white

T-shirt and a pair of panties and socks, but she also looked beautiful.

This is your house?

It is.

I like it.

It's a house. We should go in.

Lily nodded.

Though he had been gone for less than twenty-four hours it felt strange to be back. Everything was exactly as he had left it yet the place seemed different. It was like being in a stranger's house. So much had happened since last he was here.

He carried the suitcase upstairs and into his bedroom. He set it on the bed. Lily followed him into the room and stood by the door. She looked very tired, though not nearly as tired as he felt. Yet she'd been through a lot tonight – last night – particularly on an emotional level. She must be feeling very raw indeed.

You should take a shower, he said. I'll find something for you to wear.

She nodded.

The bathroom is at the end of the hall.

Okay.

She turned and stepped out of the room. Not long after this water began splashing into the bathtub. He wished his bathroom weren't so dirty – wished he scrubbed it more often – but supposed it didn't matter. Probably the girl wouldn't even notice. In a way, after the night the two of them had had, it was absurd to even think about such things. It was strange to have killed three men and yet be able to think about his unsightly bathtub ring. You would think matters of life and death would overwhelm everything else and push small things to the back of your mind. But daily matters remained whatever else happened. Your father might die but you still had to pay the electric bill. That was simply how things were.

He thought about calling Abigail Mosley but decided it could wait. He was exhausted and did not want to have to speak to her, did not want to have to speak to anyone. The world had in the last day been very hard on him and he was not eager to invite any part of it into his home.

He stood motionless for a very long time and looked at the suitcase on the bed and thought about nothing. He walked to the suitcase, unzipped it, and flipped it open. The amount of money within it was overwhelming. He picked up one of the bundles and riffled through it. Ten thousand dollars: close to half of his average annual income. Yet there were over four hundred bundles within this suitcase just like it. It was strange to think about it. It was impossible to think about, impossible to think about clearly, at least if one was as tired as he was now.

He wondered what price he might pay for all that cash. After what had happened at the compound tonight – last night – he would almost certainly spend time in prison. It was true that there were mitigating circumstances. It was true that he had rescued a young woman from a dangerous situation. But it was also true that he had killed three men and burned down a house in order to do it. A jury might not believe the ends justified the blood. He was not even certain he believed they did. He knew only that he'd had a job to do and had employed whatever means were expedient in the moment to accomplish that job, and he regretted his decisions not at all.

Even if he had regretted them there was nothing to be done about it now. He had done what he'd done and would face what consequences were coming. This was all anybody could do, really, though they might wail and cry.

You could not unshoot a gun.

He listened to the water running in the bathroom. Lily would probably be done with her shower soon. He walked to the dresser and pulled out one of the drawers.

He was putting the suitcase in his closet when Lily stepped into the room wrapped in a white towel. Her dark hair hung wet around her face which was pink and freshly scrubbed. She smelled of pine tar soap and Head & Shoulders shampoo and Old Spice deodorant. She should have smelled like him, should have smelled like a man, but did not. These products smelled different, better, on her. Her feminine scent came through.

I used your toothbrush.

That's fine. I put a T-shirt and a pair of sweats on the bed for you.

Thank you.

No problem.

She allowed the towel to drop to her feet and looked at him in silence for a long time. Finally she broke the silence with seven words:

You can have me if you want.

There was something like desperation in her eyes and it broke his heart to see it. She was young and beautiful and broken perhaps beyond repair. Her body was a woman's body with full breasts and hips and yet the face was a girl's and it made him feel strange to be looking at her standing before him as she was. It felt wrong.

You don't have to do that.

I want to.

Put your clothes on.

Her eyes welled with tears at these words. Why don't you want me?

You've been used enough.

I'm not used up.

That isn't what I meant. I don't think of women in that way.

I want you to have me.

He walked to her and put his arms around her and held her there for a long time. She wrapped her arms around him as well and put her face into his neck and didn't move.

You don't have to fuck people to be loved.

I'm sorry, I just wanted to feel—

Don't be sorry. You didn't do anything wrong.

I feel embarrassed.

You shouldn't.

Then what should I feel?

He pushed away and looked her in the face. She returned his gaze, her eyes moist and full of uncertainty.

Feel whatever you feel. There's no such thing as a wrong feeling. I meant only that you needn't be embarrassed. I think I understand.

She shook her head. You couldn't.

Not completely. But I understand emptiness and the need to fill it. Some people do it with booze or pills. Some people do it with violence. Some people do it with sex. Some people do it with all of those things. Too few people get to fill it with love. There isn't enough of that in the world to go around. But I'm telling you – I'll be here for you and you don't need to fuck me to ensure that fact. I'll be here because I care about what happens to you. Do you understand?

She nodded.

Do you really?

I think so.

Good. He kissed her forehead. I'm going to take a shower.

Okay.

Once he'd undressed in the bathroom he peeled away the dirt- and blood-covered gauze – unwrapping it from his hands and feet, balling it up, throwing it into the trash can

– and when that was done he examined his wounds. He thought he had never before suffered so much physical damage – not outside of a warzone. In Iraq he had been hit by an IED. A vehicle at the front of the caravan he was part of had broken down and he was working on it, trying to knock dirt out of the air filter, when a child walked up carrying the device. He'd ended up with bolts and screws in his left hip, between two of his ribs, in his neck, and in his right shoulder – the shrapnel of a home-made explosive – and this had required four separate surgeries. Yet he'd been one of the lucky ones. Three other men, men standing around smoking Newports while he worked, had died. This damage was not as bad as that, and he'd lost no friends, but even so the pain had been nearly as great.

His arm was torn to shreds where the dog had bit him. His hands and feet still screamed with pain. His muscles were tight and cramped. His brain ached. He dreaded stepping into the shower and washing for he knew it would only increase his suffering, but he knew also that it was necessary. He needed to wash and dress his wounds in order to avoid infection. They were sure to be filled with dirt and grime after the night he'd had. Besides that he felt utterly foul and wanted to clean himself of blood and sweat and memories though the last of these he knew would not swirl down the drain. Those seemed to stay with you most when you wanted them gone and leave only when you wished to cling to them.

He stepped under the hot spray of the shower and

simply stood there unmoving for a very long time. He watched the filthy water drain away only to be replaced by more filthy water. He looked at the holes in his feet, black and crusted with blood. He looked at the raw pink skin that surrounded the holes. He felt the throb of pain work its way up his legs from his feet, as though some invisible hand were rhythmically squeezing them. He picked up a bar of pine tar soap and began washing, starting with his armpits so he would not have to smell his own stink, which he hated, and then moving on to his wounds.

Tears of pain streamed down his face as he did so.

When he stepped into the bedroom after putting on a pair of boxer shorts and dressing his wounds he found Lily asleep in his bed. She looked beautiful, almost angelic, as she lay there on her side atop his comforter in the warm morning air with her dark hair spread across a white pillow. Her face was calm and still, her knees pulled up nearly to her chest with her arms wrapped around them. She breathed low. Her eyes did not move beneath their lids.

Morning light was splashing in through the windows so he walked to them and drew the curtains. Then he took a pillow from the bed and dropped it to the area rug that covered his hardwood floor and lay on the rug, resting his head on the pillow. He watched the ceiling fan spin slow, the front edge of each blade gray with dust. His body he thought had never before been so tired and though his mind was tired too he also felt wired both from pills and the activities through which he had lived.

He focused on one of the blades and counted revolutions while trying not to think about anything at all.

He thought it might be some time before he managed to fall into sleep but exhaustion overwhelmed him and he was gone before he counted thirty.

It was almost three o'clock in the afternoon when he woke. He sat up on the floor feeling hungry and sore and disoriented, then twisted his neck to the left and to the right, cracking it a half dozen times. He glanced over to the bed and saw that Lily still lay asleep. Her face was calm and he was glad of it. She deserved a little peace. Her life had been a nightmare, so she ought not to have to face more of them while she was sleeping.

He got to his feet, walked to the dresser, and found a pair of Levi's and a T-shirt. He slipped into them as quietly as possible, not wanting to wake the girl, and once he was dressed he picked up his cigarettes and his cell phone from the nightstand and stepped out of the room.

He made his way downstairs.

Sat on the couch in the living room and lighted a cigarette. Took a deep drag, exhaled, and looked at the ceiling. Someone had wallpapered it once and though it had been painted over it was now peeling and sagging. The seams were visible. He wondered how long he had before the police came knocking at his door. He wondered what he should do with the money. He had to do something if he hoped to have it still when he finally got out of prison, and the more he thought about it the more certain he became that he would in fact end up doing time. He dialed Abigail Mosley and waited for her to pick up. He supposed he could simply leave the country and live the rest of his life elsewhere. He'd heard that Costa Rica was an inexpensive place to live and beautiful as well. He didn't speak but a few words of Spanish but he supposed he'd pick it up eventually. If you immersed yourself in a language you almost had to pick it up, unless you were tungsten dense. The phone rang three times before Abigail answered.

Lamb.

She's here.

Lily.

Yeah.

Where is here?

My house.

You got her?

I'll either spend the next ten years in prison or have to flee the country to avoid it but yeah, I got her.

Is she okay?

She is. Or she will be – I think.

What happened?

She's been through a lot.

How are you?

We both have.

I'm coming over. Can I bring anything?

Clothes for Lily.

Anything for you?

No.

Okay. I'll see you soon.

Abigail ended the call and left Lamb to listen only to silence. He pulled the phone away from his ear and set it on the coffee table.

He took another drag from his cigarette.

The knock came only fifteen minutes later. Lamb got to his feet and limped to the door and pulled it open. Abigail Mosley stood on the other side with nervous hope in her eyes and when she saw him she pulled open the storm door and kissed him on the mouth and thanked him half a dozen times in a single breath. I can't believe you did it. I really can't.

I told you I would.

People say a lot of things.

I do what I say I will.

And God fuckin bless you for it. Where is she?

Sleeping.

Can I see her?

Of course.

He walked her to the bedroom – though she knew the way – and they stood in the doorway looking at the sleeping girl. Abigail's eyes were moist and wide with awe.

I can't believe she's really here. What happened?

It's a long story.

Tell it to me.

It's an ugly story as well.

I want to know everything.

Okay.

For the next hour and a half, while Lily lay sleeping, they sat in the living room drinking his last two beers – he drank a Newcastle and she drank a Red Stripe – and he told her what had happened at the compound. She listened wide-eyed with horror and interrupted only to mouth an exclamation or to ask for clarification when she did not understand something he'd said. When his story was finally finished she sat silent for a very long time. Then she took a swallow of her warm beer, opened her mouth to speak, hesitated, and after a long moment asked the question she wanted to ask.

Do you really think he's dead?

I think so, yes.

But you aren't certain.

It was dark.

If he's still alive he will come after you – he'll come after all of us.

I don't think he is.

But what if you're wrong?

What if he's wrong about what?

They both looked up from the couch to see Lily standing at the foot of the stairs in an oversized Cardinals T-shirt and a pair of gray sweatpants. Her hair was tangled and her eyes were red and swollen from sleeping, but she looked all right nonetheless.

Hi, Momma.

Abigail got to her feet and walked to her daughter and wrapped her arms around the girl. Lily hugged her back, putting her face in the older woman's neck.

I missed you so much, sweetie.

I missed you too, Momma.

He felt them dragging him through the tunnel, the heels of his shoes scraping along the concrete floor. He was coming in and out of consciousness and did not know who they were but did know there were two of them. They spoke but what they said did not sound like words to his ears; the voices barely sounded human at all. It was almost as though he were listening from underwater.

Then light hit his eyelids and he saw red, saw the blood under his skin. He moaned in an attempt to speak but even he did not know what it was he was trying to say. Words did not come to him, just this feeling that everything was falling apart, that *he* was falling apart, and somehow he wanted to express that.

But he could express nothing.

Do you think he'll pull through?

He has to pull through. We'd be lost without him.

We should take him to a hospital.

You know he wouldn't want that.

He might if it meant survival.

He'll pull through.

How can you be certain?

God is on his side.

He opened his eyes and found himself looking at a bright white ceiling. It hurt his eyes and they watered and the water ran down his cheeks. There was a great pain in his right hip, a radiating pain which seemed to spread out through his entire body in ripples. A similar pain though less severe throbbed also in his left shoulder.

How do you feel?

He looked toward the sound of the voice and there saw Chloe, born of Eunice some twenty years ago, standing with her hands behind her back and looking at him with concern in her eyes. Her blonde hair was pulled back into a ponytail. Her blue eyes were beautiful though empty as promises. She was his child, as were sixteen others who lived here, though he did not believe she knew it. None of them did. That his seed had helped produce her meant nothing to him. Everyone here was his child. He loved them all equally.

Eunice had birthed her when she was fourteen years old and when she fell back into drugs three years later abandoned her here. He had given Eunice everything she needed to find happiness and yet she had chosen the streets.

Several women raised the child here.

I heard you talking with Abigail. Has she returned to me?

I've been caring for you myself.

Who carried me here?

Daniel and David.

He remembered the voices he had heard, the voices of two women speaking, but perhaps he had simply dreamed it, he did not know, or perhaps the girl was lying for reasons he did not fully understand. People did that. They lied and they betrayed you. You gave them love and a home and salve for their souls and you shared your bed with them and still the devil could convince them of the truth of lies and have them walk away with him willingly while you lay bleeding on a concrete floor. He had believed her pure but it turned out that she was like the others. There was no place for trust in this world. Even God might abandon you.

What happened?

You've been shot – twice.

He remembered the tunnel, his struggle with the private investigator, a great pain slamming into his right hip and another into his left shoulder. He remembered the feel of warm blood pooling beneath him, the sound of more shots being fired, bits of concrete hitting his face as the bullets broke them away. He remembered the sounds of the struggle in the garage reaching him faintly before he lost all consciousness. He remembered hoping that his men—

Did they kill him?

Who, Father?

The devil.

I don't under—

The interloper. Did my men kill him?

She shook her head.

Naked I came from my mother's womb and naked shall I return. The Lord giveth and the Lord hath taken away; blessed be the name of the Lord.

He spoke those words but he did not believe them, not in the moment. He felt alone. He felt abandoned. He had not felt so helpless since he was a little boy and he was now almost sixty-four. It was both horrible and somehow nostalgic to feel this way, to feel this utterly isolated, especially when surrounded by people.

How long was I unconscious, girl?

Almost a full day. It's nearly dark again.

He nodded and looked down at his body and saw an IV feeding into the back of his hand and bandages wrapped around his hip and shoulder, and scrapes and bruises on his arms. He felt weak and tired and not at all the man that he knew he was. The devil had hurt him. But he had not defeated him, not yet in any case.

How bad are my wounds?

The bullets hit no organs, nor did they hit bone. God must have been looking out for you. You have torn muscles and some blood loss but I think you'll be okay.

I doubt that very much. He gave her a look which dared

contradiction and she replied to the look wisely with silence. How are my people?

They're worried, Father.

What are the rumors?

There are no rumors. They know you've been shot and are concerned.

There are always rumors.

Then I haven't heard them.

Help me to my feet.

You should rest.

I must address my people. I must take care of what needs to be taken care of. Help me to my feet, girl, and do not argue.

She helped him to his feet.

It was a painful process but eventually and with assistance he found himself standing.

He stepped out into the evening, feeling hollow and raw. His legs were weak. His right hip ached when he used it. He felt dehydrated. He limped toward the place where his house once stood and found there nothing but a black hole in the ground that had once been his basement and within it a pile of charred rubble, all that was left of his belongings. Somewhere among the ashes were what remained of several million dollars burned almost to nothing. He had a safe-deposit box with enough money in it to take care of his people for a couple of months with careful budgeting, but that was it, and when that was gone it was over. He had told his men that what they had built could not be destroyed but he believed now that he had been lying to them, and to himself, for he had believed the words as he spoke them but believed them not now. It already had been destroyed.

Everything was lost.

His people had counted on him and he had failed them. He had been proven weak and ineffectual, not a spokesman for God but a mere fragile human as were they. He did not know how he could face them and presume to speak wisdom when he had so easily been undone.

Yet neither could he abandon his people as God had so clearly abandoned him. Neither could he leave them to the wolves of the world. They would be destroyed and those who were not destroyed would be drawn into evil, which was worse. This he could not allow to happen.

Which left him only one clear option. If he could no longer take care of them, if God had left this place, then he would have to send them to be with the Lord where the Lord was, and the Lord was in Heaven. It broke his heart to do such a thing. It broke his heart to even consider it. It was an admission of absolute failure. But he did not see that he had a choice.

The end was here.

No longer will there be any curse. The throne of God and of the Lamb will be in the city and his servants will serve him. They will see his face and his name will be on their foreheads. There will be no more night. They will not need the light of a lamp or the light of the sun for the Lord

God will give them light and they will reign for ever and ever. The angel said to me that these words are trustworthy and true. The Lord, the God of the spirits of the prophets, sent his angel to show his servants the things that must soon take place.

Behold, I am coming soon.

Everything he had built had been destroyed and it was time to send his people home.

The end was here.

Tears streamed down his cheeks as he thought about this, as he thought about what he must do, and he allowed them to flow freely and did not attempt to hide them from anyone who might be watching, and though he could not see them for his back was turned, he felt many eyes upon him and heard the unspoken questions in their minds.

Soon he would have to answer but for the moment he would simply stand here and look at that black hole in the ground in order that he might fully understand the extent of his failure, the extent of his loss.

It was total.

V

You should both stay here until we're certain this is finished.

Lily and Abigail were sitting on the couch, both turned toward him as he was them. They looked so much alike it was uncanny, despite the age difference, despite Lily's long hair and Abigail's short. They both sat with their knees together, their palms flat on their thighs, their shoulders slumped. They both had the same wide-eyed receptive expressions on their oval faces. Their mouths were narrow but full-lipped. Their skin pale and nearly flawless with a few freckles dotting the areas beneath their eyes.

He supposed it made sense that they should look so much alike. They were more closely related than most mothers and daughters, for they were sisters as well. What had been done to them would never leave them. It was in their blood. He liked them both and did not want to think about such things – it made him think less of them despite the fact they'd had no real choice in the matter – but sometimes the mind went where it wanted.

If they could live with it he supposed he must as well.

Are you sure?

He wouldn't have said it otherwise, Momma.

He looked from Lily to Abigail. I'm sure. You should go to your apartment and pack a suitcase. Do you have anything Lily can wear?

She's wearing my clothes now. I have others she'll fit.

Lamb nodded.

Lily can stay with me while you go. We'll make lunch.

Abigail got to her feet. She dug her keys from her purse. She kissed Lily on the corner of the mouth and hugged her, clearly hesitant to leave the girl now that she'd got her back. She kissed Lamb on the mouth. He tasted cigarettes and peppermint on her breath.

Thank you – for everything. Whispered into his ear before she pulled away.

Go get some clothes and hurry back.

Okay.

She turned toward the front door. She walked to it. A moment later she disappeared through it, closing it with a click behind her. Lamb looked at the door for a long moment. He did not know why – he didn't know Abigail very well – but there was a tight feeling in his chest at the thought that he might never see her again, and it made a strange melancholia wash over him, like a wave coming to shore.

Let's make some food.

Lamb turned toward the kitchen and walked into it. It was long and narrow, too narrow really for two people to work in simultaneously, neither the oven nor the fridge opening all the way before their doors banged against the counter opposite, but even so the two of them made do. Lamb pulled three cans of tuna fish from his cupboard, and while Lily opened and drained the cans, he got mayonnaise and mustard and celery and capers from the refrigerator. He scraped the cans of tuna into a blue ceramic bowl and added the ingredients as well as salt and pepper and celery salt and Lawry's seasoning salt and paprika. There had been a time in his life, after his baseball career had died, and with it his dreams, when he'd considered going to culinary school. He liked to cook a great deal, liked even the simple task of making tuna sandwiches, but almost never prepared food in this kitchen unless he had a girlfriend. He found preparing food for one a depressing task; it reminded you that you had no one with whom to share your meals.

But he did have someone with whom to share this meal – two someones.

Lily found a loaf of Bunny brand sandwich bread sitting atop the refrigerator beside two boxes of cereal – Cheerios and Cap'n Crunch – and pulled it down. She untwisted the metal tie and removed six slices of bread. She twisted the bag and put the tie back on.

Is it stale?

Lily shook her head. Still soft.

Lamb went about making the sandwiches, but while he did he thought about Abigail. He wondered why he had this tight feeling in his chest. There was no reason for it so far as he knew. Mosley, even if he was alive, could not possibly have tracked her down yet. He might have been able to track down Lamb himself. Lamb had lived in the same house since his return to Louisville over a decade ago. But Abigail was barely an inhabitant of the city. She would be hard to locate. Which meant she was almost certainly safe.

He supposed part of him was simply dreading her eventual, inevitable, departure. For he knew she had been lying to him about her motives and the money. He'd known since the lie left her tongue, though he had not acknowledged it even to himself. Of course he hadn't. Nor had he admitted his own motives. The fact that he was himself doing it for the money. The fact that he did not give a solitary dry turd whether Lily lived or died, much less whether she escaped the compound.

Things had changed since he took the job. He met Lily and saving her became his real priority rather than merely his stated one. The pain in her eyes broke his heart and he wanted to take it away, crush it with the heel of his shoe. He wanted her to understand that she could be free.

But he did not think Abigail's motives had changed.

He thought she would hunt for the money he had taken, and when she found it she would disappear. She'd take Lily with her if she could, but if the girl refused this betrayal, as she might, she'd go it alone. He hoped he was wrong. Wanted to be wrong about this more than he'd wanted anything in a long while. But he knew people and doubted very much that he was.

It made him sad to think about. He wanted her to stay with him. He wanted both her and Lily to stay with him. When they were here he felt as though he had a family. A wife and daughter. It filled up something within him that he'd not even known was empty.

Do you want to eat now or wait for your mother?

Let's wait.

Lamb nodded, stacked the sandwiches on a plate, and covered them in cellophane. He lighted a cigarette and looked out the window to his backyard. He needed to mow.

Abigail slid in behind the wheel of her car and pulled the driver-side door closed behind her. She put the key into the ignition and turned it clockwise. The car whined, sputtered. She pumped the gas pedal. The engine coughed, then roared to life. She thrust the shifter into reverse and backed out of the driveway. Put it into drive and started down the street. The asphalt was faded. The sky deep blue. Clouds like pulled cotton stretched across it.

While she drove she thought about Lamb and what he had done for her and Lily. He risked his life for them. Almost got himself killed for them.

Yet she was going to betray him and had known that she would since this began. She'd be a liar if she did not admit – to herself if to no one else – that she felt some guilt about it, but it was a small guilt and her hunger for money was large. Still, depending on how much he had walked away with, she might leave him something.

She pulled the car to the curb in front of her building and stepped out into the summer heat. She looked across the street at Central Park and the people there. It seemed to her that they lived in a different world than she did, a world that overlapped with her own but was separate nonetheless. But then maybe everyone lived in his or her own private world, a world that overlapped with all the others. You could see one another. You could speak to one another. You could touch one another, pushing against the membranes that separated your worlds. But you could never step from your own world into someone else's. There would always be that membrane through which you could not break completely. Every person had their own private world, and while they might rule it, it could be very lonely indeed.

She turned her back to the park and walked toward her building. Walked across the tall green grass, feeling it give softly beneath her feet. Walked up three concrete steps and through a red-painted door, into the air-conditioned building. Walked up three flights of stairs, hoping she did not bump into Michael, who had called her another half dozen times since yesterday. Unlocked her front door and stepped into her apartment, which she could afford for another month.

But that would change.

She walked to her bedroom and pulled a burgundy canvas suitcase out of her closet. She set it on her unmade bed and opened its zippered jaw. She filled it with clothes, folding them neatly before stacking them. Pants and blouses and underwear and socks and bras. Once the clothes were packed, she gathered her toiletries and packed those as well.

As she zipped the suitcase shut it occurred to her that she might never return here. If Mosley found them and came for them, if he managed to kill them, this last six months might have been the only time in her life she would ever live that belonged only to her.

Thirty-three years she had walked this earth and six months had been hers.

It made her sad to think about it in such a way.

She pushed the thought into the back of her mind, to the shadowed corners unlighted by conscious thought, and hefted the suitcase off the bed. It was heavier than she'd anticipated and pulled down her right side. She reached out with her left hand, gripped the handle with it, so she was holding it with both hands in front of her. She walked with it toward the front door, her knees banging against it, struggled her way out of the apartment, and looked back over her shoulder before pulling shut the locked door. She fought her way down a flight of stairs, grunting and banging her knees and shins against the suitcase, cursing as she went.

Then Michael's door opened. He stood in the open doorway in slacks and a white button-up, his tie loose around his neck, his sleeves rolled. He looked at her for a long moment, blinked.

I thought I heard you.

I don't have time for this right now.

You never seem to have time. I just want to talk. You going on a trip?

I'm moving some things into my boyfriend's house.

You don't have a boyfriend.

I do.

But you spent the night with me.

I hadn't met him yet.

You told me you didn't want a relationship.

I didn't – and don't – want a relationship with you.

You're so cold.

I'm honest, Michael. You should appreciate that. A lot of girls would string you along.

I wish you'd string me along.

Life's too short. Now, excuse me, but this suitcase is heavy.

She started walking down the stairs, struggling with it, but Michael stepped from his apartment, reached out, and tried to take it from her. She pulled back, refusing to let go her grip.

I got it, Michael.

Let me carry it for you. He pulled.

I said I got it. She pulled back.

But he managed to wrest the suitcase from her grip.

Fine, she said. Let's go.

She started down the stairs and Michael followed, hauling the suitcase with him. She knew he was doing this not to help but to continue a conversation she did not want to have, and as she walked down to the street she waited for it to continue.

Finally it did: What does this guy have that I don't?

A personality that doesn't make me want to punch him.

What does he do?

None of your business.

You embarrassed?

He's a private detective.

Didn't all the private detectives go extinct in the 1950s? They're like dinosaurs or wooly mammoths or something.

Abigail pushed her way out into the sunshine. She squinted at the bright daylight, tears standing out in her eyes, and wished she hadn't left her sunglasses hanging from the visor in her car. She wiped the tears away and walked across the yard, through the open wrought-iron gate, and out to the street. Michael followed, grunting as he hauled her suitcase. She unlocked the trunk and motioned for him to put the suitcase into it. He did so. She slammed shut the trunk.

Say what you want – Damien's twice the man you are.

His name is Damien?

This conversation is over, Michael.

She walked to the driver side, pulled open the door, and slid in behind the wheel. She started the engine, pulled the shifter down, putting the car into drive. She looked in her rearview mirror and saw Michael standing there, looking through the back window at her. She checked traffic, saw the street was clear, and pulled away from the curb.

Soon she was on her way back to Damien Lamb's house, on her way back to her daughter.

On her way back to the money which soon would be hers.

L ess than an hour after she had left Abigail returned with a suitcase full of clothes. She did not knock but simply walked through the front door as if this were her home and had always been. Lamb liked this, though he did not know why exactly. He was not a man who examined his feelings, merely one who felt them.

She set the suitcase down by the front door. It's heavy. Do you mind carrying it upstairs?

Yeah, I'll get it.

Until it was confirmed that Rhett Mosley was dead they would stay together. Lamb wanted to be able to protect the women. He had promised Lily that things were going to be okay and he was going to do everything in his power to ensure that what he'd said had not been a lie. He had a great many flaws, but he was a man who kept his promises.

He carried the suitcase upstairs and tossed it on the bed, then emptied two dresser drawers for her to use. He unpacked her suitcase, putting her clothes into the drawers he had cleared out for her.

This done, he headed downstairs. He found Abigail in the living room standing over the piano. She was randomly pressing keys, sending discordant notes into the air. It was clear that she didn't play.

She looked up at him as he reached the first floor. Is it just furniture?

I play a little.

I'd like to hear you sometime.

Maybe. Let's eat. I made some tuna-fish sandwiches.

Abigail scrunched up her nose.

You don't like tuna fish?

It's okay. I'll eat it.

I have pimiento cheese spread if you'd rather have that.

No, tuna's fine. Where's Lily?

In the backyard.

What's she doing?

Just standing in the backyard.

Why?

To see what it feels like to stand outside and know you can be anywhere you want to be but you are here – I think.

Abigail nodded. Then locked her eyes on his eyes. Why are you doing this?

Doing what?

All of this. I asked you only to get Lily back, and you did. You could wash your hands of us and if you did your life would probably be a lot easier.

He'll come after me too.

He might be dead.

He might not be dead.

But you think he is – and if he's not it would be easier to take care only of yourself.

Easy has nothing to do with right.

I just want you to know I appreciate it. She walked to him and kissed his mouth. It means more to me than I can say.

But you're still going to take the money and leave. He thought this but did not say it. He knew it was true but did not want to ruin what time they had together.

You're welcome, he said.

They sat at his dining table and ate tuna-fish sandwiches, and as they did Lamb realized that though the table had been in place for over a decade – since the day he moved in – he had never taken a meal there. Even when he had girlfriends. Most of the time he sat in front of his television alone, scooping microwaved dinners into his mouth without enjoyment, merely giving fuel to the machine that was his body. Salisbury steak and corn and mashed potatoes. Chicken and peas and mashed potatoes. Meatloaf and sliced apples and mashed potatoes. When he had girlfriends he sometimes ate with them in bed, or by his side on the couch. But never had he taken a meal at the dinner table. It had instead become a receptacle for mail and work papers and random objects for which there was no home. It felt good to instead be eating this way with Abigail and Lily. He knew it was ridiculous. This woman and this girl were strangers to him, or nearly so, yet he allowed himself to pretend otherwise. He allowed himself to pretend they might be something more – might *become* something more. The dream filled a hollow inside him, and though he knew it was being filled only with smoke, which would blow away, he allowed himself to feel whole.

Under different circumstances they might talk about what their days had been like. Lily might tell them about a class at university. Abigail could talk about what had happened at the hospital where she'd picked up a PRN shift. He might talk about a case that had just walked through the door. What they discussed wouldn't matter. The comfort and familiarity they felt with one another would. Even their shared silence might be nice as they sat together on the couch and watched situation comedies while eating buttered popcorn.

Most of his adult life he had been alone. Even when he had lived with someone he had felt alone. But he did not feel that now and it was nice to pretend that this might continue even after circumstance did not demand it.

Abigail and Lily could move in permanently. He could come home to a hot meal and warm conversation. He could sleep beside a woman whose mere presence calmed him. He could be a father to a girl who, though seventeen, desperately needed a father.

But of course these thoughts were ridiculous.

More likely than not he would have to spend time in prison, and without any threat to their lives Abigail and Lily would have no reason to stay here. They would leave like everybody left. They would go on with their lives apart from him. They would promise to stay in touch but they would not stay in touch. Lily might at first but the phone calls would taper off until there were no more phone calls at all. Ten years from now he might see her at Kroger or picking up a San Francisco melt at Steak 'n Shake and it would take her a moment to recognize him and when she did she would say hello but there would be an unbearable awkwardness about the encounter that made it worse than no encounter at all.

He would step through the prison gates five or eight years from now and be utterly alone. He would reside in a halfway house for a time and find work as his parole required, probably as a short-order cook or something along those lines. He would die alone.

He smiled at his own self-pity – the mind was a vicious dog that blah-blah-blah – and told himself to knock it off. It did not matter that this situation was temporary. Of course it was temporary. Looked at from a distance every situation was temporary. In the end, come the big crunch, even the universe was temporary, and it was everything there was. What mattered was that he was in it for the moment and for the moment it was enjoyable, however terrible the reason for its existing in the first place.

What do we do now?

He looked at Abigail for a long moment before responding. Finally, though, he answered:

We wait.

I hope we're waiting for nothing.

I do too. I want this to be over.

He scratched at the back of his bandaged left hand knowing that he was lying. He would be happy to wait forever.

Before they lay down for bed he went through the house to make sure it was secure, starting in the basement and working his way up, checking every door and window and securing those that might allow entry. He knew there was no such thing as a perfectly secure home, any place with windows and doors was a place that could be broken into, but he wanted the place as tightly locked as he could get it.

He cleared off a bed in the guest room that had been covered for years with paperwork and once-read books – mostly old paperbacks he bought from Harry White at Dog-Eared Books out on Bardstown Road – and boxes of pens and pencils and other knickknacks he did not know what to do with. He took off the blanket and the sheets which smelled of dust and changed them so that Lily would have a room to call her own if only temporarily. He carried a television up from the basement so that she could watch it if she chose. He stood in the doorway and looked at the room and felt very glad that someone would finally be sleeping there.

He wished that he had a daughter. He wished he had known Lily from childhood and had the opportunity to raise her. He would have picked her up from school and taken her to get ice cream at Graeter's and talked with her about childish things. He would have read her bedtime stories and kissed her goodnight. He would have put Band-Aids on her booboos.

Instead she had lived with Mosley. The man had not deserved her – had deserved neither her nor Abigail – but somehow he had got her all the same, and been allowed to share her company while Lamb himself had been alone in his life or felt alone, since all his prior companions had been companions of convenience. Even those he loved had not loved him in return. Their eventual actions proved this.

He showed Lily her room and she hugged him and thanked him and said goodnight and went into it and shut the door behind her.

He walked into his bedroom and found Abigail already in bed, wearing nothing but one of his old T-shirts, her breasts visible through the thin white fabric. She smiled at him when he walked into the room. He smiled back and began undressing. He removed his shoes and his socks and his pants and his shirt. He pulled back the covers and slipped into bed. He looked at the ceiling.

Abigail moved toward him and put a hand on his chest

and told him again that she appreciated what he was doing. She kissed his neck and his cheek and his mouth.

He kissed her in return. He combed fingers through her hair. He stroked her right breast, the skin smooth and soft beneath the touch of his callused fingers. Her nipple became hard.

What do you think will happen when this is all over?

We don't need to talk about that.

Do you think—

She silenced him with another kiss and then worked her way down until her head was hidden beneath the covers and he could concentrate on nothing but her mouth.

They had gathered in the church all of them and were sitting now with their eyes upon him as he stood at the front of the room in a white linen suit and white leather bucks with brown soles. His hair was combed and his face was shaved and he looked as put-together as he ever had but for the blue sling holding his left arm in place. But there was a hole in him that would never be filled. That *could* never be filled.

He looked out at the dozens of faces tilted toward him white and pale and trusting as newborn babies, eyes all wide with awe and wonder. He did not want to say to them what he had to say to them, but would say it nonetheless. Sometimes a thing was difficult *because* it was necessary and the fact it was difficult let you know it must be done.

Early yesterday – he began quietly, with little more than a whisper – early yesterday we were visited by a beast disguised as a lamb. I saw through him from the beginning

– Satan himself masquerades as an angel of light – yet was unable to stop him despite making every effort to do so. I should have been able but I was not. I – I have failed you. I promised you safety here. I promised you a table next to the Lord. But I fear now that the Lord has left us. That His light has been extinguished here on earth. Had he not left us the devil would have been unable to destroy all that he has destroyed. We are still children of God but our home is no longer here. The earth has been taken and we must flee. This is a sad day for the world but it is not a sad day for us. God's people have always been nomads. God's light moves and we move with it. Yet we hunger and thirst for righteousness, which means we shall be filled. We are pure of heart, which means that we shall see God. We are persecuted for our righteousness, which means ours is the kingdom of Heaven. It is now time to go home to the kingdom. The Lord has left this place which means only that we must go to the Lord. We must take our place at the table beside him and sup our holy meal. Do not mourn for this earth we will leave behind nor for the life you may have lived on it for it would have been no life at all but only an imitation of life. The world is unholy and riddled with temptation designed by the devil only to draw you from the path of the righteous before you might perish, so that upon that day you will be delivered unto the gates of Hell rather than the kingdom of Heaven. That is no place for children of God to make their home. Yet in our Father's house are many rooms. If it were not so would I have told you that I prepare a place for you there? I would not, nor would I tell you now that that place has been prepared, but I do tell you this and in my heart I know it is true. God spoke to me in a dream last night and asked me to bring His people home. You are His people. You are the righteous and the faithful and the meek. You are little children and it is time for you to step into His holy arms and be embraced fully in spirit, and in order that this might happen you must first shed your mortal skins. So I ask you now to go back to your houses and prepare yourselves. Write letters to your families telling them that they should not mourn for you. You will be in a better place while they remain on unholy soil. Tell them that you are standing in the light of God now while they must contend with darkness. Tell them that if they find their way back to the narrow path you shall see them in Heaven when the time is right. Tell them you love them and that they should rejoice in your decision to be with the Lord for only the Lord finally can protect us from the evils that lurk in the midst of darkness. His light as you know is the only light that will never burn out.

Now let us bow our heads before we go.

He watched each of his people – man, woman, and child alike – lower their heads and hood their eyes. He looked out at them each so pure and trusting. He had told many truths tonight but he had also lied – he believed he had – for he had said *we* with no intention of leading his children home. He would not leave this earth until the devil that had destroyed his home and driven the Lord from it had paid with his life. Nor would he allow Lily or Abigail – for she had almost certainly sent that devil here – to breathe while the lungs of his faithful swallowed no air. They had betrayed him and they had betrayed the Lord. Unlike the devil they pretended to be children of God. He would send them home as well though theirs would not be a place of light but one of darkness, one of eternal night from which there would be no reprieve. Night replaced by no morning.

He began to pray.

Oh Lord, I have heard thy speech, and was afraid: Oh Lord, revive thy work in the midst of the years, in the midst of the years make known; in wrath remember mercy. God came from Teman. His glory covered the heavens, and the earth was full of his praise and his brightness was as the light; he had horns coming out of his hand: and there was the hiding of his power. Before him went the pestilence, and burning coals went forth at his feet. He stood, and measured the earth: he beheld, and drove asunder the nations; and the everlasting mountains were scattered, the perpetual hills did bow: his ways are everlasting. I saw the tents of Cushan in affliction: and the curtains of the land of Midian did tremble. The mountains saw thee, and they trembled: the overflowing of the water passed by: the deep uttered his voice, and lifted up his hands on high. The sun and moon stood still in their habitation. Thou didst march through the land in indignation, thou didst thresh the heathen in anger. Thou wentest forth for the salvation of thy people, even for salvation with thine anointed; thou woundedst the head out of the house of the wicked, by discovering the foundation unto the neck. Thou didst strike through with his staves the head of his villages: they came out as a whirlwind to scatter me: their rejoicing was as to devour the poor secretly. Thou didst walk through the sea with thine horses, through the heap of great waters. When I heard, my belly trembled; my lips quivered at the voice: rottenness entered into my bones, and I trembled in myself, that I might rest in the day of trouble: when he cometh up unto the people, he will invade them with his troops.

Yet I will rejoice in the Lord, I will joy in the God of my salvation.

The Lord God is my strength, and he will make my feet like hinds' feet, and he will make me to walk upon mine high places. To the chief singer on my stringed instruments. Amen.

He asked five of his men to stay behind while everyone else left the building and once all but those five were gone he sat down, the pain in his hip too great to allow him to stand a moment longer, though he wished to project strength and determination. They stood watching him, concern in their eyes.

Now that Elijah has passed you are my most faithful servants, which is why I trust you with things I could not tell the rest. Our home here is a home no more, which I believe I made clear to everyone tonight. Our home is in

Heaven. Yet I fear that there are those among us who may try to flee their fate, not having faith enough to carry them through. I want you each to retrieve a weapon and stand on the perimeter of our land and ensure that no one leaves. Do your best to avoid the necessity of death, do your best to convince them of their error, but fire if you must. I want none of my people to step foot off this land. They shall soar into the heavens while their bodies stay behind but shall not walk this vile earth. Though some may not know it, what I am doing is best for all. I am sending my people home to be with the Lord. Do you understand?

They expressed their understanding.

Good.

For the rest of the day he sat on his porch eating pain pills and watching his land. People brought him letters to mail and the letters stacked up. Many of the bearers had tears in their eyes. Sometimes they were tears of sorrow while other times they were tears of joy. The tears of joy pleased him. It was a joyous thing to go home to the Lord. If they expressed their doubts he tried to calm them; if they expressed their joy he attempted to share in it.

A large part of him wanted to make the journey with them, and did he not have things left unfinished to which he needed to attend he would. He wanted free of this cursed earth. But he must stay behind for a time and meet them in Heaven at some later date.

Occasionally the country quiet was interrupted by the

sound of a gunshot or a series of gunshots. There were screams and there was crying and sometimes there was mourning. He had his men carry the bodies to one of the feed sheds and pile them there.

People did not always know what was best for them. Often they did not. But fortunately for them he was here to show them the way. He would bring them to the Lord if they were unwilling to carry themselves to Him and kneel in His presence. He would allow none of his people to be left behind.

And when his time came he would kneel before Him as well, believing he had done right and holding up his palms in supplication.

L amb awoke the next morning in a panic. He sat up, confused, looking around the room in order to get some sense of where he was, for at first he did not know. To his right he saw his dresser pressed up against the wall, and behind it a mirror that revealed to him his own reflection. His face was pale and sweaty. He needed a shave. His eyes looked tired and there was a fading green bruise below one of them. To his left was a large painting of a flower, a painting a girlfriend had made for him some years ago. She had been beautiful. She had also, as it turned out, been needlessly cold in her dealings with other people's hearts.

He looked down and saw Abigail asleep beneath the sheets. She was turned toward him, her face still and calm. Her shoulder was bare and pale and smooth and he wished to reach out and touch it but did not for fear of waking her.

Instead he slid out of bed, picked up a pair of pants from the floor, and walked out of the room, cringing when the floorboards creaked beneath his bare feet. He made his way downstairs and into the kitchen, intending to make coffee. But when he walked into the room he found Lily sitting at the table, his French press and a mug of steaming coffee in front of her. She was flipping through a copy of the *Courier–Journal*, apparently reading headlines. When she heard him enter the room she looked up.

I hope you don't mind.

I don't – but you did use my favorite mug.

You can have it. I barely took a sip.

I don't take cream in my coffee. He smiled, then walked to the cupboard and pulled it open. He found within it a black mug he'd stolen from the Ritz Carlton in Naples, Florida, some years ago – although stolen might be the wrong word: they'd charged his credit card $16.95 – and made his way with it back to the table. He poured himself a cup, took a sip. It was good and bitter and strong. He sat down.

Is that today's paper?

It is.

Do you mind if I grab a section you aren't reading?

She handed him the entire paper. I was just looking at the headlines.

Anything interesting?

Nothing about what happened at the compound.

Interesting.

Why?

Because if Rhett Mosley was dead that would be news. Would anybody there have covered up his death?

Lily shook her head. Elijah might have, but . . .

But he's dead himself.

She nodded.

Mosley's survival – if in fact he had survived – meant two things so far as Lamb could tell. First, it meant that the man would almost certainly come after them. Second, it meant that Lamb might not end up in prison. Mosley would want police around even less than Lamb would. In the past, after all, he'd actually paid them off in order to keep them away. He would cover up what had happened there. The deaths could be concealed. The fire could be a terrible accident.

What is it?

Lamb looked up at Lily, startled by her presence. He'd been lost in thought and forgotten she was there.

Nothing.

She looked at him for a long time, seemed to actually study his face. It made him feel uncomfortable, as if he were under a microscope. He looked back at her for a long time, however, before finally dropping his gaze. He took a sip from his mug.

You think he's still alive.

I do.

What does that mean for us?

I wanted you here because I knew it was a possibility. Because I wanted to protect you if he decided to do something stupid. That hasn't changed.

Do you think you can?

I know I can.

What if you're wrong?

I'm not.

But what if you are?

What if he is what?

Both Lamb and Lily looked toward the kitchen doorway. Abigail stood there in nothing but panties and one of Lamb's T-shirts. Her pixie hair was mussed. There were lines across her right cheek from where it had pressed against wrinkles in her pillowcase. Her eyes were swollen with sleep. But she looked, to Lamb, absolutely beautiful.

Coffee?

Abigail shook her head. Do you have any sweet tea?

Refrigerator.

Abigail padded barefoot to the cupboards and started opening them randomly, looking for a glass in which to pour her tea.

On the left.

She opened the cupboard on the left and found the glasses, a random assortment he had collected over the years. She selected a Coca-Cola glass, walked to the fridge, and poured sweet tea into it from a blue plastic pitcher. She took a sip and turned back toward him.

What if you're what?

There's nothing in today's paper about either Mosley or the Children of God.

Abigail was silent for a moment, thinking about this

information. Then she spoke. You think that means Mosley isn't dead.

Lamb nodded.

Then it's good we're here. If he's alive he'll have figured out that I'm involved, and he'll come after us.

I know – and it will probably be soon. Lamb took another sip from his mug. Do either of you want breakfast?

Mosley watched by the doors in the dining hall as his people stood in a long line waiting for their medicine. Once they had each collected three tablets and a cup of water they took their seats at cafeteria benches and waited. They did not speak except in whispers. It was a quiet, solemn time. But despite the lack of words he saw many of them share looks with one another. As well as their own pills, mothers and fathers collected those for their children. A few babies wailed. Within twenty minutes the cafeteria benches were full, the last people to sit his men who had been patrolling the perimeter to ensure no one escaped. Many people were silently weeping and a few were weeping loudly.

Mosley put a chain through the doors and then a padlock through the chain. The key he slipped into the right hip pocket of his white linen suit. He did not expect trouble. Those who would be a problem were already stacked up like cordwood in one of the feed sheds. But it never hurt to be prepared. He walked slowly to the head of the room – he had to walk slowly because of his hip but made an effort not to limp: he could not appear weak before his people – and stood there still as stone for at least a full minute allowing the implications of all this to wash over him like tidewater rising.

The outside world was certain to misunderstand what was about to happen here. He knew that but did not care. The outside world was a vile place and its people were godless and incapable of understanding anything beyond the reality-television programs they subjected themselves to and their latest McDonald's cheeseburger.

This, on the other hand, was a holy moment.

He began to speak, and as with all his speeches it began softly:

I see that many of your eyes are wet with tears but you should not cry except for joy. Tonight is a night of great happiness. For years you have lived on this dark and godless earth and now you are going home. You are going to hear angels singing. You are going to visit with those you have loved and lost. You will get to hug your grandparents and your great-grandparents. You will get to meet ancestors you did not even know you had. You are going to get to gaze upon the face of God Almighty and know finally what He truly looks like. How hollow your lives here will seem once you have been wrapped in His warm embrace, how utterly empty. I ask you now to raise your cups and take your medicine and while you do, say a silent prayer of thanks, for the Lord has given you salvation in Jesus Christ, who sacrificed himself that you might be saved.

At first no one moved. Then Mosley put three aspirins on his tongue and swallowed them back, his people watching. Following his lead now, one by one, they began to put pills on their own tongues and the tongues of their children and he watched them as they washed them down, and many of them said *hallelujah* and many of them said *amen*, and when it was over silence once more filled the room and the wait began. There was a sense of anticlimax in the room. It seemed that something should happen immediately after such a commitment was made but nothing happened at all. They continued to sit and wait and the wait went on for far too long.

You may say goodbye to those you love here, and you may embrace, but know that you will soon embrace again, only next time you will have shed your physical bodies and will be embracing in spirit. What wonderful things you all have to look forward to. What magical things.

People began to speak to one another, and they hugged, and when children cried they were comforted. It was beautiful to watch their combined faith. There was so much belief in this building: enough, one would think, to move mountains. Had the Lord not fled this infernal planet their faith would surely have been strong enough to overcome anything. But God was gone from here now. He had abandoned this place as hopeless and Mosley saw that He had been right to do so. It had been foolish to believe his world apart could hold off indefinitely the ugliness that existed outside his fences. The Children of God had had their time but their time on earth was finished. They must move on now to the next level of existence.

Now was when their journey truly began.

He watched them die but felt no sadness. One by one they fell into a sleep from which they would never awaken. They put their heads down on tables. They held one another. They held their children. They became statues and grew pale as the blood stopped flowing through their veins and their lips turned blue and their eyes stared blank. Wipe away the life. It was strange and somehow awesome to witness as a room full of living, breathing human beings became a room full of corpses. As whatever was special about them left behind only cooling meat and rose into the air to be among the holy. He saw fear in many eyes, fear in the faces of those whose faith was not quite strong enough. More than one person ran for the door, but the doors were locked and others went to them as they struggled with the chains and pulled them away, telling them it was all for the best, they would soon be with the Lord. Another two or three tried to induce vomiting but they too were stopped in their actions. Do not fight it, brother, for you are fighting God's will. Father has spoken and the words that came from his mouth were the Lord's as the Lord speaks through him. Soon your body will perish and your spirit will ascend.

Have faith, have absolute faith, for those with faith can accomplish all things.

Within an hour the room was completely still but for Mosley who stood looking at what he had done. His people had all fled this earth. The room felt very cold and he felt very cold both inside and out.

He was, as he had not been for many a year, utterly alone.

He thought of the way he felt after his mother had disappeared – after his mother had been killed. He thought of how he'd sat alone on his bed with the door shut and stared at the wall, the blank white wall holding no promises. He thought of how empty he'd felt. A husk with nothing in him but the need to be filled by something. And then he'd found God and been truly at peace for the first time in his life. That swirling emptiness within him, that vacuum craving something – hunger pains of the soul – had finally been sated, and he had known, finally, what he was and who he was and what mattered most in this world.

But God had abandoned him when he'd needed Him most. He'd searched for His light and found only shadows. And now too had his people abandoned him, and though he had initiated their actions and had his men destroy those who had attempted to flee this fate, he felt a great sadness sink into his heart like a lead weight and settle at the bottom of it. It wanted to pull him down, not to the ground, for one could always sink lower, but under the earth itself, so that he would lie amongst the worms and the tree roots.

He had not felt sadness while it was happening but he felt sadness now. He wanted so very much to be with those he loved but only their bodies remained.

Finally he left that place and all the corpses that filled it. He unlocked the padlock and pulled the clanking chains from the door. He let them fall from his hand and land in a pile, like some coiled metal snake.

He walked out into the night and looked up at the moon and wondered whether his people were beyond it yet or were their spirits even now ascending in its direction. He wished that spirit had color. He wished it gave off light. He would like very much to watch those hundreds of beautiful people rising into the night sky like paper lanterns all red and green and blue and white and flickering with light, and he would cry at the beauty of it and know with certainty that what he had done was right. He believed it now but he wished he could know it. He wished he could rely on something other than mere faith. He wished that God would speak to him in His great voice and let him know that though he was alone he would not be alone forever. He wished God would tell him that his own time would be soon and when it came he would get to stand by His side.

Goodbye, children. I love you all.

He looked at the sky for a very long time and wondered if any of his people were looking down. Then after what felt like several minutes he ceased to look at the sky. He turned in a circle and scanned the empty compound. The empty buildings so hollow now that they were uninhabited. He had been out here on other nights and believed that he encountered silence, but never before had he heard a silence as great as the one he heard now. Every building was empty of life. They held clothes and hair brushes and keepsakes and Bibles but the brushes would never again run through hair and the keepsakes meant nothing.

The Bibles would go unread.

This world he had built apart from everything outside his fences, this world was dead. The apocalypse had come and it had been decidedly soft but was wholly destructive for all of that. His house was gone. His people were gone. His God was absent.

Soon the world would discover this place.

His people's letters would reach their recipients and those people would want answers and the answers they found they would not like. They would not understand.

This is the way the world ends.

The beast that thou sawest was and is not; and shall ascend out of the bottomless pit and go into perdition: and they that dwell on the earth shall wonder, whose names were not written in the book of life from the foundation of the world, when they behold the beast that was and is not and yet is – and yet is, and yet is.

He walked to his truck and pulled open the door and stepped up into it. He stared through the windshield at the hole in the ground where his house once stood. He looked to his right and saw the blue backpack that contained seven thousand dollars and a good supply of heroin. He had forgotten about its existence and now what he had done for that money seemed ridiculous. The world was ending and he had been counting pennies.

He turned the key in his ignition and started the truck's engine. He drove up the driveway to the place where his gate had once held out the world and there he stopped a moment. He looked at this land in his rearview mirror and he thought about what he was leaving behind and finally decided he was leaving behind nothing. Everything he had loved about this place had already left. It left before he did.

He turned onto the street and drove away from there.

He drove to Louisville and checked into a motel that did not require he show identification of any sort. Tomorrow when he had access to his safe-deposit box and another identity he could move but for tonight it would suffice. He paid cash and gave a false name and the man behind the counter did not seem interested one way or the other in who he was or what he might be doing here. He probably could have written that his name was Humphrey Bogart without the man so much as blinking. It was the sort of place that asked no questions and tonight of all nights he appreciated that, even if it meant he slept on a come-stained mattress in a room that smelled of cigarette smoke and mold with yellow walls and the saddest painting of flowers in a vase you'd ever seen.

He lay on the bed in pain and thought about Abigail

and Lily and their betrayals of him. Women simply could not be trusted and this had been true since God created the first. More than men they were attracted to darkness, perhaps because they were responsible for bringing life out of it. Maybe such an act required that they stand always near to that vast emptiness in which lurked the beasts of existence. They could pull life out of it and grow it in their wombs but they could also be seduced into it and had been since the first woman walked in the garden.

Can a woman forget her nursing child that she should have no compassion on the son of her womb? Even these may forget.

He thought again about Abigail sending the private investigator to the compound. The man had come for Lily and in the end he had left with her. Even after the girl had chosen to be with him Abigail could not leave it alone. He had let Abigail go but that had not been enough. She decided that she must take everything from him and now she had – with the devil in her employ. She had robbed him of everything.

But they would pay for what they had done, each one of them would pay with their lives and once he had made them pay they would be thrown into the pits of Hell where they would continue to pay and pay forever and ever. He knew that what he had done and what he had yet to do would end his life on earth but without his people here to care for he had no purpose. So when he was done with this last task he would go home to them. He would put a bullet into his own brain that his spirit might be freed of it.

He would look at the face of God and feel peace at last.

But not before he had made those cunts and their pet devil pay.

L amb stepped out onto the front porch and picked up the newspaper. On the front page he found a story about what had happened to the Children of God. He read the story while standing in his underwear and as he did a knot formed in his stomach and grew tighter there. He did not want to show this newspaper to Abigail or Lily but knew he must. It would break their hearts but sometimes broken hearts could not be avoided.

He walked inside and closed the door behind him and carried the paper to the kitchen table where Abigail and Lily sat eating scrambled eggs and toast that he had made them. They seemed almost happy. They seemed content.

Well over two hundred and fifty men, women and children had taken part in a mass suicide and another two dozen at least had fallen to gunshot wounds when they refused to participate. Police were still attempting to determine exactly the course of events that had led to this tragedy but it was clear that something had gone very, very wrong, and though bodies were still being identified and counted it did not appear that Rhett Mosley was among the dead. There were chains by the doors of the church where most of the dead had been found. The police believed they'd been chained in but the chains had since been loosed and someone had walked free.

Though Lamb was not glad of such loss he did believe now more than ever that what he had done would be buried amongst the bodies and of that he was indeed glad. The scale of the tragedy would hide his small part in it, as sorting through such a mess would be impossible. A single death could be investigated but nearly three hundred could only be counted. This was a rule of war but applied to this situation as well as any. All of the dead were part of a single story and the police would apply that story to each of them without individual investigation.

Lamb tossed the newspaper onto the table.

Abigail looked up at him and asked him what is it.

You should read the story.

Abigail set down her fork and looked from him to the paper. Something like knowledge flashed in her eyes and she pulled the paper toward her and began to read and as she did tears began to flow. When she was finished she told Lily what had happened and she said no, oh no, and began to cry as well. Though they both had left the compound willingly the tragedy had taken almost everyone either had known. All of their friends were dead and they would never see them again and it hurt them deeply. No telephone would reach any of them, nor would any letter. Not where they had gone.

Lamb felt for Abigail and Lily but knew not what to say. Perhaps there was nothing *to* say. Words could not capture such loss. The mind of someone outside the situation could not understand it. The death of a single man might be comprehended. You understood that this person had once had a mother and a father and siblings and friends and lovers and that each of those people would feel sadness now when his name crossed their thoughts. You could look at his picture and imagine what kind of person he might have been. You could discover how old he was when he died and feel something about it: had he died too young or had he lived a full life. But when nearly three hundred people died you were left with a statistic. Every face got lost in the crowd and a crowd somehow lacked the sadness of an individual with bright brown eyes and a crooked smile who now was gone.

It was a sad fact but a true one that when many people died each death lost significance in proportion to the number of dead. Somehow the heart could feel only so much and felt it for one as for a hundred, or three hundred.

So Lamb remained silent and let the women deal with the loss as they did. He simply could not understand what it might mean to them. He could not give the numbers faces. He had met few of them and those he had met he did not mourn.

The rest of that day was draped in quiet sorrow. Neither Abigail nor Lily spoke very much. They wandered the house red-eyed and seemingly unsure what to do with themselves. Abigail washed dishes despite Lamb telling her she need not. Lily vacuumed. He offered to make them turkey sandwiches for lunch but both declined.

They also skipped dinner.

When bedtime came Abigail and Lily lay together in the girl's room holding one another and he could hear them whispering sadly, talking about what had happened, but heard not what they were saying. Even if he had been able to hear them, however, he was certain he would have been unable to understand.

He lay alone in his own bed realizing that his fantasy of a family was just that. These women had experienced something he could never share with them and that something had dominated their lives for years. He would always be outside this, the most important event in their lives. They might someday become everything to him yet he would remain a footnote in their lives.

He would always be a stranger.

He stopped letting them leave the house alone, even to go into the backyard. It did not seem safe to allow them out of doors unprotected. Mosley might be watching, might be watching and waiting to make his move, waiting for a vulnerable moment. They stayed inside and he stayed with them, refusing to go to the office. He carried a pistol with him always, setting it down only when he was taking a shower and even then keeping it near to hand on the bathroom counter. He had never before felt such a need but he felt it now. When he went out to the Highlands Kroger to pick up groceries they came with him; when they needed to go out for any reason he went with them.

Neither Abigail nor Lily liked the situation – they had gone from being prisoners there to being prisoners here – but he assured them that in this case it was temporary. It was also necessary. Mosley was out there and he was dangerous. If that hadn't been clear before, what he had done to his own people had made it so. The man was utterly mad and might do anything.

Lamb sat by his open bedroom window and smoked a cigarette. He looked out at the street, at the cars parked upon it and the houses lined up behind it, each ornamented by a yard green with either ivy or grass as well as shrubbery and trees both evergreen and deciduous. People walked their dogs and washed their cars and mowed their lawns. Some of them waved. When they did he waved back lazily, wishing they would simply leave him alone. Though he knew none of them very well he had known most of them for many years. It was odd to consider how little you could interact with the people who surrounded you day in and day out. If one of his neighbors died it would mean nothing to him. He might not even learn of the death for weeks, until some other neighbor decided to stop him while he was cutting his grass and tell him all about poor Walter who'd collapsed in his kitchen while making a steak.

He looked down at his left hand and scratched it through the gauze. It was healing but it itched. Often when he changed his bandages the scabs stuck to them and he ended up having to peel them away in order to redress his wounds. Usually he changed them after his shower so that the scabs were softened by the moisture and the heat. The skin around the wounds themselves was pink. With each day that passed he saw it closing in on the holes in his hands and feet. Soon the holes would be gone, leaving behind only puffs of pink scar.

Mosley had been shot but lived long enough at least to commit an atrocity on his compound and flee and Lamb doubted very much that he had since succumbed to his wounds. The man was a survivor.

He took a final drag from his cigarette and flicked it out the window.

It might be true that he was a survivor but so was Lamb, and when they next met he was certain that at least one of them would finally succumb, and he was determined that it not be him. If Mosley craved the afterlife so much he could have it.

Mosley parked outside the private detective's house. The sky was dark. The windows of the house were yellow rectangles but everything else was covered by the blanket of night. He coughed into a handkerchief. It hurt his shoulder to do so but he was used to his shoulder hurting. He had removed his sling and been using his arm and using it hurt a great deal. Yet there was no way to avoid it. He needed both arms. He was also very tired but at least he knew that it would all be over soon. Tonight was the night it would end. When this was over he could finally lay down his head and allow his spirit to rise.

He chewed a pain pill.

The last few days had been very busy indeed.

He'd collected his new identity as well as a hundred thousand dollars. He had purchased clothes and a car. He'd abandoned his truck after removing the license plate. He had dyed his hair so that he would not be as easy to identify on the street. His face had been on the news and in the newspaper and he did not want to be recognized. He wanted vengeance. He purchased sunglasses at the Walgreens on Bardstown Road in the Highlands and wore them constantly. He had paid Abigail's apartment a visit and finding it empty had worked to discover where the private investigator lived. This had proved less than difficult. He had driven to the private investigator's house and watched it most of yesterday from a distance. The curtains were drawn so he could not see what was happening inside but he knew they were in there, all three of them who had ruined him and driven God from his land, as he had seen them leave once and return. He'd also watched as the private investigator pulled back a curtain and sat in his window and smoked. Then he had gone back to his motel room and lain in bed and dreamed of vengeance and he knew with certainty that for vengeance there would be no bloodguilt, for God was a vengeful God and he was God's servant in his actions tonight. Today he had loaded his weapon – a pistol he had taken with him when he left the compound – and gone to the range and fired it. He wanted there to be no mistakes when he did what he must do. He found that he was a good shot and enjoyed the range though with every pull of the trigger he felt a new jab of pain in his shoulder. He pictured the faces of those who must die every time he squeezed his trigger and when he squeezed his trigger he destroyed those faces.

Now he would destroy them in reality.

He sat and watched and waited. Eventually the house lights turned off and the windows went dark one by one but still he waited. He wanted everyone in the house asleep. He wanted peace to fall over that house before he broke the peace with violence.

The private investigator was soon to learn something about loss. The man had taken everything from Mosley and he was intent on reciprocation. He would cast that devil back down to the hell whence he had come and when he did he would feel nothing but joy.

An hour passed.

He pushed open his door, picked up his night-vision goggles from the passenger seat – the pistol was tucked already into his pants – and stepped painfully out of his vehicle, the torn muscles in his hip cramping as he did so. He leaned against the car and waited for the cramp to subside and once it had he pushed himself to his feet and limped across the street toward the house. He walked stiffly, pulling out the pistol and gripping it in his right hand. It felt out of place there despite the fact that he had enjoyed shooting it earlier. He was not a man who used guns. He preferred the knife and blunt force. But this man Lamb was not someone with whom he wanted to play; he was someone he simply wanted dead. That meant using the most efficient weapon available, and that weapon was the gun. Besides which he was injured and incapable of his usual actions.

He walked up several steps to the front yard and once

there decided to walk the perimeter of the property. He was not at all certain about how to enter this house. He was not at all certain about anything he was doing. He knew only that within him was a great need for vengeance and that need would be sated. It must be sated.

He opened the cedar gate and entered the backyard and walked along a brick wall looking at possible entrance points. Every window and every door held potential. He circled the house and thought about the fact that he did not want his entrance heard. He decided he must get in through the basement. After watching the house yesterday he was fairly certain the bedrooms were on the top floor near the front of the house – those had been the last lights to go off – so entering through the basement would put distance between his activities and the sleeping people above him and this distance meant that the sound of his actions would be dampened by the floors and walls between himself and those he wished dead.

He walked to one of the basement windows and sat on his haunches before it. He wished to god that he knew the layout of this house. Not knowing it put him at a great disadvantage, for he would have to learn it while walking through the dark on the hunt for a man who had lived here for years. But he would be awake while the other man slept and he would be able to see in the dark while the other man would not.

With the butt of his gun he shattered the window and then knocked away the shards from the edges of the frame in order to avoid cutting himself during his entrance. With that done he climbed through the window. It was dark down here, so he could not see exactly how far he had to drop, but he knew it was a good distance and tried to prepare himself for this. A moment later he slipped all the way through, catching his hip on what he thought was the edge of the washing machine and spinning before hitting the concrete floor and dropping both his pistol and the night-vision goggles. His hip screamed with pain and he almost screamed with it but was able to stifle his voice. He sat there a dazed moment with tears streaming down his face.

Then he went about picking up both his gun and his goggles and getting to his feet and once on his feet he slipped the goggles over his face. He flipped a switch, blinked, and took in his surroundings. He needed to find the breaker box and hoped it was down here.

He scanned the walls, pushing aside boxes and winter clothes that were hanging on a dowel and camping gear and comforters stuffed into trash bags, and finally found the breaker box in one of the corners. He pulled open its gray metal door and flipped all the switches, shoving them left with the edge of his palm, shutting down the power in the house.

He turned toward the wooden stairwell in the dark basement and found that he could see it clearly. He raised the goggles and saw nothing but absolute night, which was, he believed, exactly what the private investigator would be seeing when he awoke.

This was good. This was very good indeed.

He replaced the goggles and walked to the stairs and then up them. Every creak the steps made beneath his feet sounded incredibly loud in his ears. The pistol felt heavy in his fist.

When he reached the top of the stairs he found himself facing a white door and before he tried the knob it occurred to him that it might be locked but it was not and a moment later he stepped into the house proper and found himself standing in a short hallway that separated the living room from the kitchen. The kitchen lay to his left and the living room to his right. The curtains were drawn, so the windows let in next to no light, yet he found he could see clearly.

He thought of his people in the dining hall. He thought of them dying while holding one another and crying and praying. He thought of the little children. He thought of his own sons and daughters who died without ever knowing they were literally as well as figuratively his children. He wondered if, when they saw him in Heaven, they would forgive him his silence. Wondered if they would embrace him as their father and understand why he'd kept his paternity a secret.

He thought of the fact that the people in this house were responsible for his having to send all his children home. They had destroyed everything he worked so hard to build and they had put cracks in his faith as well, which was unforgivable. He had dedicated his life to the Lord and the

Lord had abandoned him in his time of need. The Lord had left him to deal with this devil alone. He could have cast the evil spirit into one of his pigs and allowed Mosley to simply cut its throat but He had not. The Lord had done absolutely nothing but watch from afar while everything he had built in His honor was destroyed.

He could not himself be so passive. He could not turn the other cheek.

He walked toward the living room and looked around at the couch and the piano and the coffee table and the television. This was where the devil sat and took in his entertainment, where he sat and watched television and laughed at the screen. But after tonight he would never laugh again. After tonight he would never do anything again but burn.

The stairs stood against the back wall, rising to the second floor where his future victims slept even now. He walked toward them and paused. This was about to end. This would soon be finished and for the first time in his life – with all the violence he had committed – he had murder in his heart.

Gird up now thy loins like a man.

He took a first step up the stairs. A second and a third followed and on the third the wood creaked beneath his foot and he froze and waited for a response from above but heard nothing but the beating of his own heart in his chest and his temples, so he took a fourth step.

His hand was sweaty on the grip of his gun. His stomach

ached and he felt the need to cough but he suppressed that need.

Once he had felt that he was something more than human. Once he had felt that he had the Lord on his side and with the Lord on his side he could accomplish anything. He did not feel that anymore. He felt scared. He felt like a little boy. All of the insecurities of his childhood stirred within his heart and he found that he was afraid. But the fear within him only worked to increase his anger and his need for blood.

These godless cunts had done this to him. They had turned him into something he had thought himself free of. He thought he had shed this skin and yet it clung to him still.

He took a fifth step and the floor creaked again beneath his foot.

He froze again and listened and this time he did hear a sound. He heard what he believed was the shifting of someone in bed followed by a whisper.

Then feet hit the floor above him and footsteps followed.

Let death seize upon them, he whispered under his breath, and let them go down quick into Hell: for wickedness lives in their dwellings and among them.

If murder was in his heart then he would murder. He would not be afraid. He would not shrink back from what he was and what he felt. He never had. He would not even if it meant that upon his death he would have to explain his actions to the Lord. His heart was true even if it was black. He knew that and believed that God did too without his having to explain it. For God knew all things.

He raised the gun and took another step up.

Lamb opened his eyes. At first he did not know why he opened them, did not know what had awakened him, but while he lay there in a nonsensical panic he heard the stairs creak and knew that he had heard that sound before, knew that it was what had awakened him.

Someone was in the house.

He rolled over toward Abigail and said her name. She moaned in her sleep and said a word he did not understand. He said her name again. She opened her eyes and looked at him and opened her mouth to speak but before she could he clamped his hand down on her face to block any sound.

There's someone in the house. He said this in a whisper.

Fear glistened in her eyes.

It'll be okay. Just get in the closet and don't come out until I tell you it's safe.

She nodded and he took his hand from her mouth.

What about Lily?

I'll get to her.

Okay.

Abigail rolled out of bed naked and padded to the closet. He watched her as she walked away from him and pulled open the door and stepped inside. She looked over her shoulder.

Be safe.

I'll try.

She closed the door behind her. It latched quietly. He looked at it for a moment before reaching under his pillow and removing a pistol. He got to his feet. He was naked as well and felt very vulnerable in his nudity but knew there was no time to dress. A man was on his way up the stairs and the stairs had only fifteen steps.

He walked to the bedroom door and grabbed the knob and turned it as carefully as he could, as slowly as he could. Then he pulled the door open and was faced by darkness, darkness deeper than what he should have found. There was a nightlight in the bathroom in order that he might piss at two o'clock in the morning without flipping any switches but that light was not on. The bulb did burn out occasionally but he did not believe that this was what happened. He was certain that this was not what happened and his certainty was confirmed when he carefully reached around the door and attempted to turn on the hall light. His fingers found the switch and flipped it but nothing happened.

Mosley liked to use darkness to his advantage. He liked

to work under the cover of night. Perhaps he did not want God to see what he was doing. Lamb knew that if he was such a man he would fear God witnessing actions such as his, particularly if that god was the one of the Old Testament.

He looked toward the stairwell to his left and saw nothing but darkness. He listened to the darkness but heard nothing. He moved quickly across the hallway toward Lily's room and then into it, pushing the door closed behind him. He walked to her bed and found her there already looking at him. Her eyes were wide and scared.

What is it?

Someone's in the house.

Is it him?

I think so.

What are we gonna do?

I'll take care of it.

How?

The floorboards creaked at the top of the stairs.

Don't move and don't make a sound.

Lamb turned toward the door, raised his gun, waited. He couldn't see anything but he could listen and listening he heard footsteps. They moved from the stairs and across the short hallway and into his bedroom.

He moved through the darkness himself, hoping against hope that the floor did not creak beneath his feet. He had lived in this house for more than ten years and believed he knew where the creaky floorboards were and tried to avoid them. He stepped softly. Eventually he reached the bedroom door and pulled it open and when he did the hinges creaked.

A flash of light exploded in his bedroom. The bullet hit the wall just to the left of his head and he felt chunks of plaster strike his face.

His first instinct was to step back into Lily's room and shut the door behind him but he knew he could not do this. He needed to get the man away from the girls; he would not be able to live with himself if a stray bullet hit one of them. He moved quickly across the hallway and went for the stairs but as he did he heard a gunshot and saw a flash of light and his gauzed foot slipped on the hardwood floor and he went down the stairs fast and hard, almost losing his balance completely but managing somehow to stay on his feet.

He needed to let light into the house. He was nearly blind at the moment and the power had been turned off but he knew he didn't have time to go to the basement and find the breaker box and flip the switches. He didn't even know if doing so would work. Maybe the power had been cut in some other way.

He walked to the living-room windows – there were two of them – and pulled open the curtains, and though the light they let in was not bright, the moon and the street lamps provided enough illumination by which to see. Not clearly, this was true, but sufficient to reveal movement. He believed that might be enough.

Footsteps thumped down the stairwell.

He was glad of this for it meant that Abigail and Lily

were safe for now. If Lamb ended up dead he was certain that Mosley would head back upstairs and find them but so long as the man was hunting for him the women were out of danger.

He left the living room and made his way to the dining room and in the dining room stood behind the edge of a wall and waited and listened.

The footsteps continued down the stairs.

The man walked slowly and to Lamb his footsteps sounded as if he had not a care in the world. He might have been heading downstairs to grab a midnight snack.

The slow pace was somehow disconcerting.

A man who moved in such an unrushed manner was a man without a care in the world and such a man was a man to fear for such a man knew with certainty that he would come out on top.

Mosley reached the bottom of the stairs and stopped.

The footsteps ceased.

Lamb closed his eyes and listened as intently as he was able. Darkness overwhelmed him but he could feel a draft coming in from under the front door and he could hear a dog barking in the distance – and after a time he could hear a footstep on the hardwood floor. That first step was followed by others.

Mosley was on the hunt.

Lamb peeked around the corner of the wall and looked into the living room and saw Mosley, saw him walking through the living room.

He turned to shoot but as he did Mosley turned toward him and raised his gun and fired quickly, sending out a flash of light and a loud bang.

The bullet hit the wall beside his head and wood splintered and hit his face and he pulled back quickly to avoid a second shot.

His heart pounded in his chest.

He was not a man who regularly felt fear but he felt it now. Mosley was on a mission and in his mission he had nothing to lose. He had already lost everything. His house was gone. His money was gone. His people were gone.

That made him very dangerous indeed.

Lamb peeked around the corner again, and again Mosley fired.

You will not live through this, Lamb. You might as well step out now and take what is coming to you for your fate will meet you eventually. It cannot be avoided; this is why it is called fate.

Lamb did not respond. He did not even think about the words. He thought instead about how to get out of the place he was in. He thought about how he could move from here and put himself in a better position. He did not want to die. He had been happier in the last several days than ever before in his life and would not allow himself to die.

He would live through this no matter what. He had to live through this.

He looked across the room. He looked at the dining table and wondered if he could get behind it before Mosley landed a shot. He believed he could. He believed he had to. He centered himself. He listened for footsteps and heard them nearing.

He made a run for it and when he reached the table he slid down as if he were stealing a base and stayed there behind the table unmoving. He looked through the table and chair legs and saw nothing. Mosley was no longer where he had been. The man was gone.

He was again lost. He knew where he was but not where Mosley was, and that was at least as important. His heart pounded in his chest. His hands and feet throbbed with pain. He tried to silence himself. He listened for footsteps.

Eventually he heard them. They were moving out of the living room toward the hallway. He looked toward the second dining-room door, the one that left him exposed, and knew Mosley was going to be coming through it. He thought he did at least. But before Mosley came into sight the footsteps ceased.

Silence rung loudly in Lamb's ears.

He waited.

Mosley stopped in the hallway. Directly in front of him lay the kitchen. Behind him lay the living room. Up ahead to his right was a doorway that led to the dining room in which the devil was hiding. The devil would be waiting for him to appear there, waiting with his gun drawn. He could not satisfy that anticipation. He was smarter than that. He would draw the beast out of hiding and once revealed he would take him.

Did you think you could do what you did and face no retaliation?

No – I expected you.

Yet now that you have me you hide as a child from the bogeyman. I remember when you called *me* a child.

Your people are dead and yet here you are still breathing, unable to take the medicine you prescribed. If that's not the cowardice of a child I don't know what is.

You don't know what you're talking about.

The facts speak for themselves.

You fucking cunt.

The last resort of a man with no argument.

I need no argument. My argument is the hell into which you will be thrown after I am finished with you here.

If there's a hell you'll be meeting me there.

You know nothing of what you speak.

I know that your god is nowhere to be seen.

When He hath tried me I shall come forth as gold.

The devil laughed – and his laugh sounded genuine. It made Mosley furious that this godless creature should question his heart when his heart was true. He wanted him dead more than he had ever wanted anything before. He wanted him dead but as much as that he wanted him to suffer. He wanted him to feel the same failure he so deeply felt.

The man had lured him down here but following had been a mistake, for the women were upstairs and killing them might erase the fight from this beast's heart. If what he was fighting for lay bloody on the floor then what reason would he have to go on?

The devil had destroyed everything and what he had not destroyed he had stolen. Mosley wanted him to feel the loss he felt. He wanted him to suffer before he perished.

The women were upstairs. *His* women were upstairs. Upstairs and unprotected, upstairs and vulnerable. The devil had tried to draw him away from them and in so doing had left them exposed. He would make him pay for that error. He would make him pay dearly.

He quietly backed out of the hallway and across the living room toward the stairs, watching for the beast's appearance. The floor creaked beneath his feet and he was glad of the sound, glad because it might draw the devil out.

He reached the staircase and stopped. He waited but nothing happened.

You should not have left them alone.

He took a backwards step up, and this was followed by a second.

A shot rang out and a flash of light. This came from the hallway out of which he had just walked himself and when he looked he saw the man standing there in the darkness and though the curtains were pulled open he knew the man could not see him. The shadows in the corner of the room hid him and Lamb was shooting blindly, shooting at the sound. He himself did not have to do this. He took aim and he fired and almost before the sound echoed in the room Lamb cried out and fell to the ground. The gun dropped from his hand.

Mosley moved toward him quickly, with the speed of a predator, and when he reached him he kicked him in the face. This sent a horrible pain radiating from his hip, but he ignored the pain and reached down to pick up Lamb's weapon.

First the suffering. Death can come later. The women are unprotected now.

He turned and made his way up the stairs.

Lamb lay on the tile floor and watched Mosley disappear into the shadowed stairwell. The son of a bitch was going to kill the women he had sworn to protect and then he would return and kill him. He had failed. He had made a promise and he had failed in keeping that promise.

No – he had not yet failed.

He would not give up. He *could* not give up. It wasn't in him to do so. He had been shot in the leg and did not know if he could walk but he knew he would try and if he failed he would crawl. He rolled over onto his stomach and pushed himself up to his hands and knees. He had no weapon. He had no strength. But he would not give up until he was dead.

He had made a promise.

He reached up to the wall on his left and tried to pull himself to his feet. When he put pressure on his legs he felt a great pain. He believed the bullet that had struck his right leg had hit bone – hit bone and fractured it. But he forced himself to take the weight.

He had made a promise.

He limped toward his kitchen and when he reached the kitchen he opened a drawer and from the drawer he pulled a hammer. With the hammer in hand he turned back toward the living room. The living room and the stairs.

He had made a promise.

He hop-walked toward the stairs, cringing as he did so, the hammer hanging from his sweaty right hand. He could feel hot blood running down his leg. It dripped to the floor. He almost fell as he made his way toward the stairs, but managed to maintain his balance. He stopped at the foot of the stairs and looked up into darkness.

He heard the sound of Abigail struggling against Mosley.

He heard her scream.

He wanted to rush up there but something made him hesitate.

The handle of the hammer was sweaty in his grip. His nude body was covered in goose bumps. His leg was screaming with pain.

He stepped back from the stairs.

M osley stepped into the bedroom for the second time. *Where are you, you cunts?*

He received no response but had expected none. He simply wanted them to be aware of his presence. He wanted their hearts to be filled with fear. He needed their hearts to be filled with fear. He moved not at all for a moment. They needed time to understand their fate. They needed time to understand that hope was lost, that the beast on whom they had placed their faith had failed. If he was up here alone then where was their protector? They'd certainly heard the gunshots, and having heard them could only presume one thing.

After a moment he walked toward the closet door and grabbed the knob and pulled. He heard a cry and met with resistance from the other side. The door was being held closed. He pulled harder and tore the door away from its interior grip and it swung open to reveal Abigail. She cowered away from him. Her eyes were full of both fear and tears. Mascara streamed down her cheeks.

He reached down and grabbed her by the hair and pulled her from the closet.

For whatever one sows, that will he also reap. For the one who sows to his own flesh will from the flesh reap corruption, but the one who sows to the Spirit will from the Spirit reap eternal life. Spittle flew from his mouth as he spat the words. Drool on his chin.

Her short hair tangled in his fist. Her hands trying futilely to pry his fingers away.

He threw her to the floor and kicked her stomach.

She gasped for air.

He kicked her again before reaching down once more and grabbing her by the hair and once he did he pulled her out of the room and into the hallway. He dragged her to the stairs and threw her down them. He would return for Lily but first the woman.

The sound her body made as it rolled down the stairs was wet and sickening yet he was not sickened but joyed. Every thump was pain inflicted and he wanted her to hurt.

You will witness your failure, devil, and know pain.

He made his way down the stairs to where Abigail lay at the foot of them and when he reached her he lifted her to her feet and put a gun to her head and looked to where the devil lay on the floor but he lay there no more.

Mosley's heart froze in his chest.

Then a sound to his right. He turned and looked and saw the beast coming at him with a hammer raised.

Lamb stood in the shadows with the hammer gripped in his fist. He heard something crashing down the stairs, something heavy, and then Abigail rolled into view. For a moment she neither moved nor made a sound. His stomach tightened. The fear that she was dead. She groaned. Relief flooded him. He wanted to rush to her but resisted the urge. He could not do that. Not if he wanted to live. Not if he wanted the girls to live.

You will witness your failure, devil, and know pain. This from the top of the stairs.

He awaited Mosley's descent. Listened to his footsteps thudding ever nearer. Then Mosley reached the first floor and he lifted Abigail to her feet and put a gun to her head and looked toward the place where he had left Lamb on the floor.

Lamb went at him, raising the hammer over his head as he approached in the dimly lighted living room. The man turned toward him at the last instant but had no time to react before Lamb brought the hammer down on his face. His face for a moment was dull and empty. Then the blow struck hard and true against the temple and knocked the goggles from his head.

The man let go Abigail and the two of them fell to the floor.

Lamb fell too upon Mosley and struck him again and again in the face with the hammer. The man reached out to fight but he had no fight in him. His eyes were wide and glassy with fear and confusion both. Lamb struck him yet again with the hammer. He felt bone break beneath his blow. He watched one of the eyes roll left while the other looked at him still. He struck again – and again, and again.

He swung until he could swing no more.

He swung until there was nothing left at the top of the neck but a sack of shattered bones and the face was hardly recognizable as such, and then he stopped swinging and fell atop the corpse breathing hard and covered in blood.

After some time he rolled onto his back and managed to sit up. He dropped the hammer. Dropped it amongst shattered teeth lying on the floor like misshapen pearls. There were pieces of meat sticking to it.

Abigail during his fight with Mosley had crawled away from them and sat now several feet from him. Her nose was bloody and her eyes were moist but she appeared to be otherwise unharmed. She might have broken something in her fall down the stairs but she would be okay. Of that he was certain.

Is it over?

Lamb nodded. It's over. You should call the police.

VI

Lamb lay in his hospital bed at University of Louisville Hospital and stared at the ceiling though the television was on. The door swung open. He turned his head expecting a nurse. Instead Abigail and Lily walked in. Abigail was wearing a clean set of clothes. Her face was made up. She looked beautiful, despite the yellow-green ring of fading bruise around her left eye, almost but not quite hidden by her make-up. Lily stood pretty and innocent beside her.

They're letting me check out today.

Lamb smiled. Good. I'm glad you're okay.

How are you feeling?

I've been better.

You'll be better again.

Lily walked to him and wrapped her arms around his neck. Thank you.

I keep my promises.

She pulled away from him, tears moist in her brown eyes.

I love you, she said. I wish I would have met you sooner.

I've wished the same thing.

When will they let you go home? From Abigail who remained by the door.

Another week at least.

She walked to him and took his hand. Hers was cool and smooth in his grip. He held it tightly despite the pain. His hand throbbed with it, and it sent waves up his arm, but he ignored this. He wanted to touch her one last time. Needed to touch her one last time. He was afraid that once she walked out the door he would never see her again. He was, in fact, almost certain of it.

You'll never know how much I appreciate what you've done for me. For us.

I see goodbye in your eyes.

Abigail was silent for a long time. He could see her thinking as she looked at him. She bit her lip. She sighed. Under different circumstances—

Don't do that. Don't insult me. Despite everything I'm glad I got to spend the time with you that I did. I wouldn't trade it for anything.

I wouldn't either.

But you aren't going to stay.

Would you really want me to?

Of course I would; I think I love you.

It wouldn't last.

What wouldn't?

The love. You'd get tired of me. We'd fight. Eventually there'd come a time when just the sight of me would annoy you. The way I held my fork or drank from my water glass. It's best to end it now. To end it on a high note. Then we can think about each other with longing. We can miss each other. It never has to turn sour – as it inevitably would.

Does that mean you feel the same?

It doesn't matter.

Lamb pulled his hand away, looked toward the ceiling again, the white acoustic tiles there and the fluorescent bulbs behind opaque plastic sheets. He thought of the calm that had blanketed him as he lay beside her at night. He thought of that hollow within him finally filled. He knew it mattered. But he knew too – and had always known – that it was only the moments you were promised. Nobody was guaranteed a future. You had to appreciate what you got when you got it, because everything could be taken away tomorrow.

The money's in a suitcase in the closet.

What?

When you go to collect your things. You're going to look for the money before you leave. It's in a suitcase in the closet.

She looked at him with wide eyes, a hurt expression on her face. She was somehow offended that he thought she was going after the money. Yet she did not correct his presumption. Did not attempt to tell him she wasn't. For she was. But for some reason she did not want him to think of her in that way. She'd wanted his image of her to be the one she projected. At least until after she had parted. But people were his business. He could not help but see beyond the facade, through the windows and into the heart.

It's okay, he said.

How long have you known?

Since you lied to me in my office. Not entirely true. He knew consciously that she intended to take the money only after he had left the compound with Lily. When he had seen her at his front door. But somewhere deeper, in the dark shadows of his mind, he thought he had known since the beginning.

What are you guys talking about?

They both looked toward Lily. She turned from one of them to the other, a searching expression on her face, unhappy that something very important was happening in front of her without her understanding it.

Abigail opened her mouth as if to answer, but instead turned back toward Lamb. Why did you take the job if you knew?

Because a girl needed saving.

For a long time Abigail said nothing. She simply looked at him in silence, some emotion related to regret passing over her eyes like the shadow of a cloud on a windy day. It was there and then it was gone. Finally she spoke. We should go.

Lamb nodded. Okay.

Abigail leaned down and kissed him on the temple. Despite how this is ending, what you did means the world to me – you mean the world to me.

Your words are empty vessels. Can you close the door behind you?

He picked up the remote and turned up the volume on the television. An old episode of *The Shield* was on. He'd seen it before – Vic Mackey would soon be killing another cop during a police raid – but that was hardly the point. He was not particularly interested in what was onscreen.

Lamb.

He turned the volume up louder.

Let's go, Lily.

Abigail started for the door.

After it had latched he looked toward it. It sat there, an inanimate slab of wood with no significance at all. Piece of shit.

Abigail stepped from the hospital and into the daylight hot and bright. Lily stepped out behind her. They'd exited through the emergency-room entrance, and several people were standing and smoking to their left, despite a posted no smoking sign. She glanced toward them, then walked across the asphalt to the sidewalk. Continued on toward the street where she had parked.

What happened in there?

Abigail reached into her purse and removed a pack of Marlboro Reds. She tapped a cigarette from the hard pack and slipped it between her lipsticked lips. She thumbed the wheel on her S. T. Dupont lighter several times. Come on, you fucking thing. Finally an orange flame erupted and burned on the blackened wick. She held it to the end of her cigarette and inhaled deeply. Her hand was shaking, though she tried to ignore it. She pulled the red-stained cigarette from her lips and exhaled. Held the cigarette pinched between thumb and index finger.

What happened in there?

Not now, Lily.

She pulled a key ring from her purse and thumbed the fob. Her car unlocked. She pulled open the driver-side door and fell in behind the wheel. She took another drag from her cigarette and went about trying to pull her seatbelt strap over her shoulder, but the goddamn thing kept locking, refusing to unspool. After several attempts she slammed the heel of her hand against the steering wheel and cursed. Fucking thing. Fuck.

Lily pulled open the passenger door and got into the car.

What's wrong?

I don't want to talk about it.

Maybe you should though.

Shut the fuck up, Lily. The words spit out in anger.

Lily looked at her a wide-eyed moment, and then turned toward her window. She looked at a black fellow walking along the sidewalk, pushing a stroller in which he had stacked several bags of groceries. He wore tattered jeans and a too-large white T-shirt and a dark blue University of Kentucky hat crooked on his head.

I'm sorry. It isn't your fault.

She put her key into the ignition and started the engine. She slammed the shifter into drive, pulled her foot off the brake, and turned out onto the cracked and faded street.

Lily.

The girl turned toward her, looked her in the eyes. It was like looking at an enchanted mirror. A younger version of herself staring back at her.

I'm sorry.

Lily nodded, then turned back toward her window. Bitch. Spoken under her breath.

Abigail supposed the girl had a point.

When they reached the house she pulled into the oil-spotted driveway and killed the engine. She looked at the two-story Cape Cod with its brick exterior, its green-painted porch and front door, its unlighted windows. In another life she might have called it home.

Let's pack our things.

Where are we gonna go?

I have an apartment.

I want to stay here.

We're not staying here.

You're not staying here. I am.

I'm your mother.

You don't care about me.

After all I did for you. I can't believe you can say that.

After all Lamb did for me, you mean.

I'm talking about birthing you, feeding you, raising you.

I never asked to be born. You took on those responsibilities when you got pregnant.

You little slut, you have no idea what you're talking about.

You weren't a whore who got knocked up? Mosley told me all about it. I finally understood why you'd never told me about my father.

I've made a lot of mistakes in my life, but I won't own that one. I was raped, and I didn't want you to grow up knowing you were a product of that. Why do you think I tried to get you away from Mosley? I didn't want to see you – she blinked away tears – I didn't want to see you damaged the way that I was damaged. Goddamn it, can't you understand that?

Lily looked at her in silence for a long time. Finally she said, I'm sorry. Let's go pack our things, Momma.

Abigail nodded, pulled the keys from the ignition, and pushed open the car door.

She stepped into Lamb's bedroom, walked across the area rug rolled out on the hardwood floor, and pulled open the closet door. Several suits hung from the rod, as well as button-ups both light-blue and white. A pair of brown dress-shoes, a pair of black dress-shoes, and two pairs of Nikes sat on the floor, as well as a worn pair of canvas boat shoes, the white soles of which were stained dark green. Abigail assumed those were Lamb's yard shoes.

Five nights ago she had been huddled on that floor while Lamb fought a madman in order to keep her alive.

This after he had been nailed to a floor for hours by that same madman.

But that was something she was not interested in thinking about. It was something she refused to think about.

She pulled the cord which hung from the ceiling. Light flooded the closet, as well as splashing out of it and blending with the light coming in through the bedroom windows.

In the back of the closet, still hidden partly in shadow, she saw the suitcase to which Lamb had been referring. It was burgundy. She reached to the back of the closet, shoving aside the clothes hanging from the rod, and pulled out the suitcase. It was heavier than she had expected, but she hefted it up and tossed it onto the unmade bed. The bed she had last seen just before being thrown down a flight of stairs. She unzipped the suitcase and flipped open its canvas jaw. Her heart was suddenly beating faster. Her mouth went dry. Never before had she been in possession of so much money. She had been around this much and more, but it was not hers to touch. Money that is not yours is somehow oppressive. This she could take and keep and live on for the rest of her life. This money would offer freedom.

She zipped up the suitcase and pulled it off the bed.

Abigail and Lily made their way up the apartment building stairs, each of them hauling a heavy suitcase. The suitcases thumped loudly against each step as they walked. But finally they reached the third-floor landing. Abigail set down her suitcase, removed her keys from her purse, and unlocked the front door. They made their way into the apartment, setting the suitcases down in the entrance. Abigail swung the door shut and slammed the deadbolt into place. Then she faced the apartment and looked at the empty living room.

It had never before felt as lonely as it did now, despite her daughter being here with her. She hated herself – part of her did – for feeling as she felt. She wanted to be self-sufficient. She wanted to live a life reliant on nobody. After years of living under Mosley's dictatorial rule she was finally free to be her own person, to own herself wholly, and yet when she thought about sleeping alone in her bed she felt empty. After only a week she had come to depend on Lamb lying beside her. She'd wake in the night and reach out. She'd feel his naked hip, warm against the palm of her hand, and that warmth offered a comfort that allowed her to fall once more off the cliff of consciousness and into the welcoming darkness below.

She walked to the kitchen and pulled open the refrigerator. She pulled out a bottle of Red Stripe and popped off the lid. She took a swallow. It was cold and bitter and good.

After a few moments Lily stepped into the room. She stood in the doorway.

It's a nice apartment, Momma. Better than the motel we stayed in after we left the first time.

It only has one bedroom.

I saw that. But it has a queen-size bed. We could sleep together.

I thought I'd sleep on the couch, but that's a good idea.

A knock at the door.

Abigail jumped. Beer foamed up the neck of the bottle and began to pour out the top. She brought it to her mouth and sucked at it.

Fear lighted Lily's face. Her eyes went wide.

Who is that?

I'm not sure. But it isn't Mosley, honey. Mosley is dead.

Lily nodded. I know – I know that.

Abigail set her beer on the counter and walked to the front door. She looked through the peephole. A sigh escaped her mouth. She pulled open the front door.

I heard you come home.

I thought I made it clear that I don't want this to continue.

What's the bruise from? Did he hit you?

Who's at the door, Momma?

Abigail glanced over her shoulder and saw Lily step into the room.

Just a neighbor.

Who's that?

My daughter. Not that it's any of your business.

You didn't tell me you had a daughter.

I didn't tell you because you have no right to know anything about me. My life is mine alone and I don't want you in it. I thought I made that clear.

I thought we could be friends.

No you didn't. You thought you could get close to me by pretending to be my friend. You thought if you could hang around long enough you'd be able to become something more. But I don't want you as my friend. I don't want you in my life at all. I've said it every way I know how. I don't want anything to do with—

Shut your mouth, you fucking bitch.

A hand whipped out and slapped against her cheek.

Abigail stood stunned for a moment, simply staring at the man standing across from her.

I'm sorry.

Don't ever come back here.

She pushed the door shut and locked it. She put her back against it. She slid down to a sitting position and wrapped her arms around her knees.

Lily stood across the room looking at her.

She felt alone and she felt worthless. She was worthless. This was why she attracted men who thought they could use her. Who thought they could own her. Because things of little value could be got cheap.

There was an exception. He was as damaged as she was, but he was also good and true. He treated her like a human being. The only man who ever had. But she'd walked away from him. She'd turned her back on her own feelings and walked away. She asked herself why, but did not know the answer to her own question.

Are you okay?

Can you get me my cigarettes?

Okay, Momma.

Lily stepped back into the kitchen.

Abigail watched her disappear. She thought about the money in the suitcase sitting on the floor to her right. For the first time in her life she realized there were things more valuable than money – far more valuable.

And she had turned her back on them.

Two weeks after being driven to the hospital in an ambulance Lamb checked out. A nurse wheeled him to a taxi and helped him into it, sliding a pair of crutches into the car after him. He told the driver his address. Looked out the window pensively as the car rolled out of the parking lot and into the street. He did not know for certain what he would discover upon returning home but he did have an idea. He had called both his home telephone and Abigail's cell phone on several occasions but she had not picked up. Her refusal to answer told a story, but it was one he did not want to hear.

Over the course of the last two weeks the police had paid him several visits. He told them the same story every time. He told them the truth every time. Leaving out, of course, his actions at the compound that might put him in prison. They seemed satisfied with his story and one of them had even told him he was a regular goddamn hero.

Lamb knew better than that but did not contradict the man.

When he thought about the chain of events that had unfolded he felt a strange sadness overwhelm him. He was very glad that Lily had escaped that place but he also could not help but feel responsible for the deaths of all those people on the compound. Had he never set foot on that land they would be alive still. He knew this for a fact. He had not poisoned those people but he had pushed Mosley to do what he had ended up doing and those people were dead because of it.

Yet he told himself that he could not hold himself responsible. The man had been insane and one could not take responsibility for the actions of such a person. One simply could not. Mosley had made his own choices and many people were dead because of it, and because of Lamb's actions Mosley was dead and the world was a better place. If Lamb had not pushed him to his actions, someone or something else would have done so. It might not have happened so soon – it almost certainly wouldn't have – but it would have happened eventually.

All Lamb had done was ensure that one innocent girl had not died with the rest of them. That had to be a good thing. Didn't it?

The taxi pulled to the curb in front of his house and he asked the man to wait.

Keep the meter running.

He stepped from the vehicle. He had no money on his

person. He had nothing of his on his person. He wore clothes the hospital had given him, clothes they'd retrieved from a lost-and-found. A red Coca-Cola T-shirt and a pair of beige cargo shorts.

He crutched across his lawn to his front porch and when he reached his front porch he removed a hidden key from beneath a potted plant and unlocked the door. He stepped into his living room and found it a mess.

A bloodstain covered a large part of his hardwood floor.

He crutched upstairs to his bedroom.

Then to his nightstand where he picked up his leather wallet and unfolded it. He looked inside and found two twenty-dollar bills and four ones, more than enough to pay for his taxi. He made his way back downstairs and outside and paid his cab driver. The man thanked him and drove away.

He turned back to the house and headed inside then upstairs. He leaned his crutches against the nightstand and lay on his bed. He aimed the remote at his television, turning it on. He looked dumbly at the flickering screen. Though it was still early in the evening he fell into a deep sleep.

The next day Lamb limped to his dresser and pulled out one of the bottom drawers. On the floor within the dresser he found several stacks of cash. He reached into the open space where the drawer should have been and began removing the money and tossing it onto the bed behind him. When he was done he had counted just short of $300,000. He got to his feet and limped to the bed and began stuffing the money into a duffel bag but for ten thousand dollars which he put into one of the dresser drawers that Abigail had emptied out when she left. He tried not to think about how that empty drawer made him feel. He tried to ignore the aching hollow in his center. The woman had lied to him and betrayed him. He should be angry. But he had known what her plans were before she followed through on them, and he had done what he'd done anyway, so it felt less like a betrayal than a simple fact. Something he'd known would happen did happen. That was all.

He hefted the bag and carried it downstairs and waited on the front porch for his taxi to arrive. It pulled to the curb five minutes later and he limped across his lawn and slumped into the backseat, throwing the duffel bag down beside him. He had the taxi driver take him to a Sam Swope dealership where he purchased a pre-owned 2010 Nissan Sentra for cash without bothering to test-drive the vehicle. He drove the Nissan to a PNC bank where he got a safe-deposit box. He piled his money into the safe-deposit box and closed it and locked it. He stuffed the duffel bag into a trash can on his way out.

He drove to Steak 'n Shake and bought a San Francisco melt, cheese fries, and a Coca-Cola, then headed home to eat his food. He sat on his green couch, turned on the television, and went about unpacking his food from its brown paper bag. He dipped a few thin fries into the cheese sauce and shoved them into his mouth. He unwrapped his sandwich and took a bite, Thousand Island dressing getting smeared on the corner of his mouth. He licked it away.

Then came a knock on his door.

He cursed to himself, set his food down on the coffee table – knowing it would be cold by the time he returned to it – and got to his feet. He walked to the front door and pulled it open.

Abigail stood on the other side of the storm door, facing him. She blinked. The suitcase sat at her feet like an obedient dog.

You probably hoped you'd never see me again.

Lamb pushed open the storm door. Come on in.

She hefted the suitcase and walked into the house. She set the suitcase down to the right of the door, then stood in the doorway awkwardly.

Finally, after a long moment, she spoke. I couldn't do it.

Couldn't do what?

Steal from you.

Lamb smiled. I already took my cut out of the suitcase. That money is yours.

I don't want it.

You don't want to feel guilty about it.

That too.

So don't. It's yours. I don't consider it stolen. I've been well paid for the work I did. You had to live with that son of a bitch for nearly twenty years.

I also— She cut herself off, looked at her shoes. Never mind. Forget it. I should go.

You also what?

I guess – I also wanted to talk to you again.

I called.

I was embarrassed – and ashamed of myself.

You don't owe me anything.

But I lied to you.

I knew you were lying, which means it wasn't a lie at all.

That's one way to look at it.

I care about you. I want you to be happy. Take the money. Go live your life.

What if I said I thought I'd be happy with you? I think about the time we spent together and when I do I know it was the only time I ever felt safe. It was the only time I ever felt loved. I know you don't really love me – you couldn't – but that doesn't change the way it felt. I shouldn't have done what I did. I shouldn't have lied to you. It doesn't matter that you didn't believe me. My intent was to use you. You're a good man and deserve better.

I don't deserve anything. Nobody does. We're born and we live the life we live, and if we're lucky we have some good times along with the bad, but we aren't owed them. That's the problem with people today. They think the world owes them something simply because their mothers pushed them from their bloody loins. The world owes nobody anything. Once the umbilical cord is cut you belong to the world; the world does not belong to you. People should understand that. Sometimes it'll beat the shit out of you. Sometimes it'll treat you kind. But you belong to it, not the other way around. I'm fuckin ranting. Sorry. I need to eat my lunch.

I didn't say you were owed anything. I said you deserved it.

Semantics.

Abigail sighed. You can be a hard person to talk to. I'm trying to apologize here. I'm trying to tell you I want to see if we might become something.

What about it turning bad?

Maybe it won't.

Maybe it will. Probably it will. It almost always does, doesn't it? We both know that. We've both lived that.

I don't care. I want to give it a chance. If you still want me, I want to give *us* a chance. Maybe it won't work out, but I think we owe it to ourselves to try.

Lamb was silent for a long time. Silent and thinking about the way this woman made him feel. She was damaged, perhaps damaged beyond repair – and with what she'd been through that was entirely understandable – but he was not exactly whole himself, and he believed he loved her. Despite her faults, perhaps in part because of them, he loved her.

Okay, he said.

Okay, what?

Let's try. Maybe we can even make it work.

Abigail smiled. Maybe we can.

*

The following Monday he got up early. He showered and dressed. He crushed an Adderall and snorted it. He packed himself a liverwurst sandwich, a yogurt, and a bag of Doritos. He stepped out into the morning sunshine and felt it warm against his face. He walked to his Nissan and slid in behind the wheel and started the engine. The Fall were on the radio, Mark E. Smith singing about how there were twelve people in the world, but the rest were paste. He turned it up and drove to his office with the window rolled down. He smoked a cigarette while he drove, the wind blowing in his face. When he reached the office he parked and stepped from his vehicle. He unlocked the office door and pushed it open. He flipped the sign to let folks know he was open for business, turned on the lights, limped to his desk. He sat down and stared at the wall opposite.

He lighted another cigarette and inhaled and exhaled and watched the smoke waft toward the nicotine-stained ceiling. He looked at the scar on the back of his cigarette hand, pink and raised. It looked like a button. He turned his hand over and looked at the scar on his palm. He felt very old today though he was not yet forty. Sometimes you went through something and it took a very long time for normalcy to resume. He felt that way when he was discharged from the army and he felt that way now. The world looked different to him. It seemed harder to him than it had before, the corners seemed sharper, but there was, perhaps, a goodness here he had not seen before. Abigail had shown it to him. She had been through so much, she had suffered more pain than he ever had, and yet, somehow, she was still able to open herself up to more. She was able to open her heart and feel love, despite the fact that an open heart was a heart that could be broken. It took bravery and it took faith to do such a thing. It was much easier, much safer, to keep yourself closed off, to keep yourself protected. He knew that himself. But perhaps the benefits were worth the risks. She seemed to believe they were, and he was inclined to agree.

Life was supposed to be felt. If you lived it closed off from the world, you might not get hurt, but you weren't really living at all.

Around three o'clock a man in a pair of Levi's and a green T-shirt, which was tucked into his pants, walked through his fingerprinted office door. The door swung shut behind him but he remained standing there for a very long time. He was a large man, over six feet tall and easily two hundred pounds. He had a crew cut. His head was a block atop his thick neck.

You in the right place?

I'm not sure.

Then maybe you aren't.

I lost something and it's important that I get it back.

Then maybe you are. Have a seat.

The man walked to a chair and sat down. He looked across the desk to Lamb who looked back expressionless. The man was in his forties with black porcine eyes and a mouth like a gash, lipless and angry.

It's probably best if you just tell me about it.

The man did tell him about it, and Lamb found that he was glad to be working again.

A man needed an occupation.